T0171696

THE KING

RULER OF ISRAEL

CHARLES DAUSE

WESTBOW
PRESS®
A DIVISION OF THOMAS NELSON
& ZONDERVAN

Scripture taken from the New King James Version. Copyright © 1979, 1980, 1982 by Thomas Nelson, Inc. Used by permission. All rights reserved.

WestBow Press books may be ordered through booksellers or by contacting:

WestBow Press
A Division of Thomas Nelson & Zondervan
1663 Liberty Drive
Bloomington, IN 47403
www.westbowpress.com
1 (866) 928-1240

ISBN: 978-1-5127-2796-8 (sc)
ISBN: 978-1-5127-2798-2 (hc)
ISBN: 978-1-5127-2797-5 (e)

Library of Congress Control Number: 2016901142

Print information available on the last page.

WestBow Press rev. date: 2/22/2016

I am deeply grateful to my wife, Tracey, for her help and encouragement, to my kids, Ella, Jack, Noah and Anna for their motivation, and most importantly to Christ, for His salvation.

Prologue

Surely the Lord's anointed stands before me, thought the old man. The young man was tall and strong, handsome, with the regal bearing of a ruler. He was the eldest son of his father, a soldier, and obviously held authority among his family. Few men bore the look of a king so much as this young man.

Do not look upon his countenance, or his stature, for I have refused him, came a Voice that only the old man could hear. *I do not see as a man sees. A man sees only the outward appearance, but I look upon the heart.*

"The Lord has not chosen him," said the old man. The handsome young man's face fell, and he stepped away. His father, who stood behind him, spoke up.

"Shall I present another to you, Samuel?"

"Yes," answered the old man. The group stood at the top of a small hill outside the family's village, with the father and mother and their children all gathered together to meet with this old man, the leader of God's people. Samuel sat on a stool a short ways from the family. The father beckoned to another son, not so tall or handsome but very soldierly. This young man also came and stood before the prophet.

This one has also been refused, came the Voice to the old man.

"Neither has the Lord chosen him," said Samuel without hesitation. This young man also stepped away, and the father motioned for another. Four more sons were brought in front of the prophet, only to receive the same response. The father was at a loss for words.

Samuel was not. "Have you any other sons?" he asked.

"There is still the youngest," answered the man. "He has remained at home to keep the sheep."

"Send and fetch him. We will not sit down to eat until he comes."

"Ozem," spoke the father to the second youngest, "hurry and take your brother's place with the sheep. Have him come here immediately."

"Yes father," replied the lad, who turned and ran down the hill with all he could muster. The family lived close by, and was not long before

v

another boy came running hard up the hill towards the group. He was not nearly so tall or strong as the others, perhaps around fifteen years of age. The boy was breathing heavily as he reached his father, who reached up to wipe the dirt from his son's face and brush off his clothing.

"Have the boy come to me," said Samuel. The father pointed the boy towards the old man and the son obeyed, coming to stand before the prophet.

Rise and anoint him, came the Voice, ***for this is a man after My own heart.***

1

The sound of the trumpet rang out clearly through the air. It was the battle call for the army of Israel. Men shouted orders, and soldiers began falling into their formations. Small rocks and loose dirt tumbled down the hillside as men ran to and fro, picking up weapons and strapping on armor. The men began assembling at the base of a high ridgeline, sparsely populated with small trees and shrubbery, which ran along behind them from the southwest heading in a northeasterly direction. In front of the camp, to the north, a wide valley spread out before them. Most of it was covered with tall grass, swaying in the gentle breeze. On the other side of the valley, almost a mile away, stood another ridge, not quite so tall, which capped the horizon. The most important detail, however, was another army, well-equipped and professional looking, and quite a bit larger, marching resolutely southward across the level ground. Behind the southern camp, a young man began hurriedly trotting down a dirt path than ran diagonally from the top of the ridge all the way to its base. He was about average height with a lean, muscular build. He had shaggy black hair and short scraggly beard, the kind that teenage boys get when they try to grow facial hair and can't quite get enough of it to grow in. His skin was a deep tan, darkened from long days in the outdoors. He wore a brown linen loincloth that hung to his knees, and a shirt, both dirty and stained with sweat, with a belt around his waist. He carried a large sack on his back, with the strap slung across his chest, and had a shepherd's staff in one hand. He quickly made his way to the bottom of the steep, rocky path. Coming around a large outcrop of boulders, he came into view of a company of soldiers covering the flank of the army. About thirty soldiers were spread out in a line, facing along the side of the ridge, with the path running between them. Most wore leather armor over their shoulders and chest, armed with a bow and quiver of arrows. One of them spoke up and pointed at him. Next to the path was a tall, solidly built man with a thick beard, and held a long staff-like weapon in one hand. The young man headed towards him.

"Whoa there, boy. Who might you be?" asked the tall armored man, holding what looked like a sharpened ox goad level with the boy's head.

"Sir, I am a servant of the king, called David. I'm returning from my father."

"Oh yeah, you're the harpist, aren't you? Lot of good you'll do here. What you been doing?" The tall man pointed to the staff in David's hand. "That doesn't look like a harp."

"Sir, I've been home with my father, keeping his sheep. He sent me with some food for my brothers and their commander. They're serving with Judah."

"They are, are they? What about you? You look almost old enough, especially with that beard. If anything, you could play us a tune," the tall man snorted. There were more laughs from the others nearby.

"Sir, the king prefers that I stay with him. If not, I would gladly fight."

"Don't call me sir, boy. Take that bag of yours to Judah's supply man." He pointed toward a group of tents, back away from where all the soldiers were assembling. "If he doesn't eat it himself, he'll give it to your brothers. Hurry up, now." The tall man waved him on, and the young man jogged on in the direction of the tents. Behind him, he heard another soldier yell, "Don't forget the harp, boy!" By now, the majority of the men had assembled in formation, broken up in companies of approximately one hundred. Each group had four ranks, with the men facing out across the valley. There were about thirty companies or so, spread out over nearly a third of a mile. Behind them, a large number of officers congregated in small groups, discussing strategy. The approaching army was still a good ways off, but showed no sign of slowing down. As David reached the supply tent, a short, portly man came out, carrying an axe and a quiver of arrows, looking very stressed. The man nearly crashed into the youth.

"What?" the portly man barked.

"Sir, I have some food to give to my brothers, they're-"

"Not right now." The portly man cut him off. "Leave it here, I'll deal with it later."

"Where?" he asked.

"I don't care. Anywhere." The portly man shuffled off, at the quickest pace he could manage. David set his sack just inside the tent, thinking he'd come back when the excitement was over to make sure it got delivered to the right place. His father was worried about his boys, and would want to know they'd received their package. Suddenly, the trumpet sounded again. The approaching army was now only a few hundred yards away. Soon the battle would start! He had to find his brothers, quickly. Glancing down the line of companies, he noticed that they must be grouped according to tribes. About every other company had a bannerman in the front, holding the banner for its tribe. Every third bannerman stood next to a standard-bearer, with a standard twice the height of the tribal banners. In the middle of the whole formation was a red standard, with a golden lion on it. Recognizing Judah's standard, the youth bolted toward it. The companies were stacked two deep, so as he reached the company in the rear he began to scour the lines for his brothers. He spotted two of them close to where he was standing.

"Shammah!" His brother turned and looked with surprise. Directly in front was the other. "Abinadab!" He ran over to them. For a moment they both just stared at him.

"What are you doing here?" asked Shammah, the younger of the two.

"Father sent me. What's happening? Are you about to fight?" David asked excitedly.

"What do you think boy?" answered Abinadab. "Why did Father send you? You can't fight."

"He sent me with some food for you. I left it in a tent behind the lines."

"You should've brought it down here. Haven't had a decent meal in a month. I'd like to eat something good before I get killed." Shammah grinned. "You never know-"

Abinadab interrupted him. "You've got to leave. You'll get killed out here."

The soldier next to them, quite amused with the little reunion, piped up. "Let him stay. Maybe he will go fight the giant for us."

Abinadab looked at the soldier angrily. "Quiet you."

Suddenly, a different trumpet sounded. The opposing army had come to a halt, less than a bowshot away. There were so many, all well armored and ready to fight. The mid-morning sun glinted off their helmets and steel weapons. They looked impressive. The trumpet of Israel sounded again. All the captains had made their way to the front, and stood ready for any orders. Across the field, a soldier made his way out from the lines. Even from so far, he looked huge. He wore a helmet and a coat of mail, and had brass greaves on both legs. He carried a long spear, and had a sword sheathed at his side. Next to him, barely half his height, stood another soldier, almost hidden behind the great shield that he carried. The giant walked to within a stone's throw from Israel's lines, showing no fear. In a deep and mighty voice, loud enough so all could hear, the giant shouted a challenge.

"Hear me, you men of Israel. We are Philistines, and you are servants of Saul. You cannot overcome us. You are too weak. Your God will not fight for you. Choose a man to fight me. If he kills me, we will serve you. But when I kill him, you will serve us. Choose a man for me. Are you all as soft as women? Choose a man, Israel, or we will march across your land and destroy you. Choose a man, Israel! This day I defy you and your God!"

With that, the Philistine army began to shout and bang their shields together. The Israelite army, almost to a man, cringed and felt their knees weaken. They were filled with dread, knowing there was no one who could defeat the giant.

David, standing among his brothers, was in shock. The excitement he had felt was gone. For a moment he could not even think. Then, deep in his stomach, he felt a great anger welling up inside him. Who was this man to speak so of the God of Israel? This wretched, uncircumcised creature was attempting to defy the Almighty God of all creation. He must not be allowed to get away with that.

"Who is this? How can he be allowed to speak such a way?" he said.

"Are you going to stop him?" said the soldier next to Shammah. "Go kill him, and Saul will let you bed his daughter."

"What are you talking about?" he asked.

Abinadab spoke up. "The king will marry his daughter to the man who kills the giant, and free his family from taxes. At least that's the rumor."

"I'll fight him, if no one else will. He can't be allowed to speak like that." All those close by were listening to him. Suddenly, a tall, handsome soldier stepped up with an angry look on his face, and grabbed him by the shirt.

"What are you doing here?" It was Eliab, the oldest of the brothers. "You should be watching the flock. Now they will all be lost and Father will be ruined."

"No, Eliab, they are with Ozem. Father sent me with food for you," answered David.

"Don't lie to me! I know how selfish you are. You came to see the battle."

The Philistine army stared across at the Israelites. Out in front of Judah, Nahshon, the tribe's war captain, stood next to his second in command. He was a hard man, slightly taller than average, thick-chested, with a graying head and beard. He was in his forties, and had spent most of his life fighting for Israel. Never before had he seen his men so demoralized. This giant had taken their spirit. If he wasn't killed soon, he would take many of their lives. From behind him, over the sound of his leaders barking instructions to the men, he heard something that seemed out of place. It sounded like an argument, or maybe back-talk from some of the troops. That he couldn't have. If these cowards weren't going to yell at that Philistine, they certainly weren't going to yell at Nahshon's troop leaders. This was not the time for this sort of thing. Irritated, the captain about-faced and marched toward the rear of the formation, where it was coming from. As he got closer, he realized not only was there back-talk, those worthless men had broken formation. Wait, there was a civilian in the formation. He was just a boy, arguing with Eliab, from Bethlehem. Eliab was a fine soldier, but he was way out of position; he belonged in the first rank.

"Eliab, what is this nonsense?" asked the captain, and everyone's mouth shut.

"Sir, this is my brother," Eliab pointed to the youth. "He's a servant of the king. He's just about to leave."

"What are you doing in my formation, boy?"

David looked at him, as serious as death. "Sir, let me go fight the giant. Our God cannot be defied."

Nahshon was taken aback. Who was this kid, this dirty shepherd boy, who thought he could fight with that monstrosity? "All of you get back in formation, and be quiet. Come with me, boy." He led David behind the formation, out of earshot of the troops. "Tell me again. You want to do what?"

"I will fight the giant."

"But you're just a boy."

"The Lord will fight for me. I know it."

"Who are you?"

"I am a servant of the king, called David."

Nahshon hardly believed he was going to go with this. But there was something about this boy, something different. "Haggith," he yelled toward the front of the formation, and the soldier he had been next to up front turned around. "Take command." And with that, he led David away from the army, back up the hillside toward the tents. They passed the tent where the young man had left his food, and continued farther up to where a large tent stood alone, set up under a tall tree. Outside the tent stood a big man, wearing armor and a mean look on his face. His name was Josheb, and he was the king's bodyguard. He growled under his breath when the two strode up.

"What is it, Nahshon? Shouldn't you be in the front, waiting for orders?"

"They won't be orders from you, you're not that smart. This boy has a message for the king," replied the captain, with obvious disdain.

"I know this boy. He's the harpist. What is it, boy?"

"It's for the king, not his guard," Nahshon answered.

"Have it your way. Wait here." Josheb pulled the tent flap back and stepped inside. Several moments passed. The captain and the young man waited silently, listening to the sounds of the two armies in the background. Then Josheb reemerged, and held the tent flap open. "Come on then, just leave the staff." David set it down where he stood. As they stepped forward, the guard laid his hand out toward Nahshon. "Just the boy, old man."

David stepped inside the tent, and Josheb dropped the tent flap behind him. It took a moment for his eyes to adjust. Four men stood inside, three in full armor. They stood in a semi-circle at the other end of the tent, looking at him. The man to the left was a stocky, powerfully built man with a thick black beard. Next to him was a very tall, strong looking man, with a graying beard and a heavy look on his face. He was standing over a small table with a scroll on it, and as David came forward he rolled it up and held it down at his side. There was also a man who looked very much like the tall man, only not quite so tall and leaner. He had a short, well-groomed beard with brown hair, and must have been at least twenty years younger. The fourth man, who was obviously a priest, was shorter and older and wore a linen ephod. They appeared to be in a disagreement about something, and there was a tense feeling in the tent. The stocky man addressed him first. "You have a message for the king?"

"Yes Sir," he replied. "I've come to fight the giant."

"What?"

He didn't answer. The stocky man, who happened to be the general of the army, didn't like that.

"Is this a joke? I'll tell you, the king doesn't have time for this nonsense."

"It's not, Sir." They could all see the seriousness on his face. Then the tall man spoke up.

"David, I brought you on as a servant, not a soldier. Tell me, what makes you think that I should let you go and fight him? Don't you realize the very lives of my people will be riding on the outcome?"

David had bowed toward the ground upon being addressed by King Saul. "My lord, I am no one, and not worth risking your people's lives on. But the God of Israel will not be mocked. He will defeat this giant, by my hand if no other, and this uncircumcised filth will never speak against Him again."

"Stand up, boy, look at me." David rose, and the king looked straight into his eyes. "The God of Israel has listened to this giant for forty days, and has yet to strike him down. Why will He do so now because of you?"

"I cannot speak for God's timing, my lord. I only know that He will do it."

"You cannot fight this giant. You are not even a warrior, just a dirty young man. This monster has been killing men since before you were born. I've heard tales of him, of his great strength. The Philistines say he could've beaten Samson had he been around," said the king.

"My lord," David spoke up quickly, "I am not a warrior, I am a shepherd. But the Lord has given me victory before. Twice I have fought beasts as deadly as the giant. Both a lion and a bear have attacked my sheep, and I killed them both. I will do the same to that Philistine, because the battle is the Lord's, and He gives the victory."

The priest spoke up, "My lord, I admire the boy's courage, but I do not think this is wise."

"Is that so, Ahijah?" Saul said flatly.

"The battle is the Lord's, that is true. But it is also man's responsibility to use what God has given him wisely. This is certainly not wise." The priest gave David a condescending look.

"No, it is not," remarked Saul. The king looked at the young man's face. It seemed uncommonly strong. There was something else different about it, as well. The stern look in his eyes did indeed make him look like a warrior, and made him seem ten years older than he was. But that wasn't it. The king knew there was something else about this boy that he couldn't quite put his finger on, something powerful. Was it powerful enough to risk his people on? He had little other choice. No one else would fight the giant, and if it came to outright battle most of his men would die. Already he had lost many men, and only small skirmishes had broken out. Perhaps this boy could do it. It was worth the risk. "Very well."

"What?" asked the general, named Abner.

"Let him fight."

"What? My lord, are you sure?" Abner looked at the king incredulously.

"Yes. He will fight the giant. Give him some armor, Jonathan." The tall young man, looking somewhat in awe of the David, turned to the king. "Father, we have none extra here."

"Right here's some, but it won't fit him. It's your spare," said the stocky man, pulling some out from the corner of the tent.

"Try it on him," said the king.

Abner and Jonathan tried unsuccessfully to fit the king's spare armor on the young man, but it was pointless. The king was a good foot taller than he was, and thicker in build. In protest, David said, "My lord, I've never used armor or weapons. I have a sling, which I used on the lion and bear. It is all I need."

"We're wasting time. If this boy's going to fight, he's got to get out there," said the general.

"Fine," said the king, "Abner, go tell the giant his challenge is accepted." With that, the general hurried out of the tent. "You want only the sling?" The king looked at David with raised eyebrows.

"Yes, my lord."

"You have stones?"

"No, my lord."

"There is a little stream that runs out of the hillside behind the tent. There should be some there, it's very rocky. You have a bag to hold them in?"

"Yes, my lord."

"Very well. Go get some."

"Yes, my lord." David turned and walked swiftly out of the tent, and Saul let out a deep sigh. Ahijah watched him leave and then turned to the king.

"That boy's going to die, and Israel will serve the Philistines," said the priest.

"Maybe."

"Then why are you letting him fight?" piped up Jonathan.

"I'm not sure." After a long pause, the king added, "I don't think he's going to lose."

Nahshon had left the area, probably going with Abner back to the army. Josheb remained, growling to himself. David ran behind the king's tent, looking this way and that. Then he saw it: a little stream coming out of the hillside, directly behind and slightly higher up than the tent. It was very small, but coming steadily, and it bent away to his right and flowed downhill until it could no longer be seen. It was probably the only fresh water close by. Between the stream and the large tree, it was as good a spot as any for the king's tent. There were many rocks to pick from. He quickly sorted through a few, picking out five that were smooth and round, and big enough to fill his palm. A small bag and his sling were both tucked into his belt. David pulled out the bag and filled it with the stones, then tied it so it hung from his belt, with the opening at the top so he could quickly grab the stones. He took a deep breath, then got down on his hands and knees and leaned his face close to the ground and prayed.

Oh Mighty God, oh Rock of Israel, how I need You now. This giant blasphemes You, and wishes to kill Your people and enslave them. I need you, oh God. I will go out against this man, but I cannot fight him. It has to be You, oh Mighty God. Make my hands fast and strong, oh God. Oh Mighty God, You can defend me, You can defend Your people, for You are mightier than all, and I know that You will, for You have said so, and Your words are true. Help me, oh Mighty God. Help me, oh Rock of Israel.

David rose, wiped the dirt from his hands and knees, and readjusted the bag on his belt. When he turned around, Saul stood outside the tent, looking at him. "Time to go David." They joined Jonathan, Ahijah and Josheb in front of the tent, and David retrieved his staff he had laid down. Then the group began making their way down the hillside. They walked in silence. It was eerily quiet, despite the fact that nearly ten thousand soldiers, armed and ready for battle, stood only a short distance away. As they passed the lower group of tents, the silence suddenly gave way to shouting. The Philistines were in an uproar. Abner must have delivered the message. The general and Nahshon both stood out in front of Judah, right in the middle of the army. As they reached Israel's formation, Abner began to shout, "Here's your king, Israel, and God's warrior! The Lord fights with him!" Israel, somewhat encouraged by their commander, joined in the shouting. The king led the small group to the front where Abner stood. The stocky general grabbed David's hand and raised it high, leading to more shouting. Then he let go David's hand, grabbed him by the shoulders and looked him square in the eyes. "Be strong, boy," said the general. "He's a man, and he can die just like the rest of us." Abner squeezed his shoulders tight, then released them and turned to face the battlefield. The king stepped up to him. David waited for some instruction, but none came. Saul looked at David intently, as if trying to read the young man's face. Finally, the king said, "The Lord fights for Israel, David. Go now."

Across the field, the Philistines stood in rigid formation. They looked sharp, and ready. Directly across from where David stood, the formation parted and out came the giant. The shouting, which had died down some, erupted again from the Philistines as their champion came forward. He was enormous. He stood over nine feet tall, and was as broad across the shoulders as any two normal men. His upper arms, which were bare, were as thick as David's waist. He wore a bronze helmet that covered the top of his head down to right over his eyes, and a coat of mail that was so heavy any normal man would barely be able to walk with it on, much less fight. He had long black hair reaching past his shoulders, and a thick black beard that covered the top of his chest. He carried a spear in his right hand that was over seven feet long, and had a huge longsword sheathed at his side. In front and slightly to his left, a soldier came on before him carrying a huge shield. The giant looked nearly double the size of the shield-bearer, but the soldier must have been strong for the shield was nearly as big as he was. The heavy footsteps of the giant stamped loudly as they approached, and the Israelite soldiers went quiet in fear. The giant reached the middle of the field between the armies and stopped. David, with a dreadful feeling in his stomach, strode out to meet him. As he approached, the giant stared at him, uncomprehending this raggedy boy on the battlefield. David stopped a short distance away, and stood silently. Suddenly the giant roared with laughter. "Are you the champion of Israel? How long have you been off of your mother's teat, boy?" Looking past David toward Israel, he yelled to the king, "Saul, have you become a nurse-maid?" Behind him, the Philistine army jeered. With the butt of his spear, the giant poked his shield-bearer. "Go away." The soldier stumbled forward from the force of the giant's spear, then circled around well behind him and waited. Then without warning the giant's laughter turned to rage. His face became red with anger, with veins throbbing in his neck. Looking right at David, he yelled, "Am I a dog, boy, that you come at me with a stick? Dagon will curse your soul. I am Goliath, the Philistine, and there is no god in Israel that can save you from me. Come to me, and I will give your stinking carcass to the birds of the air, and beasts of the field."

The dreadful feeling in David's stomach passed, flushed out by hot anger. It was time to silence this fool. "You come to me with a sword and a spear, but I come to you in the name of the Lord of hosts. There is a God in Israel, and you will know Him today. No, Goliath, now you will die, and I will give your carcass to the birds of the air, and the beasts of the field."

As if they almost believed it, the Israelite soldiers cheered, shouting encouragement to the shepherd boy who had dared to face the monster. In a fury, Goliath raised his spear and came forward. David, gritting his teeth, dropped his staff and ran toward him. Slipping a stone into his sling, David raised it overhead and whipped it in circles, building up speed. Goliath reached back and hurled his spear. David pulled down the sling and leaped to his left as the spear flew past. With a roar, the giant drew his sword and rushed at him. Again David began to whip his sling overhead. As Goliath closed the distance, David planted his left foot in front of him and threw his right arm forward, releasing the sling and sending the stone flying at awesome speed. The stone met its target. With a thump, it sank deep between the eyes of the giant. Bellowing, Goliath stumbled and dropped his sword. With a heavy thud, the giant crashed down with his face toward the dirt.

Silence reigned. Both armies became speechless in utter shock. Every eye was glued on the center of the battlefield. Goliath lay completely motionless. David ran toward the fallen monster, picking up the massive sword that lay beside him. With both hands, David raised it over his head. Using all his strength, he brought the sword down on the giant's neck. It passed cleanly through, and the enormous head rolled away from the body. David dropped the sword and slid the helmet off Goliath's head. The long hair that had not been cut away was soaked in blood. David picked up the head with both hands. He planted one foot on the giant's back and lifted the head high so all could see. Then he shouted, "The Lord! The Lord fights for Israel!"

The Israelite army erupted in a roar. Abner was ecstatic. The boy had actually done it! Now it was time to finish this. The general drew his sword and held it high, shouting, "A sword for the Lord! A sword for the Lord! Standby to move!" Each captain called his company to attention, preparing them to attack. Soldiers readied their weapons. Abner pointed his sword at the Philistine army. "Forward, Israel!" With the general leading from the front, the entire army charged forward in disciplined formation. Their earlier fear was gone. Goliath's shield-bearer, who had been standing by in amazement, dropped his shield and ran back toward the Philistine lines. With their champion dead and the sight of an energized army rushing at them, the Philistines lost their courage. Almost the whole army turned and fled, stampeding like a crazed herd of cattle. Several companies near the front held their ground and formed themselves up to meet the Israelite charge. To their rear, a large Philistine threatened death to any who would flee. Abner, seeing the courageous few, directed the charge into their center. The two armies clashed with the sound of metal on metal. The weight of the mass of Israelites immediately pushed back the Philistine line. The large Philistine in the rear rushed forward, hacking his way through the lines. Abner fought his way toward him. Out of the corner of his eye he saw David. The young man was completely unarmored fighting in the middle of the melee. He was wielding Goliath's giant sword with great effort, ploughing it through one Philistine soldier after another. That kid was astounding. The general slammed his sword across a soldier's helmet, knocking him to the ground, and came face to face with the large Philistine. This one was a warrior, and bigger than Abner. They repeatedly clashed swords together, with the Philistine using his size to move the general backward. Abner quickly stepped to his rear to let his adversary gain momentum, then side-stepped the Philistine's strike and drove his own sword straight through the soldier's belly. The general pulled it out and the man fell to the ground. By now nearly all of the remaining Philistines had been killed. Abner held his sword high. "Reform the line, Israel, reform the line!" The Israelites had shown good discipline, and most were not far out of the original formation. It took only a few moments to reform. David came running up to Abner, breathing heavily. "Boy, you are a wonder! Fall in next to me, you'll help me lead."

The Philistine army had run back across the valley toward their camp on the north side, but had not stopped. They were heading west along the base of the ridge, toward the road that ran around its edge, which would take them to the city of Ekron. The general led the Israelites quickly, moving diagonally across the valley, toward the edge of the northern ridge. The Philistine army was still much larger and slower, and the Israelites would be able to overtake them. The Philistines needed a sound beating today. For too long they had been a threat to Israel. Abner and David jogged along briskly as the army, which was still stretched out in a line formation, kept pace slightly behind them. Nahshon ran alongside the formation, shouting encouragement. The Philistines had fallen somewhat back into formation and slowed to a fast march, unable to keep up a run with all their heavy armor. The end of their line trailed far behind the front and had just now reached the camp area. The entire Philistine army was stretched out in front of the Israelites. Abner headed for the center. As Israel drew near, the Philistine commanders in the rear shouted for their men to set in and prepare to fight, passing the word to the front that they were under attack. Those farther to the front failed to heed the message. Instead, nearly half of the Philistines started into a run again, heading out of the valley. As they drew near the Philistines, Abner shouted again, "A sword for the Lord! A sword for the Lord!" The Israelites plunged into the remaining Philistine line. The Philistines were exhausted from the long run in full armor, and put up a poor fight. David, still wielding the giant sword, fought right through the middle of the opposing line. Abner fell back toward the rear. He had several companies of archers that had yet to be included in the action. Shouting directions to their captains, the general ordered them far out to the left of the formation, shouting for them to engage the fleeing Philistines. Israel had some excellent marksmen, and more than a few Philistines fell from their arrows despite the armor. The Philistines had begun the day with nearly six thousand men. Less than half that number escaped the valley.

Saul stood at the base of the southern ridgeline as the sun began to set. Josheb and the king's other guards, as well as Ahijah the priest, stood nearby. The army had begun to return, and many companies had already arrived and settled in. They had spent the remainder of the day looting the Philistine camp. Now they marched back in companies, carrying weapons, food and clothes. The king felt a sense of relief. Perhaps now he could have some peace. The Philistines had been a thorn in the king's side his entire reign. After today's victory, maybe they would leave Israel alone for awhile. As the last of the companies made it back, Abner found his way to the king.

"Abner, you've done well," said Saul, greeting him.

The general was elated. "My lord, today is a gift from God. We have not had a day such as this, not while I have been here."

"Where is David?" asked Saul.

"Probably with his brothers. He returned with Judah."

"He is from Judah, isn't he? Who is his father?"

"I don't know, my lord."

"I only sent word to him when I was told David was a harpist. I never met the man. Surely, to have such a son he must be a valiant man."

"All the valiant men of Judah are here, my lord. I've been through all the tribes. All the fighters are here."

"Find David. Bring him to me."

"Yes, my lord." Abner trotted off in the direction of Judah's tents. Saul waited in the gathering dusk. Only a few minutes had passed when Abner returned with David following at his heels, still carrying Goliath's sword. As they reached the king, David bowed his head.

"David, you were amazing today. All of Israel will sing about you." Saul was beaming.

"My lord, it was not me. It was the Lord," David said humbly.

"Tell me, who is your father?"

"I am the son of your servant Jesse the Bethlehemite."

2

J onathan looked around, surveying the scene around him. He stood inside his father's compound at Gibeah. It was one of the largest walled towns in Israel, built into the highlands west of the Sea of Arabah, and to the north of the Jebusite capital of Jebus. In the center of the compound stood the king's house, a large unadorned building of two stories made out of hewn stone. All around it were more stone buildings, many of them other homes, some military barracks, supply and metal-worker rooms, kitchens, stables, and an armory. Around the entire perimeter ran a stone wall that was more than twelve feet high and nearly five feet thick, with two gates on opposite sides. The wall ran for nearly two miles all the way around. At the moment, Jonathan was preoccupied with the training yard, where a company of Ruebenites were training with wooden swords. Less than a decade ago, the only swords in Israel had belonged to himself and his father, for the Philistines had controlled the use of iron. Recently, the victories over those uncircumcised fellows had not only freed up the use of metal-workers, but had also yielded many weapons from the plunder of defeated Philistine troops. Now there were very few Israelite companies not completely outfitted with proper arms. This group would be one of the last to receive this training. Jonathan was an excellent sword-fighter, and his father had chosen him to lead the instruction. He had several other experienced soldiers with him to help. About a hundred soldiers had drilled with the dummy swords all day, repetitively striking and blocking each other. It was hot, mid-afternoon, and the air was full of dust kicked up by the fighting. Now they were engaging in their final drill. In ten separate areas, one soldier fought two others, while a small group looked on and caught their breath, preparing for their turn. Abner stood a little ways away outside the barracks, looking on. He had already told them this drill would continue until he saw a single man dominate his two opponents, and had promised punishments to whoever was defeated, as a deterrent to any who may just want to give up. None so far had been victorious to the standard the general held.

Jonathan paced along, wandering from one group to the next. He was relatively pleased with what he saw. This group still had a ways to go, but they had made some great improvements. Three days ago, more than half of them had never even held a sword. Today most of them used their dummy swords with confidence. This was their last day of instruction. After the drills were completed, they would each be issued a real sword. Jonathan kept a close eye on the men. This final drill was very productive. The soldiers were getting some good, realistic training, but it would be hard for any of them to defeat both of their opponents. It had been a long day, and they were tired. This was the kind of training that separated the strong from the weak. It might be quite a while before Abner was pleased enough to release them.

In one of the groups close to the center, a tall, strong looking Ruebenite squared off against two others. The tall soldier had a grin on his face. He welcomed the challenge, and he looked as though he may be able to succeed. His adversaries split and moved to either side of him. Wanting to land the first blow, the tall man stepped quickly toward one, slamming his wooden sword into his opponent's weapon, nearly knocking it out of the soldier's hand. Then, just as quickly, he turned and struck at the other soldier. Continuing to move from one to the other, the tall soldier kept the other two on their heels, slamming his wooden sword into theirs like it was a sledgehammer. Several of the other groups next to them stopped to watch the tall man work. Finally, he grabbed the wooden blade with his non-sword hand, and brought up level with his chest. He stepped into one soldier with all his weight, pushing him to the ground, then spun around and slammed the dummy sword onto the other soldier's helmet, dropping him as well. A cheer went up from those watching. The tall Ruebenite held his sword high and gave a yell.

Jonathan was not impressed. He walked over to the tall man, and the soldier lowered his sword, grinning. Jonathan took his own wooden sword and cracked it against the soldier's knuckles so hard that the tall man dropped his weapon. He gave a grunt and stepped back, holding his hand.

"Excellent work, if you were still using an ox-goad. You just grabbed a sharpened blade with your bare hand. Now, it's all cut up and bleeding. It's useless." Jonathan looked at his nearest assistant. "Bind his left hand to his belt, and they can continue." The assistant complied, and the tall soldier, looking rather sheepish, submitted to his punishment. After opening and closing his right hand, which was going to be bruised but not broken, he picked up his dummy sword and stepped back into the drill. This time he didn't fare so well, taking a pretty solid beating at the hands of the same two he had just pushed around.

Jonathan resumed his pacing. The last session he had resided over, David had been one of the instructors. That young man was a natural warrior. Only a few years had passed since he had killed the giant, which was the first time he had ever faced battle. Now he fought as if he had been doing it his entire life. Saul had given David command of a thousand men, which gave him equal authority as himself. The standing Israelite army numbered nearly three thousand soldiers. Jonathan commanded a thousand, David commanded a thousand, and Jonathan's younger brother Ish-bosheth commanded a thousand. Abner was over them all. Today David was out with his troops, probing Philistine posts to check their strength. He was due to return soon, perhaps today. Jonathan glanced over in Abner's direction. The king was making his way over toward the general, with Josheb the bodyguard trailing along. His father was a good king, and a good soldier, but Jonathan would run things differently if it were him on the throne, he often thought. His father didn't always use enough common sense, and he spent too much energy worrying about his reputation with his people. Early in Jonathan's military career, Saul had forbidden a division of soldiers from eating during an active campaign against the Philistines. How ridiculous an order that had been. It was his pride, Jonathan had thought, and his desire to look righteous in front of the army that drove him to make that decision. A very poor decision. Yes, Jonathan would make some changes when he came to rule. His father now stood and talked with the general, keeping an eye on the training.

Jonathan turned back to the drills. No one was making a great fight of it. They were very tired. He paced toward the first group in the drill, closest to where the king stood with Abner. One of the soldiers there seemed to have more energy than the rest. He wasn't very tall, and had a lean build. He stepped into the drill, matched against two soldiers that were both slightly larger than he was. He was patient, waiting for them to make the first strike. When one finally did, he blocked it and slipped around behind them. He was quick. He started striking, one at a time, then darting away. His footwork was excellent, and it kept him out of his opponents' reach. He also used his wooden sword with considerable skill. For several minutes the short man kept it up, striking in and darting out. His opponents began to slow, and he began to get some good licks in to their body armor and helmets. Finally, he landed a solid blow to one soldier's helmet that left him slightly dazed. Sensing his opportunity, he drove hard at the other soldier, battering him time and again until he had disarmed him. Grabbing his opponents' shoulder with his free hand, the short man swept his leg behind the soldier's leg, knocking him to the ground. He then spun around, just as the other soldier regained his senses. The short man drove at him with a fury, knocking the soldier's sword out of his hand and cracking him on the helmet, so hard that he fell in a crumpled heap on the ground. The short man gave a yell. Those standing by shouted their approval.

"Well done." Jonathan said as he strode up to the short man. "I'm sure that met the general's expectations. What's your name?"

"Hezron, my lord."

"Excellent job. Maybe the rest of this company needs to become as well conditioned as you. Then we could wear out the Philistines."

"Yes, my lord."

Jonathan raised his voice, "Assemble! On me!" As the soldiers started to fall in, Saul and Abner came walking up, and Jonathan stepped over toward them. "He is a good instructor, is he not?" Saul said loudly to no one in particular. The king looked at Jonathan and grinned. "Thank you, son. You have done a good job with this group. I saw them a few days ago, and they are much improved."

"They are. Several here I would use in my guard, if need be," Jonathan agreed. By now the company had fallen into their ranks, and quietly stood by awaiting instruction.

"I have a task for some of them, now that training is finished. Dismiss them, let them clean themselves up, then send twenty or so to the steward. I need some work done on the feasting hall. A runner has arrived, and David will be returning shortly. We will eat there tonight." Saul seemed pleased with the idea. Jonathan, however, was not.

"Father, training is over, but they still have to receive their weapons. I need them all at the armory, then they have to go to the metal-worker. Plus, they've been at it all day. They don't need to be laboring for some feast."

"They'll have water and rest first. The armory can be taken care of tomorrow."

"Tomorrow they have to return home, and my smiths have to see to other business. It needs to be tonight."

"Then send the rest to get that done, and send twenty to the hall."

"Father, that won't work-" Jonathan started, but Abner cut him off.

"Jonathan, listen to me." The general drew very close to the tall prince, speaking in a low voice, so only Jonathan could hear. "The king has just given you an order. You will not fail to give him the proper respect, especially not out here in front of my troops. Do I make myself clear?"

Jonathan's face tightened. "Yes, sir," he replied.

"Very well. Dismiss them."

"Yes, sir." Jonathan gave a curt nod to the general, then about-faced and strode back to the company. Out in front of the formation, in charge, stood the tall soldier who the prince had scolded earlier. Jonathan approached him. "Elizur!"

"Yes, my lord?"

"I need twenty men, I don't care who. Send them to the steward in the feasting hall. They have work to do. Take the rest to the armory, you'll be outfitted."

"Yes, my lord."

Jonathan turned and faced the troops, looking for Hezron. Elizur called them to attention. The Ruebenites snapped to and looked at the prince.

The king turned and waved to Josheb, dismissing him, and the bodyguard strode off. Saul and Abner walked away in the other direction. As they walked, they could hear Jonathan talking to the Ruebenites, encouraging them so they might leave confident, ready to fight when called upon. The king and his general walked toward the main gate of the compound. The training yard was near the rear of the compound, a good five minute walk from the main gate. As they walked, people walked to and fro around them, going about their business. There were women carrying clothes to wash or mend, others carrying bread or water cans, and several young men who looked like smiths carrying weapons. There were also many children running around, some playing and others doing chores. The compound was relatively full of people. When David and his troops arrived, the place would be packed. Saul was in good spirits. Things were going well for the king and his nation. His army was beginning to shake off the yoke laid on them by the Phillistines. They had achieved many recent successes against Philistine troops, and that had benefitted all the Israelites. Much of the credit belonged to David. That young man had so much personal courage and battlefield intuition, and he had yet to lose a battle. His troops had complete trust in him. But he was not the only thing on the king's mind this afternoon.

"Jonathan is doing an excellent job teaching swordsmanship, don't you think, Abner?" Saul asked.

"He is an excellent swordsman. There are few who would do a better job," replied the general.

"I believe he only has two or three companies left to train. That's good. We need a fully outfitted army. We have done very well in the field recently, and this will make us better."

Abner gave a grim smile. "We need to be better. We have fewer soldiers than either Achish or Adonizedek. And we have fewer weapons. If we want to keep what we have earned recently, we have to get stronger. Both the Philistines and the Jebusites are doing that now."

"David should be able to give us some information on that shortly," said Saul.

Abner continued, "I don't need to hear it from David that Achish is gearing up to come after us. The Philistines have always hated us, and wanted our land. Nothing would make Achish happier than taking your head and your kingdom."

"True. But he is less capable now than he has been in the past. And Adonizedek is no true threat. He does nothing but watch the world from his tower. It has been a long time since I have seen him on the battlefield. The man is a coward," the king said with disdain.

"That may be, but he is also smart. The Jebusites have the best defensive position between here and Egypt. He does well enough simply by sending his troops to raid the passing caravans headed for the coastline. He doesn't need to take the risk of sending his army out against us, not yet. But he wants you dead as much as Achish does, believe me. He's biding his time, waiting for us and the Philistines to wear each other down. He's an evil man, too, judging from some of the stories that come from Jebus. Mutilations and child sacrifice, all kinds of disgusting things."

Saul looked at his general and smiled. That's why Abner was in charge. He didn't trust anyone and was always ready to fight. "You're right Abner. We need to keep improving. And we will. But ease your mind for tonight. I am confident David will bring us good word. Then we will feast and relax, if only for tonight. Try to enjoy it."

"I will, my lord."

"How has Ish-bosheth been faring, have you heard?" asked the king about his younger son.

"Well enough. He is not the natural leader or fighter that Jonathan is, but he seems to have earned the respect of his men. Elishama, of Ephraim, is with him as second in command. Elishama has been fighting his whole life, and he is older than me. His father died at Aphek, when the ark was lost."

"I know the man. He fought for me at Jabesh-gilead, when you were still too young to fight. I am glad he is with my son. Ish-bosheth needs the help," said the king.

"Anyone would benefit from having Elishama around." Abner looked up at the sky. It was cloudless and bright. The sun had passed the hottest part of the day, and a breeze had picked up, making the air feel somewhat cooler. The two men marched along silently for a few moments, and the general let his thoughts go. The plodding of his steps against the rocky, hard-packed dirt filled his ears. Looking ahead, he could see the main gate, manned with several soldiers, getting bigger with each step. Beyond the gate, he could see the road running east going downhill, toward the town of Nob, the city of the priests. Then he shut his eyes to dull the glare from the sun.

"Heard anything else?" Saul broke the silence.

Abner opened his eyes. "Yes, I have, and I've been meaning to tell you. Ish-bosheth received word of some Philistine troops near him. He took about three hundred soldiers and killed about half as many Philistines, west of Mizpah. He said it looked like they had been looking to plunder and burn some areas of Benjamin, but hadn't yet. They killed all of them. I had a runner tell me that earlier today."

"I don't like the way that sounds. Mizpah is farther east than they should be," said the king.

"I wonder if they may be targeting Benjamin because of you, to get you to react."

"Maybe."

"I also have some word from David that he came across a small squad of Jebusites in Lehi. This just happened yesterday. They seemed to be scouting out some of the Israelite villages in the area. David questioned them, but I don't think he found out anything useful."

"What did he do with them?"

"Killed them. Apparently they attempted some kind of suicidal attack, after they had been caught and questioned. I'm telling you, something isn't right with those people. And they are obviously planning something, for them to be scouting out Judah's towns." Abner was angry at the thought.

Saul began to respond, when suddenly a trumpet blast filled the air. A watchman at the top of the gate yelled down to Abner and the king, who now stood just inside the gate.

"Troops returning, my lord!"

"Is it David?" yelled Saul.

"I think so, my lord."

"It must be," said the general.

"Yes, my lord," the watchman continued. "I can see Judah's standard."

"Very well. Sound the victory call, for David has been victorious in his mission," said the king with a smile. The watchman sounded the trumpet again, several times, in short blasts. The two men looked down the road,

23

waiting for the troops to come into view. The road ran downhill, and the watchman's viewpoint, from nearly fifteen feet in the air, was obviously better than theirs. People began to gather around the gate, mostly women and children. With many of the soldiers away, there had been many more women in the camp than men. It took quite a while still, for the watchman could see a long way away. Abner decided to continue the conversation.

"So we have enemy troop movements both to the south and to the north of Gibeah, and both are well within a day's march. I can't believe they'd be working together, as much as they hate each other, but if they both moved on us at once, we'd fall. We can't defend an attack from them both."

Saul answered the general, "They won't attack at once. Neither Achish or Adonizedek trust the other, and they wouldn't work with each other if it meant the death of their people. The Jebusites haven't mobilized their full army in years, not since I first gained the throne. The Philistines don't have the ability to overrun us anymore. So long as we continue to protect our towns as we have been, we should be fine. Every time David or Jonathan are sent out, we gain more information about them. If anything is coming, we'll know."

Abner growled under his breath. The king was satisfied, and had no more interest in this discussion for now. Saul turned to some of the people who had gathered nearby and began to talk to them. He wanted his people to like him, and trust him. Some of the women started to sing and dance. Some brought out instruments, singing praises to God and praises to the king. Saul was pleased. His people were happy, and his favorite soldier was returning victorious. Abner turned back to the road. The breeze blew in through the gate, and the general closed his eyes again. For a few minutes the general just stood there and enjoyed it. Maybe he could just forget about things this evening and enjoy the meal. Suddenly a cheer went up. Coming up abruptly over the crest of the hill were David and his standard-bearer, followed by all of his men marching in two columns, making their way toward the gate. Saul stepped up next to Abner, grinning. David and his men were dirty, and though they must have been tired, they marched in with as much discipline as they had when they marched out days before. As they reached the gate, David spoke to a tall, muscular soldier with a dark beard and short dark hair that marched alongside him. The dark bearded soldier shouted for a halt. The troops came to a stop, and David approached the king. The singing had momentarily died down. Saul yelled out to David as he approached.

"Victorious, my son?"

"By the Lord we have run through our enemies! He is a shield to all who trust in Him!" David said for all to hear. Another cheer went up, and the singing resumed, now louder. Saul clapped David on the back enthusiastically. "I am glad you're back, David. We'll feast tonight, and you can tell us all you have done. Let your men get inside and clean up, and you as well, then we can get started."

"Yes, my lord."

Abner grabbed David's shoulder. "Good to see you made it back in one piece, boy."

The general smiled and let go of him. David turned back toward his troops, and the women began to sing a new song. "Saul has killed thousands of men, but David has killed tens of thousands." They sang it repeatedly, loudly for all to hear, and there was an air of excitement about the crowd. Abner turned to look at the king. Saul looked suddenly different. The smile he had moments ago was gone, and it was replaced with a very troubled look. The king listened to the song of the women, and his face seemed to harden. He and the general remained standing by as David marched his troops into the camp. By the time the troops had made it inside, Saul's face looked like a stone.

3

The sun hung low near the horizon. The sky blazed a beautiful reddish color as the setting sun's rays filled the air. David squinted to see the road in front of him. He and one of his captains led a hundred soldiers westward down from the central highlands of Israel's territory. The captain's name was Abishai, and he was a big, tough looking man, slightly taller than David with a thick black beard and shoulder length black hair. He carried a long spear and wore a short sword on his belt. He was around the same age as David but looked older, something in his face that gave the impression of hardness. Ahead of them lay the rolling hills and scattered woods that reached into Philistine and Amalekite territory. Long ago, God had granted all this land to Abraham and his descendants. Yet due to the Israelites' hardness of heart and lack of faith, they had failed to subdue all the area that had been given them. The majority of David's troops remained at the city of Zorah under the command of Joab, Abishai's brother and David's second in command. David was on a special mission for his king. Saul had graciously offered his daughter Michal to David in marriage. The king had earlier offered his eldest, Merab, to David, but the young man had no money for a dowry, and felt that his family was not honorable enough to be related to the king, so she was given to someone else. But Michal loved David greatly, and David also loved her. When Saul had offered her to David, the king had told him the only dowry needed was to fight the Lord's battles, and kill Philistines. "Kill one hundred of those pagans," the king had said, "and bring me their foreskins. That'll be dowry enough." David had happily agreed. Michal would be a good wife for him. Being the king's son-in-law may also improve the relationship David had with the king. Saul had grown increasingly disgruntled toward him in the last few months, though David couldn't figure out why. For several weeks now he and his men had traveled throughout the highlands of Judah and Simeon, looking for any encroaching Philistine troops. He had decided to double the king's order, and with another twenty or so foreskins he would have two hundred offerings for Saul. David was ready to finish the job.

So was Abishai. "This time tomorrow, we should have enough. Then we can head back to Gibeah and relax a few days," he said.

David agreed. "This time tomorrow, we should already be heading back. If that patrol leaves Ekron before dawn, then it won't be long after sunrise when they pass our position. We should be able to handle them easy enough. We'll be back at Zorah by nightfall."

"You've been to this spot before?"

"Yes. Abner took me on patrol there a few years ago. Judging by what we heard yesterday, it hasn't changed. There is a slight hill on both sides of the road that runs from Ekron to Gath, and there are trees that cover the area. It's a perfect spot for an ambush. We'll line up on both sides and catch them in the middle. It's not real far from Ekron's gates, so it should still be somewhat dark when they reach it."

"That Philistine yesterday was definitely telling the truth, although I'll give it to him, he held out for a while. Should've just spoke up, he'd have been better off."

"You seem to enjoy that kind of thing," said David with a grim look.

"It's got nothing to do with enjoyment. I'm good at making people talk, and he knew something we needed to know," Abishai said flatly.

"Right." David nodded curtly in agreement.

"So, we've got over one hundred and eighty foreskins, so even a small patrol will probably be enough." The captain started laughing to himself. "I'm sure Sibbechai won't mind clipping a few more foreskins for me. I sure as anything won't be doing it."

"Sibbechai is a very obedient soldier. I could use more like him."

"He's too soft."

"He's only soft in his speech, not his actions. He's never backed down from any assignment. He killed more against that Gittite company than any in his line. And he's never shown any insubordination."

"True. I am glad to have him," said Abishai, who chuckled again. Then he added, "Thankfully we hit that big company last week down near Lachish. That gave us almost all we needed."

"God sets all our paths, Abishai. That company would have undoubtedly caused destruction to some of Simeon's villages. I'm more thankful that we stopped those attacks than we got so many foreskins," said David.

"Right, God sets our paths. Everyone don't follow the paths He sets, though."

"No, everyone doesn't. But the Almighty's plans will be carried out, of that you can be sure."

Abishai grunted in agreement, and David continued. "Anyway, by God's oath this is Israel's land. Philistine troops have no right to it."

"We should chase every last one of them into the sea."

"That is what having a king and a standing army can do. Before Saul, the tribes failed to work together. Now that we are united, we can finish driving these heathens out of here. And the sooner the better. The longer we wait, the more their evil practices will separate us from God." Abishai smirked. David was an amazing fighter and a great battlefield commander, but sometimes he sounded more like a prophet.

The sun continued to descend toward the horizon. The troops marched on, kicking dust in the air with each step. It was rolling country. They marched down one hill and up another, then back down again. It was more down than up, however, as they left the highlands behind. The foliage also increased, with trees and undergrowth replacing the bushes and brambles that covered the higher ground. By the time the sun had set, they were marching across relatively flat ground. The road was clear and well kept, so even in the dark David had little trouble navigating it. Though there were no people or towns near, the troops marched in silence, in order to draw as little attention as possible.

Abishai had never traveled this path before. As the night wore on, he began to get impatient. He trusted David, but it was very hard to see. Trees lined the road. Above them, the night sky was clear and bright with stars, but nothing below the tree line could be seen. David knew of a road that branched off the main route and ran north, but it would be nearly impossible to see it in this light. As the hours passed, even David began to feel unsure. It had been a long march, and he could feel sweat dripping through his hair and beard. His beard had thickened since his encounter with Goliath, and he had filled out some in the shoulders and arms, too. Between his physique and the longsword sheathed on his hip, David was really starting to look like a war commander. But whether he looked like it or not, he had to find his way. He was looking for a huge landmark, and it would stand out against the night sky, but he could not quite remember how far it was. Finally, after what seemed an eternity, a huge object rose high above the tree line, blocking out the night sky.

"There. That's it," said David.

"What is that?" asked Abishai.

"The stone of Abel."

"It's huge. I've never seen it before."

"The stone is big, but most of what you can see is the hill it sits on. The stone is at the top. During the day, you can see this place from miles away," said David.

"So where do we go from here?" asked Abishai.

"There's a smaller road just on the other side of it that runs north. We'll follow that until we get close to Ekron."

David led them along the edge of the road until after they had passed the hill. Finding the road, they turned and headed north. They continued to march in silence, with the only sound that of the heavy footsteps of the troops, and the occasional grunt as the men bumped each other or stepped in a hole in the poor light. After about an hour, they came to an intersection with a larger road. It ran passed them on a slight diagonal, oriented roughly southwest to northeast. This was the road that ran directly from Ekron to Gath. David directed them toward the right, northeast toward Ekron, and the silent march continued. This road, too, was thickly lined with trees, and not much could be seen, even in the daylight. The road also weaved back and forth, and the land on both sides rose higher than the road, which further prevented visibility. Maybe half an hour had passed when the company began to see torchlights of a city, high above the tree line and off in the distance. It was now close to midnight, and the moon shone brightly. David led on until coming to a bend in the road, where steep hills covered in trees rose on each side. He uttered a low, "Halt", which was quietly echoed through the ranks. Abishai left David's side to gather several of his squad leaders to the front. The troops remained in formation, each facing outward except the men in the back who faced the rear, looking for any threats. After several minutes, Abishai along with ten soldiers clustered around David.

"This is it. Ekron is no more than a twenty minute march from here." David's voice was low, but stern and clear. He spoke with authority as he laid out the battle plan. "I want first and second platoon spread out here on the south side of the road. Keep everyone as on line with each other as you can, and close to the roadside. Third platoon will line up on the north side. Same thing, keep them close to the road. Who's got the archers?" A soldier raised his hand. "Give me five of your men. They'll stay here with me. You take the other five to the far end on the south side. Make sure no one from third platoon is lined up directly across from you. Now, once the entire patrol has passed by me, I'll have the archers with me fire on their rear. You," David pointed to the leader of the archers, "make sure to fire on their front but only if you have clear line of sight. I don't want to shoot any of our men on the other side. After the first volley, first and second platoons will charge and engage. Who's in charge of third?" Another soldier raised his hand, named Helez. "Wait until first and second has them engaged, then charge their rear. Any questions on the attack?" No one spoke up. "There shouldn't be more than fifty in this patrol. We've got more men and we're in a good spot. Stay disciplined and we'll be fine. We've got probably five or six hours until sunrise, so sleep in shifts until then. Everyone needs to be awake by sunrise. Make sure your men are drinking water, and eat if they have anything. It's been a long night. Any questions?"

Abishai spoke up. "You're going to be at the far end of formation?"

"Yes. I will make the call to start the attack. You will be at the center of first and second. I'll join you there after it starts. No one does a thing until I make the call." David looked again at the lead archer. "I'll call out when the firing starts. If you don't see or hear it start, don't shoot. Understand?"

"Yes sir," answered the archer.

"Very well. You men know what you're doing. That's why I brought you. As I've said, this is Israel's land, given to us by the Almighty. I want those foreskins. But I want the Philistines off our land more. That's what we're doing tonight. Be strong and courageous, for the Almighty is with us."

In unison the soldiers spoke up. "The Lord fights for Israel."

"Now go." David dismissed them, and they returned to the formation. Quietly, each squad leader gathered his men and went to find cover in their positions. Abishai followed, checking each platoon to make sure they were in the right spot. Only David remained where he was. He stood at a bend in the road. To his right, running almost due north, the road ran straight on toward the city lights, which could be seen a ways off. To his left, the road bent back to the west. From here, David would be the first to see the patrol. After a moment, five of the archers came walking up.

"There are five of us sir," said the first to arrive. His name was Abiezer and he looked excited, despite the long night.

"Good. Come with me." David led them into the tree line south of the road and set them into position. Coming back towards the middle of the road, David looked around to make sure all his men were set in. Seeing no one, he returned to the tree line, behind the archers. He took first watch, settling into a notch in the hillside that made for a seat. It felt good to be off his feet. He could hear the archers settling in as they all went to sleep.

"It's time sir." David awoke suddenly to Abiezer shaking him gently on the arm. "Sun will be up before long."

"Okay. I'm up." Abiezer returned to his position. David sat up, very sore. The ground that had felt so comfortable hours earlier after a long march now felt cold and hard. Somehow, he had ended up lying on his sword, sheathed at his side. Now his hip was killing him. David stood up and stretched. He drank from the skin of water attached to his belt. It was nice and cool, and felt good on his dry throat. He returned the skin to his belt and readjusted his gear, then stepped down toward the road. The archers were all up and ready. The sky above the tree line was starting to lighten, but everything below was still very dark. Along the edge of the road something seemed to be moving. After a moment, David recognized a familiar stride, and Abishai came walking up.

"Everyone's up and ready," the captain reported.

"Good. It'll probably be an hour or so, but make sure everyone stays put and keeps quiet."

"Those pig-eaters need to hurry up. It's cold out here," Abishai snorted.

"Yeah, I could use a little action too. Soon enough."

"Right. Let me go make sure all these women don't forget what we're doing," said the captain, referring to the troops. With that, he walked back toward his position. David walked back into the tree line past the archers, relieved himself, and returned to his uncomfortable piece of ground. He spoke quietly to the archers, giving some last minute instructions. The sky continued to lighten. It was quiet, except for the occasional chirping of a bird. The bright lights of the city, which had been so clear during the night, began to fade away, and then disappeared. Now, the far end of the road looked like a grainy mix of trees and hills which the gates of the city merely blended in to. After what seemed a long time, David noticed movement far off down the road near the city. He strained his eyes, but couldn't quite make it out. "Something's coming," he said to Abiezer, who was closest to him. Abiezer echoed it quietly to the other archers. David continued to watch. After several minutes, he could make out soldiers, marching in formation. "It's them. Pass the word down the line." David said. Abiezer told the other archers, who quietly passed the word down to the rest of the company. Still David sat and waited. As the soldiers marched closer, he could see the morning sunlight glinting off the bronze helmets worn by the troops. They were definitely Philistines. No other warriors in Israel's territory were so well equipped. They were also exceptionally trained. Soon David was able to distinguish two columns marching abreast of each other. The air felt tense to the young warrior, and his heart was pumping with adrenaline.

"Ready your bow, and wait for my command," David said to Abiezer.

"Yes sir," he replied. The Philistines were marching quickly. In a short time they had reached David and the archers, and continued on past them down the road. David counted twenty-five men per column, for a total of fifty. All soldiers, all wearing heavy armor and carrying swords and spears. This would not be easy. Philistines were never easy. The Israelite soldiers knew that. Every one of them crouched behind cover, tense and ready for action. David's heart was racing. Without taking his eyes off the Philistines, he sent one more silent prayer up to the Lord.

Almighty God, how great You are. Gird us with strength and courage. Make your servants as quick as deer and stronger than bronze. Protect your servants from these heathen. Help us to carry out Your will, that Your great name may be exalted among these uncircumcised men and glory be given to You only.

David took a deep breath. As the last soldier passed by, he reached forward and grabbed Abiezer's shoulder. *Here we go,* David thought. Then, with a loud voice, David shouted, "Israel!" Abiezer and the four with him loosed their arrows and shouted. On the far end, the five other archers followed suit only a split-second later. With the attack commenced, all the troops in the southern tree line rose and rushed forward, swords raised, shouting at the top of their lungs.

The Philistine troops, caught completely off guard, reacted perfectly. Though all the archers hit a man, not all got past the armor. In the rear, four of the five arrows dropped a Philistine. In the front, three of the five. Seeing their comrades go down, the Philistines called out to each other, "On the left! On the left!" Immediately, they all faced to their left and charged. They were superbly trained, and not one of them hesitated. Israel had the jump on them, and had twice their numbers, but the Philistines would not go down without a tough fight. The two lines clashed in fury. Abishai, directing the action from the middle, moved forward and met a tall Philistine hacking into his men. As the Philistine turned toward him, the captain took his spear and drove it through the Philistine's chest. Pulling out the spear, Abishai held it high and yelled out "Now Helez!" From the opposite tree line, Helez led third platoon into the fray. Several Philistines turned to their rear to meet the oncoming rush.

Meanwhile, David had fought his way toward the middle of the battle. Sword out, he slashed through one Philistine after another. He was an excellent fighter, and often did more damage than any of his troops. But today he had a test coming. Somehow, they must have recognized he was in command. As he reached the center, three of the uncircumcised heathen descended on him at once. David ducked one sword and blocked another, using all of his strength and agility to fend them off. The trio managed to back him away from the lines, pushing David toward the trees. Moving backward, David stumbled and went down to one knee. As he went down, the trio quickly encircled the young commander to finish him off. For the slightest moment, David looked up and saw a Philistine sword coming down to take his head. Suddenly, a big Israelite soldier came crashing forward, blocking the Philistine's sword and slamming bodily into him, knocking the Philistine to the ground. David leapt to his feet and took out the other two, bringing his sword down hard on the head of one and driving it completely through the chest of the other.

After taking out his Philistine, the big Israelite soldier turned around, and David recognized Sibbechai. David nodded his thanks, and the two turned back toward the battle. It had been only minutes since the arrows had been shot to start the attack, but the fight was nearly over. David spotted Abishai and jogged up next to him. The captain had stepped back from the line, trying to get a view of the whole scene. He shouted to the archers to set up security at the ends of the line, making sure there were no more Philistines coming. He also ordered several of his men that had finished fighting to check for live Philistines among the corpses and to gather the Israelite wounded. David reached him as the last Philistine fell.

"Well done, Abishai," David said.

"I should be saying that to you. You fared pretty well against three. If it had been two they wouldn't had a chance," said the captain with admiration.

"You should be saying that to Sibbechai. Without him I would've lost my head."

"He was lined up next to me when I saw you get pushed out. I grabbed him and we went for you, but he made it over there and I didn't." He pointed with his sword to a dead Philistine lying on his back with a spear pinning him to the ground. "He got in my way."

Nearly a third of the Israelite soldiers had suffered some type of injury, but only about a dozen were serious. No one had been killed, which was a first against the Philistines. Only a handful of Philistines had survived, and most were so badly injured the Israelites executed them in mercy. Only one remained without a serious injury. Abishai walked among the troops, assigning some to cut foreskins and others to tend the wounded, make liters for those who couldn't walk, and collect lost or enemy weapons. It all needed to be done quickly. They were in more danger now than before the fight, being so close to Ekron and the army that waited behind the city gates. Sibbechai, who was a big, barrel-chested man with a reddish brown beard, had found the lone unharmed Philistine. The big man took his weapons, tied his hands behind his back and brought him to David.

"Sir," Sibbechai said as he walked up.

"This is the only one?" David asked as he looked at the Philistine.

"Yes sir. He must be someone important, too. He was carrying this," Sibbechai handed David a scroll, rolled up and tied with a leather strap.

"Something important, I take it?" said David nonchalantly. The Philistine remained quiet. David unrolled it and gave it a long look. Meanwhile, Abishai walked up to see what was going on. After a moment David looked back at the Philistine. "Where were you taking this?" Again the Philistine refused to speak. Instead, Abishai spoke up.

"He's forgotten how to speak. Help him remember Sibbechai." The big soldier, who had been standing directly behind the Philistine, grabbed him by the shoulders and slammed him face down in the dirt. Then Sibbechai dropped his knee straight down, landing high on the Philistine's back, bringing all his weight behind it and smashing him into the ground. The uncircumcised soldier groaned and struggled, but to no avail. Abishai went down on one knee and looked the Philistine in the eye. "Listen here you wretch. You'll speak when you're asked or I'll cut out your godless tongue."

David stepped closer to the Philistine. "Tell me about this."

"What about it?" he answered, gritting in pain.

"Where are you taking it?"

"Nowhere. We always keep it with us so we know where not to go."

Abishai stood up. "What is it?" he asked. David handed the scroll to the captain. On it was a map of the central highlands of Israel's territory. It had posts of Saul's troops clearly marked, as well as the king's compound in Gibeah and those unwalled towns that were farther from the soldiers. More surprisingly, it had David's troops marked down at Gibeah, and had their recent movements written down. "He's lying." Abishai handed the map back to David. "Stretch out his right arm, Sibbechai." The big soldier leaned down and cut the ropes which had bound the Philistine. Then he pinned the left arm under his other knee and stretched out the right along the Philistine's body, palm down. Sibbechai was strong. The Philistine fought to hold his arm in, but was helpless. Abishai took his spear which he had retrieved and drove it through the Philistine's palm. The man screamed in pain and the captain pulled out the spear. "Don't lie to me, boy."

"Gath. It's going to Gath." The soldier wailed and tried to pull his hand back, but Sibbechai held it steady.

"I know the patrol's going to Gath. Who's the scroll going to?" David asked sternly.

"The king. The king is in Gath."

"Achish?"

"Yes. Achish." The soldier began to calm down some, still gritting his teeth from the pain.

David knelt down near the soldier's head. "Look at me." The Philistine looked up. "Why are my troops singled out on this?"

"Because, you're David. You killed Goliath. You embarrassed us. Now you're killing us. We want you dead." He spit in David's direction, but could not lift his head enough to reach him. Sibbechai let go of the soldier's hand just long enough to punch him in the back of the head, driving his face back into the dirt.

David stood up. "Who's in command at Ekron? Tell me his name."

The Philistine spit, trying to get the dirt out of his mouth. "I don't know."

"Stretch out his other arm," Abishai said to Sibbechai.

"Wait! Wait. His name is Abimelech," the Philistine cried out.

"Very well. Pick him up," ordered David. "Get someone to bind his hand." Sibbechai sat him up, and Abishai called to a nearby soldier, who came over and treated the Philistine's hand. David stuck the map in his belt and crossed his arms on his chest, waiting in silence. No one else spoke. When his hand was wrapped, David said, "Get him on his feet." Sibbechai obliged. "What's your name?"

"Ahuzzath."

"Alright, Ahuzzath, here's what you're going to do. You're going on to Gath. Achish wants to know what I'm doing, and you're going to tell him." David's eyes were bright with anger. "You tell him, all this land belongs to Israel. The Almighty God has given it to us. You tell him I'm going to drive every last one of you away from here, until all Israel's towns dwell in peace, and there are no more heathen to separate us from the Lord, and worship abominations on His land. You tell him that." David looked at Sibbechai. "Don't let him return to Ekron. Take him west down the road toward Gath. At midday you can let him go on alone, and come back to meet with us. If he gives you any trouble, kill him."

"Yes sir," answered Sibbechai. Then David pulled Abishai aside, away from the Philistine. "Pick one more to go with him. Have them meet us at the stone of Abel. We'll wait for them there."

"Got it. I'll send Elhanan," said the captain.

"And get every else ready to move."

"Yes sir." Abishai walked away to get the troops ready to leave as David gave Sibbechai some instructions. By now, all the work was nearly done. The captain found the other soldier to join Sibbechai on his journey and briefed him. A soldier approached him carrying a leather sack full of Philistine foreskins. As Abishai looked inside, the soldier gave him the count. Abishai called for the troops to assemble, and all but Sibbechai and Elhanan, who stood with the Philistine, gathered into formation. David stepped out in front to address them.

"I'll keep it short because we need to leave. Good job today. We cleared out a few more heathen from our Lord's land. A special thanks to Sibbechai, who kept me alive today." A cheer went up from the ranks. "Abishai, what's the count?"

"Forty-nine sir. No thanks to Sibbechai." Abishai looked at the big soldier with a grin. "Since he saved our commander's butt, he thought he didn't have to cut any." Sibbechai grinned, and several of the soldiers yelled out in appreciation.

David spoke again, "Forty-nine. We're done, men. Headed back to your wives and soft beds." More soldiers cheered. "At least for now. Time to move. Sibbechai and Elhanan, fall in with us until we leave this road. Abishai, get them moving."

"Forward men!" the captain called out, and the entire company started off westward, headed down the road they had travelled only hours before.

The midday sun beat down on Ahuzzath as he marched down the road. He was exhausted. He had been second in command on the patrol, and had been up early preparing for it. He had also taken a few tough blows in the fight, and that was before Sibbechai had gotten ahold of him.

His right hand was swollen and throbbing, and he had emptied his skin of water. It wasn't a long way to Gath, and if they hadn't met the Israelites, the patrol would have been there already. But he was moving slow, and he still had a few hours to go. It had only been minutes before that his escort had turned him loose. Looking back, Ahuzzath could still see the two Israelite soldiers crossing a hill on the east side of the road. They had treated him well enough after leaving David's company, probably just so he would be able to keep up a decent pace. They hadn't liked the trip any more than Ahuzzath did. This was well into Philistine territory, and if anyone had found them, they likely would have been killed. When the king found out that Ahuzzath was the only survivor, and that David had gotten some information out of him, he might be killed as well. He was not the bravest soldier in the Philistines' army. Ahuzzath was middle age, about average height and build, dark hair and a scanty beard. His father had been a high ranking soldier years ago, and later became an advisor to the king. Now his father was simply an old man, who did nothing but sit around and complain. Ahuzzath had been allowed to serve in some good positions thanks to his old man, but he had no relationship to Achish, the current ruler. The king may choose to have Ahuzzath beheaded. But that possibility didn't change what he had to do. Achish was waiting for that map, and would want to know what had happened to it. Losing the map wasn't completely Ahuzzath's fault, of course, but he was the only one left to take the punishment for it.

Ahuzzath was alone. The soldier plodded along, slowly making his way down the dusty road. The trees became much more sparse as he walked, and the ground was mostly flat. The Philistine capital of Gath lay almost due south of Ekron, both of them west of the central highlands of Israel. Farther west were the three other major Philistine cities of Ashdod, Askelon and Gaza, all of which were situated along the coast of the western sea. Achish ruled them all, and his home was Gath.

As the time passed Ahuzzath's steps continued to slow. After about two hours on his own, he started to see the outer wall of Gath in the distance. He could also see several of the tallest buildings rising above it. It had been a hard walk, but at the sight of the city he renewed his effort. He was not alone any more. Coming around a bend, he saw herdsmen driving their cattle in the opposite direction. There were several villages nearby, and during the day people went in and out of the city as they went about their business. It was the middle of the afternoon when he finally drew near the walls, and the gates stood wide open. As he approached, a group of women were coming out, carrying sacks full of food from the markets. A young boy also drove a pair of cattle out behind them. All of them gave him a curious look. Ahuzzath was nearly done in. His soldier's uniform was torn and soaked in sweat, his hand was bound with bloody rags, and he could barely walk. As he limped his way up to the gate, a pair of soldiers standing guard stepped out, looking at him with suspicion.

One spoke up. "Who are you?" Ahuzzath leaned over on his knees, trying to catch his breath. The soldiers just looked at him, saying nothing. Straightening up, Ahuzzath answered, "My name is Ahuzzath. I come from Ekron, sent from Abimelech with a message for the king. My patrol has been butchered by Israelites, and I need water. Please, do you have some water I can have?"

Still somewhat suspicious, the soldiers brought him just inside the gate and sat him down, leaning him against the wall. One of them gave him a full skin of water, which Ahuzzath drained quickly. After another few questions, one of the soldiers left to retrieve their superior, while the other returned to watch the gate. Ahuzzath, still exhausted and finally able to rest, began to doze against the wall. He was awakened after what seemed just a few minutes by a different soldier, about his age with a thick beard that was already turning gray. The man seemed to know him. He was given more water and some bread, then helped to his feet.

"Come with me, Ahuzzath."

"You know me?"

"My name's Sidqa. I served under your father years ago." The pair began walking into the city. He must have slept for quite a while, for the sun was much lower on the horizon and shone directly into their eyes as they walked. Sidqa led him towards the king's house, which was the tallest of the buildings, dead center of the city.

"Is he here?" Ahuzzath asked.

"Yes. He was expecting your patrol hours ago." Then Sidqa talked without looking at him. "You guys had a little more trouble then you could handle, did you?"

"Ambushed. Not two miles from Ekron, just after dawn."

"And they were Israelites?"

"Yes."

"What were they doing so close to Ekron?"

"Not sure." Even though the day was getting late, the city was busy. To reach the king's house, the pair had to maneuver through a packed market. There were stands selling crops from the local villages, smith's selling weapons and tools, and shepherd's selling their livestock. The sounds of men shouting and sheep bleating filled the air, as well as the great amount of dust kicked up by so many feet and hooves. As they made their way through, Ahuzzath drew quite a few stares, his ragged appearance standing out even among so many. On the other side of the market, they came in view of the doors to the king's great hall. A squad of soldiers stood outside, guarding the way. The pair walked right up to them. After a short explanation from Sidqa, one of the soldiers stepped inside, only to return again a few moments later and lead them through the doors. The hall was impressive. Though mostly empty at the moment, it was long and wide enough to seat several hundred. The ceilings were high and had colorful draperies hanging from them. The walls were largely unadorned, save for a handful of weapons displayed on them. At the far end was a group of men, standing about a raised platform upon which the king's throne sat. A pair of statues stood on each side of the king's platform. On the left, stood an image of Dagon, the head god of the Philistines. It had the body of a man, with fish scales covering its back and a skirt of scales covering its legs. It had a man's face, yet the top of its head had the eyes and mouth of a fish. On the other side stood an image of Baal, the son of Dagon and the god of fertility. It was seemingly unproportioned, with wide shoulders and a very thin waist and long legs. The head had a pair of horns rising from the forehead. Both statues were twice the height of a man. The soldier who brought them in escorted them down toward the king. As they reached the group, the king looked down at them. "Sidqa to speak with you, my lord," the soldier announced. Both Sidqa and Ahuzzath bowed in submission.

"This one looks like he has had a bad day, Sidqa," said the king as he looked down at Ahuzzath. Achish was around middle age, with a thick chest and large stomach. His beard was brown and bushy, and it covered a thick neck. All the better to hold up his heavy crown.

"Yes, my lord Achish," said Sidqa, straightening up. "His patrol was slaughtered as they left Ekron this morning. He brings a message from Abimelech."

"Who are you?" the king asked Ahuzzath.

"My lord, I am Ahuzzath, son of Naveh. I serve under Abimelech in Ekron."

"Son of Naveh, are you? They tell me he used to be quite the soldier. Now he's just an irritating old man. Always thinks he can tell me my business. If he weren't so old, I'd had his head some time ago," said the king dryly.

"Forgive him, my lord. He spent many years as an advisor, and I believe he still thinks he is one," said Ahuzzath.

Achish cared little for Naveh, and Ahuzzath wasn't showing much reason for the king to care about him either. "What message did Abimelech send for me?" he said, getting to the point.

"He had sent a map of King Saul's troop positions and movements, showing where they had encroached on your land. His famous warrior, David, the one who killed Goliath, has been especially busy searching out your territory recently." Ahuzzath spoke nervously.

"Yes, I heard much about this David. I've been told he patrols our borders looking for a reason to fight. Has Abimelech tracked him?"

"Yes, my lord. He hopes to find a place where David is weak enough to attack him."

"Has he?"

"I'm afraid not. David is a crafty commander, and his men are excellently trained. They do not often leave themselves in bad positions."

"So where's the map?" asked the king.

"Forgive me my lord. Our entire patrol was slaughtered, and the map was taken."

One of the men from the group that had been talking with Achish when they arrived now spoke up. "Apparently they all weren't slaughtered. You seem to have made it through alright." The man was stocky and serious looking, with a well-trimmed beard and the bearing of a high ranking soldier. "My king, you may want to ask how it is that he survived and no one else did," the man said, while looking at Ahuzzath.

"Good question Philcol. What about it, son of Naveh?"

Ahuzzath had known he would look dishonorably for appearing to have left his troop. Any good Philistine would have fought to the death in such a situation. But it was done. All he could do now was live up to it. "I was knocked down and taken prisoner, my lord. David was in command. When the map was found, he would not allow me to be returned to Ekron and had me brought here."

Philcol, the serious looking soldier, spoke up again. "Who carried the map?"

"I did." Ahuzzath hung his head.

"So you allowed yourself to be captured, then gave up the information that was supposed to be brought to the king, is that right?" Philcol looked steadily at Ahuzzath.

After a long pause, Ahuzzath answered. "Yes."

"So you marched straight to the king to receive your punishment?"

Ahuzzath lifted his head. "I know I deserve it. But I still have a message to deliver." He looked straight at the king. "David gave me a message for you. If any other Israelite had said this, I don't think I would have been alarmed. But after what he has already done, it scares me."

"This David is just some soldier. I dare say Goliath looked at him only as a boy, and let himself get caught off guard. You people think too highly of him," said Achish.

"My lord, I've never seen a man speak like he does. He seems to have such an authority about him."

The king, clearly irritated by Ahuzzath's reverence for the Israelite warrior, growled at him. "What did he say?"

"David says the god of Israel, who he calls the Almighty, has given the Israelites all of your land, and he's going to drive every Philistine off of it."

4

A breeze came in through the open window, sending a wave through the young woman's hair. She was tall and beautiful, with long flowing brown hair, and she wore a brown dress that came down to her feet. She stepped over to the opening and looked out. She stood gazing out of a second-story room in a stone house in Gibeah. No other buildings were two-storied, so she had an excellent view. Below, the north end of Saul's compound spread out before her. It was mostly other houses on this side, except for a stable built right up against the outer wall. Beyond the wall, she could see the highlands, full of rocky hills and sparse vegetation, reaching on as far as one could see. A knock at her door caused her to turn around.

"Come in."

A servant girl, who was only slightly younger, came in, carrying a stack of folded linen. "Clean blankets for you, Michal. They are very thick and will help keep both of you warm tonight. Not that you need it," she said with a slight smile. Michal almost blushed.

"Thank you, Bethulah."

Bethulah set the blankets on the bed and joined Michal at the window. "You have such a beautiful view here. I'm so glad you were able to bring me here with you. When I heard that the king was giving you to David, I worried I would be assigned somewhere else and wouldn't be able to see you much anymore."

"It's worked out perfectly. I am so glad you've been able to be here."

Suddenly a deep voice came from behind them. "Does anyone mind if an old man joins in?" The two girls turned to see the king standing in the doorway. Saul was quite tall, and he had to duck somewhat as he stepped through the doorway. "Good morning, Michal." Bethulah bowed her head and became quiet, but Michal walked right up to him.

"Hello father." She smiled and embraced him. "How are you feeling today?"

"I'm fine. You seem to be doing well." Despite her height, Saul was head and shoulders above her. He reached over and ran his hand through her hair. "My beautiful daughter."

"Thank you, father. I am well. I feel like nothing could make me feel happier today."

"That's good, my daughter. It does me good to know you are happy."

"Of course I am, father. You've given me a wonderful husband. We live in this beautiful place you have built, and I have my good friend here to keep me company." Michal spoke almost dreamily.

"Friends are important. They watch your back for you." Saul looked over at Bethulah. "Can you do that, Bethulah? Watch out for my daughter?"

The servant girl looked up with a shy smile. "Of course, my lord."

"Good. Prove you can and we'll keep you around awhile."

"Of course she will, father," laughed Michal, "she always takes care of me."

"I dare say I will have to do a good job taking care of the girl who will be a queen." Bethulah said smiling.

"So what is this, you are expecting to be a queen?" Saul asked, looking at Michal with an amused look on his face. Michal answered excitedly.

"Oh, David told me that years ago, Samuel anointed him, saying he would be a king someday. It must be how God works, that he has married into our family. He must be going to be your successor."

Saul's face began to cloud up. "David told you Samuel anointed him?"

Michal, sensing the change in her father's mood, suddenly became nervous. "Well, yes. Isn't that good news? The king's daughter has married the next king?" Bethulah became quiet again, lowering her head to keep from looking at the king. For a moment Saul didn't answer his daughter. He sat with furrowed eyebrows, seemingly deep in thought. Then he gave a forced smile. "I'm not sure Jonathan would think of it as good.

But David would make an excellent..." Saul paused for a moment before finishing his sentence, "ruler." The king turned and walked toward the door, then hesitated. He turned back to his daughter. "I would like to have David eat with me tonight. When he returns, have him clean up and come to my hall."

Michal's voice was shaky as she replied. "Of course father."

With that, the king stooped through the doorway and walked out. He continued down a set of stairs and then walked through the front doors into the noon-day sun. He was fuming. How could this be happening? Josheb had been waiting outside, and as Saul marched away from his daughter's house, the bodyguard fell into stride next to him. "What is it, my lord?" asked Josheb in his deep voice.

Saul gritted his teeth. "David."

"Was he there? I saw him leave for training this morning."

"No, he wasn't there." The king didn't offer any further explanation. Seeing Saul's temper aroused, Josheb decided not to ask any other questions. With Saul leading, the pair headed toward the training yard, which was close by. They could already hear the shouts as the troops engaged in mock battle. Coming around a building that served as barracks, they could see a group of Benjaminites, Jonathan's men, running through line drills. A column of twenty-five men, carrying weapons and shields, pushed forward against another column, acting the part of the enemy. The prince walked in and out among them, pointing out mistakes and shouting encouragement. They were the only group on the yard.

Josheb knew who the king was looking for. "David took a group of his to the archery range this morning. He's probably still there." There was a good deal of space on the training yard, but not enough for long bowshots. Outside the wall on the western side of the compound, a range had been set up which had nearly a half-mile of open space, plenty of room for archery training. The king kept silent, still visibly angry. For the next few minutes the pair stood and watched the soldiers. The advancing column slammed themselves into the opposition, shields first, and then dug their heels into the ground to push, driving the other soldiers backward. As the two lines pushed against each other, they struck at each other with wooden swords and blunted spears. Slowly, the opposition began to give way. One step at a time, they were being forced backward. After being driven back almost ten feet, Jonathan shouted for an end to the drill, and the victorious column cheered.

Saul snorted. "Let's go." He and Josheb turned away and began to leave. "When David brings his men back in, tell him to come eat with me in my hall, but not until sundown. No one else. Make sure Jonathan doesn't find out."

"Yes, my lord."

"Go tell the steward to prepare for us."

"Yes, my lord." With that, Josheb headed toward the common hall, which was a separate building from the king's private house. Saul headed for his home, walking quickly with his face toward the ground, his troubled brow betraying his dark thoughts.

The sun was already setting when David came walking up to the king's hall, casting long shadows across the ground. The compound appeared empty, with most everyone already inside for the evening. The hall's main entrance was a pair of large wooden doors, which were standing wide open, at the top of a handful of steps. No one could be seen inside, and it was dark, giving David an ominous feel. Typically, the king feasted earlier in the day. David had been in the hall late in the evening before, but always the steward and his servants were about. As he entered, a light shone from a room in the rear of the hall. It was a private room for the king and certain guests, and David had eaten in it before. The hall was full of several long tables, running the length of the room with benches on each side, made to seat approximately one hundred. The ceilings were low and the interior was completely undecorated. As David neared the private room, an older man, about the king's age, stepped to the doorway. He was slightly shorter than David, with a gray beard and a portly build. He smiled as he saw the young man. "Hello, David. The king's expecting you."

"Hello, Ziba. I was starting to think I was invited by mistake. There doesn't seem to be anyone here."

"The king gave the servants the evening off. Said he didn't need anything special tonight. So I had a meal made and set out. It'll just be the two of you."

David stepped into the room. There was a table, built to seat about a dozen, with benches alongside. Several plates of bread and meat, as well as a pitcher of wine were set out. Saul's private guard often used this room, and next to the wall were several sets of leather armor, and a handful of weapons, both swords and spears, were stacked against the back wall, away from the door to the main hall. There was another door on the back wall that led into several other rooms used for storage and feast preparations.

"Are the king's guards here?" David asked the steward.

"They were earlier, and must have left some things," replied Ziba, nodding toward the armor and weapons, "but as far as I know they've all left."

As they stood there, the back door of the room opened and Saul walked in. He didn't appear to be in the best of moods.

"Evening, men."

"Running late, my lord?" asked Ziba.

"I'm afraid so. I've had much to do this afternoon, which is why I asked you to come so late, David. Thank you for joining me."

"Of course, my lord." David bowed his head slightly as he answered the king.

Saul nodded and looked at the steward. "Ziba, if everything is ready, you may leave. I know it's late."

"Thank you, my lord. Everything is out, and it should be plenty for you both. Leave what's left until the morning, and I'll make sure it is cleaned up." With that, Ziba left through the back door, shutting it behind him. Saul sat down without speaking and grabbed a plate of food. David had a strange feeling that he couldn't shake, but he sat down and helped himself as well. The pair ate in silence. David noticed that Saul wasn't eating much, mostly just drinking wine and pushing food around his plate. David, however, ate quickly. It was a light meal and he finished it in only a few minutes. Then he sat back and looked at the king, whose plate was still almost full.

"Not hungry, my lord?" he asked.

"No, I'm not." Saul pushed the plate away, sat up straight and looked at David. "How are you and Michal getting along?"

"Very well, my lord. You have an amazing daughter, and she makes me very happy."

"Good." Saul went quiet again for a moment. He just sat staring at David, and slowly his face became more stern. David, feeling more uncomfortable by the minute, noticed that Saul had sat next to where the weapons were stacked against the wall. Wanting to break the silence, David spoke up. "My lord, have I done something to displease you?"

The king's answer came much harsher than David expected. "Well, let's see. You've taken the loyalty of my people, you've made yourself greater than your king, you've stolen the hearts of my children, and become the hero of Israel. What else? What else have you done to displease me?" The king was nearly shouting, his face red with anger and jealousy. David was caught completely off guard, and for a moment could not even respond. Saul glared at him, breathing heavily.

"My lord, I have not tried to make myself greater than any in your kingdom. I have only tried to do what is right, and best for Israel. I have only prospered because the Almighty has allowed me to-".

Saul cut him off. "Yes, the Lord fights for you! I know. He once fought for me. But He has deserted me, and chosen you! And now you will take my throne, and my family, and all I have!" Saul stood up, so quick and forceful that the whole table shook. David remained seated on the bench, unsure how to respond. Never had he seen the king like this. Saul's eyes burned with hate, and he stood still, breathing heavily, as if unable to move. Then suddenly he reached toward the back wall and grabbed a spear. In one smooth motion, the king hurled it toward David. The young warrior rolled to his right, barely getting his body below the table. The spear crashed into the wall behind him. He leapt to his feet just as Saul reached for another weapon.

David turned and bolted out the doorway into the hall. His footsteps echoed across the walls and ceiling as he sprinted toward the main doors, which still stood wide open. Passing through the doors, David leaped the steps in a single bound and sprinted across the open ground. As he reached the house of Ahijah the priest, which stood directly across from the king's hall, he stopped and turned around, leaning close to the wall for cover. David could barely comprehend what was happening. The king had just tried to kill him! His mind raced as he wondered what to do. Should he go back and try to talk with Saul? The king was acting irrationally, maybe David could calm him down. The young warrior was hidden from view of anyone inside the hall, but he could see the main doors. After he had waited for a few moments, Josheb appeared in the doorway wielding a sword, looking large and imposing. The big guard came out, followed by four other soldiers who also served as Saul's guards. So much for rationalizing with the king. They hadn't seen him, so quickly and quietly David went around the backside of the priest's house, then took off running across the compound, headed for his own. It was very dark outside by now, and the streets were empty. David made it to his house in a matter of minutes. He was in top shape, and was only slightly out of breath after the long sprint. He knew he had only a few minutes at the most before Josheb and the guards came for him. He ran through his front door, slammed it shut and pulled the bolt to. He continued on up the stairs to the bedroom, looking for his wife. She was sitting on the bed brushing her hair as he rushed into their bedroom. She looked up, surprised. "What's wrong?" she asked.

"I don't have any time. Your father tried to kill me, and his guards are coming for me. I have to get away from here."

"What?" she stood up from the bed, unable to say more. David grabbed her and held her tight. The pair stood almost eye to eye. "If I can, I'll come back for you," he said, looking deep in her eyes.

"David, no! Why would he want to kill you? Stay, it must be a mistake!" Michal was shocked.

"Can't. I have to go, or I'll be killed." David quickly looked around the room. He grabbed the blankets off the bed and began to roll them up like a rope. "I need your help. They'll be here in a moment. When they get here, try and stall them." The blankets were long and thick. David tied the two together, then tied one end to the bed.

"What are you doing?" Michal asked, incredulous.

"Escaping. They'll be coming in the front. I'm going out the back. I'll climb out as soon as they arrive, so I need you to stall them to give me more time."

"No! You can't leave! This has to be a misunderstanding!" Michal exploded in tears.

David cinched the knots on the blankets tight, then turned back to his wife. "Michal, your father is going to kill me. Why should you help him? I love you, and I need you. Please, help me." David leaned in and kissed her. The events of the evening, which had seemed so surreal up to that point, were temporarily forgotten to him as he embraced her. The feel of her skin and the smell of her hair completely took over his thoughts and he felt tears welling up in his eyes. David let himself be caught up in the moment, until he heard a loud banging coming from downstairs. He broke off the kiss. "They're here."

"David!" Josheb's booming voice could be heard from outside the front door. "David, come out! We have orders from the king!"

"Go, David. I'll talk to them." Michal said as she tried to choke back her tears. David tightened the blankets once more, threw one end out the window and started climbing. Michal headed downstairs, wiping her face as she went. Josheb was still banging loudly as she reached the door.

"What is it, sir?" Her voice was unsteady, and she didn't open the door.

"We need David, Michal. Your father needs him," the guard replied.

"He is sick, and cannot come out. He will have to see my father tomorrow."

"No, Michal, he is not. Send him out."

"Yes, Josheb, he is. Now leave, you can see him tomorrow." Michal left the front door and went back upstairs. David was gone. She grabbed some of his clothes and a pillow of goats hair and stuffed it under a sheet on the bed, then blew out a few of her candles, hoping it may pass for a sick man in the low light.

Outside, four of the guards stood lined up outside the door. Josheb had walked across the street, where he stood talking to another man in the shadow of the opposite building.

"What do you want us to do, my lord?" asked the big guard. Saul stood wrapped in a cloak with his head down, holding a spear in his right hand. A storm was approaching, and his cloak billowed in the wind. Josheb couldn't even see the king's face for the darkness. Saul answered in a low voice. "Break down the door. He's here, or has been. She's knows something is going on. Break it down, and find him."

The big guard nodded and walked back toward the house. "Stand aside." The other guards moved away from the door. It was a sturdy door, with a well-made bolt, but it was built to keep out bad weather and stray animals, not a man as strong as Josheb. For his size, he was surprisingly agile. He reared back and kicked the door right near the handle. It shook, but remained closed. A second time, he kicked at the same place. That time it cracked loudly. A third time, and a great snap was heard as the bolt broke in two and the door swung inward. With Josheb in the lead, the guards quickly moved inside the house and checked all the rooms on the ground floor. Finding no one, they headed upstairs. Michal stood in the doorway to the bedroom, almost shaking in fear and anger. She didn't even speak as Josheb brushed her out of the way. He immediately walked up to the bed and pulled the sheet off, revealing the bundle that was meant to be David. Looking down, he saw the blankets tied together, leading out the window. The big guard stepped over to the window to look. "He's gone." Josheb turned to Michal. "Where is he going?"

Tears streamed down her face, but she was not sobbing in sorrow as she was earlier. "I don't know. But I hope he comes back and kills you."

The sound of heavy footsteps could be heard climbing the stairs. After a moment, the king appeared in the doorway, stooping slightly to come in. He still carried the spear. Saul looked around, seeing the bed and the blankets. Then he looked at his daughter. "Michal." The king spoke gravely. "You have betrayed me."

She shouted at him, full of anger. "Father, how could you? You have betrayed me! You are trying to kill my husband!"

"David has threatened my life, and plans to take my throne by force. I am doing what I must." Saul acted strangely calm.

"You're lying! He would never do such a thing! You're lying!" Michal lunged at him, trying to beat him with her hands. With his empty hand, the king struck her with the back of his fist. Michal fell to the ground.

"Take her to my home for the evening, and keep her there. Tomorrow she will go to her brother's," Saul commanded. Josheb lifted her up on her feet. The king looked to his big guard. "See that she isn't hurt." Josheb handed her off to the other guards and turned to wait for the king. Saul walked to the window and looked out into the dark night. He pulled the blanket rope all the way up and stood with the end in his hand, looking at it thoughtfully. After a moment, he let it fall. Then the king spoke softly, almost to himself. "Let the hunt begin."

David hit the ground hard, rolling forward and leaping to his feet immediately. The blanket rope had been a good deal shorter than it needed to be, and he had dropped the rest of the way from the window.

Without looking back, David sprinted away from his home and headed toward the northern wall. There was no way he would make it out the gate, and if he stayed inside the compound Saul would have his head. It was very dark out, especially in the shadow of all the houses, and though the distance wasn't very far, it took David much longer than he would have liked. He was moving somewhat carelessly in his haste, and he managed to run through a few laundry lines and step in a couple of pots as he ran through the compound. David was scared and very unsure. His entire world seemed to be turning upside down. As he neared the wall, he could see the night sky above it, dark and foreboding. The wind had picked up considerably, and he could smell the rain coming. The wall was nearly twelve feet high, much too high for David to reach without assistance. After reaching the wall, David moved right along the base of it. In only a minute or so he found his destination, a stable built right along the wall. He could hear the animals moving about inside, nervous with the coming storm. It had a roof made of wood covered in straw, and it was not very high, only a foot or so out of his reach. David jumped and grabbed ahold of the edge, then pulled himself up until his belly rested on the roof. With his legs hanging down, he shimmied himself up until his feet were under him. Once he was standing he was able to see over the wall by nearly a foot. He placed his hands on the cold stone and hopped up, placing his knees on the wall, then sliding them out and sitting down. On the other side, David could barely make out the ground below. It was a long way down, and he knew it to be very rocky out here. David turned back to look once more, taking in the compound that he had come to call home. It was a little easier to see up above the shadows of the buildings. His own house stood out, taller than most of the others. David could even make out a light in the window he had escaped from. *Oh Lord,* he thought, *what is happening?* David turned back to his front, looking down at the dark ground below. *Here goes nothing.* He grabbed the edge of the wall and lowered himself until his arms were fully extended, to lessen the distance of the fall. Then he let go. By luck or providence, he plopped harmlessly in some deep sand. He was back on his feet at once. David couldn't see very far in front of him, but he knew what was there. A large open space spread out in front for several hundred yards before a huge outcrop of boulders, known as the stone of Ezel, which jutted up from the ground.

Beyond that, the rocky hills of the central highlands ran off to the north. After dusting himself off, David took off at a jog straight across the open area headed for the hills. The rain began to fall, gently at first, and the sky thundered loudly. The field was rocky and uneven, but David crossed it quickly. As he reached the base of the hills, the boulders rose up in front of him. David ran behind them and knelt down. Though it was night, and no one from the compound could see him so far away, he felt safer hiding behind them than being out in the open. The rain began to fall harder. He wasn't sure what to do, and felt lost. He needed the Lord. David looked up to heaven and prayed.

Oh Lord, hear me. Oh great God, I need You. My life has been threatened by my enemies, who are strong. There are many who hate me wrongfully, and they render evil as good. I have tried to follow in Your ways, oh God, and they hate me for it. Do not forsake me, Lord. Protect my wife. Calm the king's madness, and soften his heart on my behalf, for I have not wronged him. I know all things are in Your mighty hands, oh God. Make haste to help me, Lord of my salvation.

David stood up, resolved now of what he should do. Farther to the north, through the hills, was the town of Ramah. It was the home of Samuel the prophet. He was the only man in Israel Saul feared, and would listen to. David would go to Samuel. The young warrior set out across the hills in the stormy night. He was weaponless, and had no food or supplies. David had nothing to carry other than a trust in his God.

5

"Where is the son of Jesse?" the king asked, looking sternly across the table at his oldest son. They sat in the king's hall, feasting for the new moon. Saul sat at the back of the large hall, at the end of a long table with his back to the wall. His spear, which had not left his side since the incident with David, was leaning against the table by his right hand. Abner and Ahijah the priest sat on either side of the king. Jonathan, his brother Ish-bosheth, and his sister Merab all sat across the table from him. Many of the top men in the king's service, as well as their families, were also present, nearly filling the hall to capacity. His sister Michal was absent. She had been moved out of her house and was living with their brother Ish-bosheth. Michal had stayed at his home today, being in no mood to attend the feast. Jonathan looked at his father, thoughtfully considering the question. David had been many places. Only two days ago, the young warrior had found Jonathan and his troops as they were returning to Gibeah. Jonathan had been conducting routine patrols throughout Benjamin's territory when David approached him outside the town of Hazor. He told the prince what the king had done, and how he had escaped to Samuel the prophet in Ramah. The king had followed him there, bringing his guards to arrest David, but had been thwarted when the Almighty had intervened. David claimed that Saul himself had been overcome by the Spirit of God, and had returned to his home empty-handed. Jonathan had not known any of this at the time. Strange, for normally the king would send out word to him in this kind of situation. David wanted to know why the king wanted him dead, and the prince had not been able to answer him. Like Michal, he thought for sure there must be some misunderstanding. Jonathan agreed to take up the matter with his father and bring an answer to him. He had yet to mention it to his father, but David's absence had not gone unnoticed to the king. Saul stared at his son as he waited for an answer.

"He asked leave of me to go to Bethlehem. He said his older brother had told him to join the family there for the yearly sacrifice. I told him to go." Jonathan watched his father's face for his reaction.

Saul's face grew tight. "Did you?" The king glared at his son. "What gives you the right to give David leave? Only Abner or myself have that right."

"My apologies, father. It won't happen again."

"No, it won't." The hall was loud, full of noisy conversation, but no one spoke at the king's end of the table. The king drained his cup of wine and poured himself another. An uneasy silence hung over the small group. Even Abner, who seldom allowed the moods of others to affect him, seemed uncomfortable. After finishing his food, the general asked both Jonathan and Ish-bosheth how well their men were faring and the state of their training and readiness. The king's sons gave short answers and returned to their meal. Saul finished his meal, then stood up and grabbed his spear.

"Thank you all for joining me, but I have business to attend to. Jonathan, come with me. I must talk with you."

"Yes father." Jonathan wasn't finished eating, but he rose from the table anyway. Saul gulped down the rest of his wine, grabbed his spear and led the prince into the private room where he had eaten with David less than a week before. They came in to find the steward giving orders to a pair of servants. All three bowed their heads as the king came in.

"Ziba, take them somewhere else. I have need of this room. And bring me some wine."

"Yes, my lord." The trio headed into the back rooms, and Saul shut the door to the main hall. A moment later Ziba brought a pitcher of wine and set it on the table, along with a pair of cups. Saul grabbed the pitcher and filled both cups. He took one and handed the other to his son.

"Drink it."

Jonathan took a sip.

"All of it, boy."

Jonathan swallowed it down. When the king went to pour him more, Jonathan turned the cup upside down. "I don't want anymore."

Saul's face was becoming flushed. "Who are you to tell me what you want? Am I not your father, and your king? I suppose you will also tell me you don't want my throne when I'm gone. That's why you're helping David, is it not, so he will be the king?"

"Father, I am not helping David become king. He thinks you are trying to kill him. After seeing you today, I think I might believe him. How can you betray innocent blood? David has done nothing deserving of death." Jonathan spoke calmly, but he could feel his temper rising. The king's temper was also rising, but he was not speaking calmly.

"You foolish, rebellious boy! Don't you know you will never become king as long as the son of Jesse lives? He will take my throne, and he and his sons will rule instead of you. I am only trying to end this threat to my kingdom. Now send him to me, and he will surely die."

Jonathan stood up, angry. "I will not help you kill David, and bring this guilt on my head. David is no threat to Israel, he saved Israel. I remember, if you do not, what you were planning to do before he showed up and volunteered to fight the giant. I saw you sign the scroll submitting to Philistine rule."

Saul leapt to his feet, shouting. "Insolent boy! I should have you beaten!"

Now Jonathan had lost his cool. "Beaten for what? Honesty? For telling you how poor of a king you have become? That a shepherd boy deserves to rule more than you?"

Saul was in a fury. He roared, raised his spear and swung it with both hands, as one swings an axe. Jonathan raised his arms and managed to block the shaft, but the force with which it came knocked him flat on the ground. Saul bellowed in anger, and threw his spear on the ground. "You have no loyalty!" yelled the king. "You and your sister, you have both betrayed me!"

The pair's scuffle had not gone unheard. The door to the main hall swung open and Abner stepped in. The look on the general's face revealed his shock. Ish-bosheth then appeared in the doorway behind him. Without a word, the general strode over and picked Jonathan up off the floor, while the king stood and looked on. The prince had a nice gash on the back of his head from where it had hit the floor, and he appeared to be in pain in both his arms. Abner sat the prince at the table and looked at the king.

"My lord, he needs to be treated."

"Then take him to be treated," replied the king through clenched teeth.

"And then?" asked the general.

"Then nothing. I'm sure the prince will do as he pleases." The king leaned over and picked up his spear from the ground. "I'm retiring for the evening. You may dismiss the others when they have finished Abner. And make sure Ziba cleans up."

"Yes, my lord." The king left through the back door and Abner turned to Ish-bosheth. "Jonathan will stay in here. Get some clothes to bind his head with, and tell Ahijah to come look him over."

"I'm alright," said Jonathan, wincing a little.

"You will be, I'm sure," said the general. "But someone smarter than me ought to check you out, and I'm not parading a beaten prince around outside. No need for that."

The boy pulled his arrow to the rear, keeping tension on the bowstring as he carefully eyed his target, a dummy made of sandbags several hundred feet away. Holding his breath, he released the arrow. It flew rapidly across the range toward the dummy, missing it to the right by several feet and smacked into the rocks behind it.

"Remember to breathe. Holding your breath affects your accuracy. Breathe normally, and try to release after you exhale." Jonathan stood behind the youth, watching his technique. The boy was called Ittai. He was fourteen years old, the son of a Benjaminite soldier named Ribai. Jonathan had taken a liking to him, and occasionally took some time to train him with sword or bow. They stood in the middle of the archery range outside the compound to the west, facing northward into the rocky hills. It was just the two of them this morning. His head still sore from his encounter with the king the night before, Jonathan had given his troops the morning off. They deserved it anyway. They had only returned to the compound three days ago, and would be off again within a week.

"Shoot another."

"Yes my lord," answered the boy. Ittai notched another arrow on the string, drew it back and aimed in, squinting in the morning sun. His chest rose and fell several times as he tried to follow Jonathan's instructions. Finally, as he exhaled he released. The arrow flew across the range, this time sinking deep into the middle of the dummy with a loud thud. Ittai turned around with a smile.

"Good shot. See what happens when you do what I tell you?" remarked the prince with a smile.

"I always try to follow your instructions," said Ittai sheepishly.

"I know. You're a good listener. I think that's enough for today. Head on back in the gate. I'm sure your father has some work for you to do."

"Should I go retrieve the arrows?" asked the youth.

"No. I want to check out the targets anyway. I'll get them," answered the prince.

"Yes my lord. Thank you." With that, Ittai took off for the compound at a brisk jog. Jonathan picked up a small sack that he had brought with him and walked out toward the line of dummies that stood at the edge of the range. Reaching them, he strode down the line, checking to see which ones needed replacing. After a quick check, he turned just in time to see Ittai disappear behind the wall as the youth rounded the south side of the compound toward the gate. The prince picked up the handful of arrows on the ground and started off toward a large group of boulders at the base of the hills, still carrying the sack. As he walked, he kept an eye on the compound, scanning the outside of the walls to make sure no one was watching. A watch on the wall was typically only kept at night, and there should be no reason for anyone else to be climbing the wall to look over. As Jonathan drew near the group of boulders, he whistled loudly. Another whistle answered him, and the prince walked around to the rear of the boulders from where it came. David stood there, looking raggedy and worn out. He bowed his head as the prince approached.

"My lord."

Jonathan walked up and put his hands on David's shoulders. "Hello, my brother."

"What did the king say?" he asked, with a tone suggesting he knew the answer. Jonathan removed the head scarf he had been wearing to cover the bandage underneath. It was wrapped around his entire head, with a thick bandage on the back where the gash was. The dressing was as much for keeping the sand out than anything, but it still looked bad.

"The conversation didn't go well," he said with a slight smile.

David's eyes widened. "The king did that to you?"

"He knocked me on the floor with that confounded spear. He takes it with him everywhere, at least since I've been here and probably since he flung it at you."

"Your father is not right, Jonathan. Something is stirring him up, making him mad. I fear for him."

"He has never acted that way toward me, that's for sure. But I don't fear for him. He's the king, he has an army to back him up. Even if he goes completely mad, Abner will still serve him. The man is loyal to a fault. No, I fear for you. My father will kill you if he can." Jonathan handed the sack he had brought to David. "Here's a few loaves of bread, some cheeses and two skins of water. It's not much, but it's all I could bring without arousing suspicion. When did you last eat?"

"Yesterday. Thank you, a little beats nothing," said David as he took the sack.

"Where will you go?"

"East. I can't go back to Samuel. Your father will probably look there first. If I go back to Judah, I might put my family in danger. West is Philistine territory. So I'll go east, and pray the Lord reveals what I should do next."

"And if He doesn't?"

David sighed as he looked Jonathan in the eye. "He will. God is faithful."

Jonathan reached out and grabbed David's shoulder. "You have such a great faith, my brother. I can see why the Almighty has chosen you over my father. You will be king. Promise me you will show kindness to my family when you are on the throne. Do not cut them off from Israel because of my father."

"No Jonathan, I would not for all Israel destroy your family. The Lord do so, and even much more to me, if I cut off your family."

The prince reached out his other arm and hugged him, clapping David firmly on the back. David reciprocated, wondering when it might be that he would see his friend again, if ever. They broke off the hug and each stepped back.

"You may find an ally in the king of Moab," said Jonathan as he replaced the scarf on his head. "He is against my father, and might see helping you as hurting him. Every man in the region has heard of you, how you have killed the giant and chased the Philistines out of the hill country. The Moabites may welcome you to fight for them."

"I have never fought against Moab."

"Another reason he might be willing to help."

"Thank you Jonathan. I am in your debt."

Jonathan smiled. "All Israel is in yours. I must be getting back now. Be safe my brother, and may the Almighty be with you." Jonathan slapped David on the shoulder once more, then walked back around to the front of the boulders. The prince looked across the field at the compound and saw no one. With long strides he marched back for the gate. David watched his friend go as he crossed the field. Finally, with a heavy heart, David turned and headed away through the hills.

The road heading east out of Gibeah ran almost completely downhill as it wound its way out of the hills toward the coast of the sea of Arabah. The view of the road from Saul's main gate was excellent. On a clear day one could see most of the way to the town of Nob, which was just under ten miles away. Nob was the city of the priests, home to the tabernacle of the Lord and the high priest of all of Israel. Shortly after leaving Jonathan, David had decided that would be his first destination. Unfortunately, what would have been an easy route was unavailable to him. David couldn't risk being seen from the compound or running into anyone who might recognize him on the road, so he had to make a long swoop to the north through the hills. There were no level roads there, and the footpaths were rocky and uneven, so the going was slow. After he was far enough from Gibeah to feel safe, he began descending out of the hills to the east. The descent offered no paths at all, and David had to carefully pick his way down. He had only stopped to rest once during the afternoon, and by the time the ground began to level out, the sun was already setting. David was tired and hungry, and his feet were sore. He found a comfortable spot among some boulders out of the wind and settled in. He ate the remainder of the food Jonathan had given him and laid down to rest. Unfortunately, it was not a restful night. The wind picked up and the temperature dropped, and David huddled inside his clothes trying to keep warm. Around midnight, the wind died down, but as soon as he began feeling a little better, David heard some kind of beast growling nearby. Though it was not very safe, David was in about the safest place around, so he kept quiet and stayed close to the ground, hiding behind the big rocks. Another beast approached, and David recognized the roaring of lions as the two predators fought with each other. He laid on the ground and shivered in fear for what seemed hours, until the noises disappeared. At long last, David fell asleep, only to be awakened a short time later by the sunrise.

David was exhausted, his face downcast. While listening to the beasts in the night, he had prayed earnestly to the Lord out of fear. Now he could hardly bring himself to do so. He doubted he would be able to continue this. He was so close to Saul's grasp, and he had no food or weapons, and no one to help him. Saul had an entire army, and all the weapons he needed. But he had no choice. David had to push on, so he set out in the general direction of Nob. He needed to hear from the Lord. He needed some encouragement. After a short ways, he came upon the carcass of a deer, which must have been the cause for the lions' midnight dispute. It was mostly eaten, and very close to the rocks where he had been hiding. Amazing that the beasts hadn't found him.

David kept on, slow and steady. He was much more tired today, but he was out of the hills and the march was much easier. It took only a few hours before he was within sight of Nob. As he drew near, he could see the outer wall and even some tents of the city standing out against the flat terrain. He could also see the road that led back to Gibeah. David made his way over to it. He didn't want to give the impression anything was wrong, if the priests didn't know Saul was after him already. He had woken up with the first light of day, and it was still well before noon by the time David walked up to the town. It was relatively small. Only priests and Levites lived here, accompanied by their families. When their service to the Lord was through, each man would take his family back to his prior home. Nob had been established after the Philistines destroyed the city of Shiloh and captured the ark of the Lord. There were no buildings, only tents. The prophet Samuel claimed that since the ark of the Lord abode in a tent, those who served the Lord could do so as well. The wall was not nearly as high as the one at Gibeah, slightly less than ten feet. The gate stood wide open, manned by a Levite guard wearing a short sword. He spoke up as David approached.

"Who are you, and what business do you have here?"

"I am a servant of the king. He has sent me here on an errand to the high priest," answered David.

"Another servant of the king. What is the errand?" David was dirty and disheveled from his journey, and the guard eyed him suspiciously.

"It is privileged information, I am afraid. I cannot share it with you."

"You don't look like much of a king's servant. Perhaps you are lying."

"I have no weapons, and Ahimelech knows me. He can vouch for me." David held his arms out to his side, palms up, allowing the guard to see he was unarmed. The guard stepped forward and gave David a quick search. Satisfied, he stepped inside the gate and waved another guard over.

"He says he knows the high priest. Take him to Ahimelech. If he knows him, he can stay. If not bring him back to me."

The other guard agreed and led David through the gate and back into the tent city. Just inside the gate was a large open space like a pasture, used for the sacrificial herds. At the moment, a small herd of cattle and a group of sheep intermingled among each other while they grazed. A pair of Levite shepherds wandered in and out through the animals, inspecting them for blemishes. At the far end of the livestock, away from the gate, was another shepherd. He stood still, leaning on his staff, watching the Levites work. He looked over as David and the guard passed by, staring intently at the young warrior. David recognized the man, but couldn't remember from where, nor did he recall the man's name. An eerie feeling passed over him as they walked away. They reached several rows of tents, and began to weave their way through them until coming out into another open space. The open area was surrounded on all sides by rows of tents, three rows of ten, on all four sides. In the middle stood the tabernacle of the Lord. It was enclosed in a short wall made of wood, about eight feet high, with one gate facing east. The tabernacle itself stood higher than the wall, and what could be seen of it was intricately colored linens of blue, purple and scarlet. The guard led David around to the gate. Outside of it stood two men talking, one of them an older man with a gray head and beard, the other a younger man of much the same look and build with a brown hair and beard. Both were dressed in priestly garments. As David and the guard approached, they broke off their conversation and turned to look at them. The younger priest spoke first.

"David? You look like you've had a rough night. What brings you to Nob?"

"It was a rough night, Abiathar." David smiled. The high priest's son was a friend of his. "I have an errand to your father." He looked at Ahimelech. "You look well, my lord."

The guard turned to the high priest. "My lord, it seems you know him. May I leave him with you?"

"Of course. This is the king's son-in-law. He will do no harm here," replied Ahimelech.

"Very good, my lord." The guard bowed his head slightly and walked away, off to another duty. The high priest looked at David. He seemed somewhat concerned.

"Did you come with the Edomite?" he asked.

"The Edomite?" asked David quizzically.

"Doeg, Saul's shepherd. He brought a herd this morning."

Ah, thought David, *that's who was staring at me*. He had met Doeg before. He was definitely a king's man. He was also known to be the type of man who would do anything to raise his own lot in life. "No my lord, I didn't come with him."

"You came alone?" Ahimelech's concern stayed with him.

"Yes, my lord."

"We've had no word of your coming." The high priest looked David right in the eyes. "Does the king know you are here?"

Suddenly David realized he had made a huge mistake. Ahimelech knew that David and the king were at odds. It had been more than a week since Saul's attempt on David's life, and Saul may have been planning it much longer. The high priest was an important man, and often knew much about the happenings of Israel. David had been planning to ask Ahimelech to inquire of the Lord for him, but he couldn't do that now. Ahimelech was a godly man, and would very likely do it for David even knowing the circumstances. But with Doeg nearby watching, word of the high priest's help would surely come to the king. That would put Ahimelech at risk. David couldn't do that.

"Yes, my lord," David answered, after a long pause. "The king has sent me on an urgent matter, which I am not at liberty to discuss. However, the errand required much haste, and I was unable to collect food or weapons before departing. Have you anything here I may receive from you?"

Abiathar answered him. "We have only the shewbread which has been removed from the Presence."

The high priest stood quiet for a moment, thinking. Then he sighed, and the concern seemed to leave his face. "David may have it, as long as you have not been made unclean, from women or otherwise," said the high priest.

"I have not been made unclean, my lord. The Lord's soldiers are holy even when the mission itself is not."

"Abiathar, go and prepare a small sack of shewbread and a few skins of water and bring it to David. Do it quickly." His son nodded and trotted off to obey. Ahimelech turned back to David. "What else do you need, my son?"

"Do you have any weapons here?"

The high priest nodded. "I have one, that I think will work. Come with me." He led David toward a tent on the east side of the tabernacle. Outside stood a pair of Levites, armed with swords. They bowed their heads slightly as the high priest approached. Ahimelech and David ducked through the doorway and stepped into the tent. There was little inside. There was a rug on the floor and a pair of chests on it. There was also a wooden post, about a man's height, which had a crossbeam at the top where the ephod of the high priest was hanging by the shoulder straps. It was richly ornamented, with a breastplate that had twelve precious stones attached by chains of gold. But that was not the reason the priest had brought him inside. Ahimelech motioned for David to look. A sword laid behind it, but not just any sword. This was a huge longsword, bigger than any sword in the Israelite army. David recognized it immediately.

"You have used this before. Do you remember?"

David stepped over and grabbed the sword by its hilt, picking it up. He unsheathed it and held it out with both hands. A ray of sunlight from the doorway caught the blade, and it shined brightly in the dark tent.

"I remember. This is the sword of Goliath."

Ahimelech put his hand on David's shoulder, and looked at him intensely. "Remember how the Almighty fought for you that day. He saved Israel through your hand. You are His faithful servant, and He will not forsake you. You have hard times coming ahead, I know. Trust in Him, and He will see you through it. I know Samuel anointed you king. The Lord has said you will be king, and you will be. His word is true."

6

The air was hot and still. The sun shone brightly down on the terrace, and Achish was sweating. The Philistine king was thirsty. That could be remedied.

"You there, bring us out some wine," he called to a servant boy standing by. The king and his head general, Philcol, stood on the terrace that was outside the king's private chambers above the great hall. The pair looked down on the city of Gath. To their left, east toward the main gate, they could see the market stretching out, full of people and livestock moving about. A foul stench rose up from the market, which the two men could smell. To their front stood the temple of Dagon, which blocked out the remainder of the city in that direction due to its height. The boy returned quickly carrying a pitcher and two glasses, which he filled and handed to each man.

"Thank you, boy. Leave the pitcher and be off," said the king. The boy set the pitcher on a small table and departed, closing the doors to the room behind him. "So Philcol," said the king between gulps of wine, "tell me what you've heard."

The general sipped his glass. "Well, you've heard Saul cast out his great warrior, this David. It's been over a month since it happened, from what I hear. Saul's house must be in disarray. Supposedly his son helped David escape, and the army is probably divided, as popular as David seems to be."

"Amazing how word travels. Saul probably went to great effort to keep from spreading such unpopular news as that. Yet here we are, nearly a week's march away in a city of his enemies, talking about it." Achish grinned.

"True, my lord. It makes me wonder how much of our news is heard over there." The general grimaced at the thought.

"Hopefully none."

"Hopefully. So, my lord, if you are thinking you want to attack Israel, the time is right."

The king's grin turned to a frown. "It drives me mad thinking that we have not been able to overcome such an insect like Saul. He has a mere fraction of our men, and a decade ago they weren't even armed. They fought with farm tools and sticks. Yet somehow they have resisted us, and grown stronger. Those arrogant fools with their one god. How I wish them destroyed."

"It burns me as much as yourself, my lord," said the general. "I fought against Saul at Michmash just after he became king. He killed many of us in those days. His son killed twenty of my men at one time, almost single-handedly. I've hated them ever since. Right now they are unsteady. It is as good a time as any to organize a campaign against them."

A loud knock on the doors made them turn around. Achish barked for them to come in, and one of the king's guards hurried in. He had a look of disbelief on his face. "My lord," he bowed his head, "David the Israelite has come to offer you his service."

"What?" The king looked at the general. Philcol had a stern look on his face, as though he had heard a bad joke. "Say that again soldier. Who is here to offer me service?"

"My lord, he claims to be David, who killed Goliath."

"That boy must have stones of brass to show up here. Either that or he's mad," remarked Philcol.

Achish sat quiet for a moment, thinking. "Did he come alone?" asked the king.

"Yes, my lord."

"Where is he?"

"He is in the hall, my lord."

"David is quite the fighter, so I hear. Better than any we've had here since Goliath."

"Should I have him brought up here?"

"No. We will come down to him. If he is to swear me loyalty, I would be on the throne."

The general was not convinced. "Perhaps this is a ploy. This may have all been a ploy, the whole story of his break with Saul. He might mean to kill you."

"Perhaps. I could use a famous warrior like David though, and I'm sure he knows much that could aid us against Saul. Let us go down and see what this is about." The guard walked before the general and the king, as the trio made their way through the private chambers down to the great hall. They entered through a doorway behind the throne. At the far end stood several of the king's guardsmen, with David in the middle. A servant had followed the trio inside, and Philcol leaned over and spoke lowly to him.

"Go find Ahuzzath. He should be in the building somewhere, probably with the counsel. Bring him here quickly."

"Yes sir." The servant nodded and left the hall. The general then stepped over to the guard that had led them down. "If David does anything threatening at all, kill him."

Achish took his seat on the throne. "Bring him," said the king. His voice resounded loudly in the hall. Philcol and the guard each took a spot on either side of the throne. The other guardsmen led David toward the king. They came to within a few paces from the throne and stopped. David bowed his head in respect.

"So this is the great Israelite warrior. To what do we owe this honor, that he might come and pay us a visit?" The king's words dripped with sarcasm.

"My lord, I have fallen out of favor with King Saul." David's face was stern. "I have come to offer you my sword."

"It doesn't appear that you even have a sword," said the king, looking hard at David. Fearing that showing up with the sword of Goliath would be seen as an insult, David had hidden it outside the city. A weapon would not help him anyway, if they chose to kill him. There were far too many for him to fight off. "How is it you will fight for me with no weapon?"

Before David could respond, the servant returned from behind the throne. Behind him followed four other men, one of them very old. One of them seemed familiar to David. Ahuzzath looked at the Israelite, and his eyes grew wide. Achish looked at his counselors and smiled.

"My friends, may I introduce David the Israelite. He has come to fight for me, though he has no weapon and apparently has no soldiers who follow him."

Ahuzzath had been shamed after his encounter with David and had no longer been able to lead soldiers. However, his father Naveh's reputation among the Philistine leaders was heavily regarded, and he was able to join the king's counselors. The former soldier led two other counselors into the room, as well as his father who still advised the king occasionally. He was shocked to see the Israelite warrior.

"Tell me, how is it we have the fortune to receive such a man? What say you about him giving me his sword, assuming we have one to spare?" said the king.

Ahuzzath was very uneasy. This was David, who had claimed he would drive every Philistine out of Israel. He had heard the very words come from the young warrior's mouth! Now he was here to join them? Something was not right. Ahuzzath was afraid of David, and the king did not seem to understand what a formidable opponent the Israelite was. He had to speak up.

"My lord," Ahuzzath spoke with earnestness, "this is David, who killed Goliath. Is he not the one about whom the Israelites sang, 'David has killed tens of thousands'? With my own ears I have heard him say he would drive all of us out of the land! You cannot trust him."

One of the counselors agreed with him. "My lord, I would not trust any Israelite, much less one who has had so much success against our own soldiers. This boy is as a prince in Israel. I cannot see any good coming from this."

Achish was clearly irked. The king did not share the deep respect and fear of David, and he had enjoyed giving the Israelite a ribbing. But he was always looking for a great warrior to join him, and David was said to be one of the best. "My counselors all have the hearts of women. What does my general say?"

Philcol didn't fear David, but he was also opposed. "I would not accept his offer, my lord. I don't trust him, nor do I want to see the effect he may have on our troops. Many of them hate him." The general looked David in the eyes. "I think he should be killed."

David's stomach turned. This was not turning out the way he had thought. *Oh Lord, how could I have been so foolish?* He needed a way out, but how? He was weaponless, surrounded by armed Philistines who hated him. Suddenly a strange idea came to his head. David began to twitch one eye, and drool just a little. He stamped his feet and let out a low guttural noise. His eye twitch grew into a head twitch, and the drool ran down into his beard. All of them watched him in confusion.

"What's the matter with him?" asked the king, bewildered. No one answered. David looked at the general. "Kill me? Bahhh!" he barked. "Kill me then! Bahhh!" Then David stopped twitching and stood still. He looked from one man to another, then stopped his gaze on a soldier next to him. "What?" he asked, spit flying from his mouth.

Achish was angry. Not only were all his men arguing against him, but now it appeared David was insane. He barked at his guardsmen. "What is wrong with this man? Am I so short of madmen that you must bring me another?"

"Kill him my lord. You have no need of him, " said the general.

"I agree my lord," piped up Ahuzzath.

Oh Lord, David prayed, *protect your servant. Stay close to me, for trouble is near.*

Finally, the old man in the rear spoke up. "My king, I know you care nothing for my advice. But I ask that you heed me now."

Achish looked over at him. "Tell me Naveh. What is it?"

"I was a soldier when we defeated the Israelites at Ebenezer. I helped bring the ark of their god back to Ashdod. I saw the statue of Dagon fallen before it, and I saw the punishment brought on our cities by it. Their god is a strong one. This boy is clearly his servant, no matter his state of mind. Do not kill him, for you would condemn us. Set him free, that he may go and serve his god, or may die by another's hand. I would not tempt Israel's god against us."

"Are you all bewitched against me?" roared the king. "Naveh, I ought to have your head. You always show more respect for this foreign god than you do for Dagon or your king. Very well, you faint-hearted lilies, have your way." Achish looked at David. "I'll not kill you, David. Not because I fear you or your god, but because it would not sit well with me to kill a man who comes peacefully into my house. I would've taken you on if not for your spell of madness." The king looked at David's escorts. "Feed him and let him go. Make sure he leaves the city safely." With that, Achish stepped down from the throne and headed back the way he had come in. The counselors also exited, leaving Philcol and the king's guards alone with David. The general was very angry. Not only had the king gone against his advice, he had also insulted him. Philcol would not forget that. He stepped over near the Israelite warrior.

"You haven't fooled me boy," he said through clenched teeth. "I'll be looking for my chance against you." He looked at the soldiers. "Get him out of here." Philcol turned and followed after the king, while the soldiers pointed David toward the other end of the hall and marched out.

The damp air felt good on David's sweaty brow. He was deep underground, away from the hot sun, and the temperature was rather cool. For several weeks now he had been dwelling here, in a system of caves and tunnels in an area known as Adullam. Several hundred years ago they had been used as a military fortress for the Jebusite clans. Joshua, the Lord's general, had led a campaign against the southern region of Israel's territory, and had conquered the area. Some of the displaced Jebusites had moved to the north, eventually taking over the city of Jebus. The caves had remained mostly abandoned, with an occasional company of soldiers or men in disfavor taking up a temporary residence. Now David was the one in disfavor. After being escorted from Gath, he had retrieved Goliath's sword and headed east. He had intended on making his way around the sea of Arabah toward Moab when he had stumbled upon this place. After a few days he had been found by a prophet named Gad, sent from Samuel to aide him. Gad was able to send word to David's family, and now they were on the way to join him in the caves. David had been against having his family come until he realized their lives were in danger. As he waited for their arrival, he knelt alone in one of the lower caves praying.

Almighty God, how great You are. I am in need, my Lord, and only You can help me. My spirit is overwhelmed. I do not know the path that I must take. I know You have called me and anointed me. I know You have a plan for me. You know the path I must take Lord. Men are lying in wait for me, to kill me. I pray You will guide my

steps, oh Lord, that I might carry out Your plan for my life. Strengthen me, oh Lord,
to continue on.

David stood up. Through a small crack in the wall of the cave came
a trickle of water. It ran downward until reaching a low-lying spot in the
floor, where it became a small pool. He stepped over and refilled an empty
water skin on his belt, then dampened a cloth and cleaned his face. Feeling
better, he turned and headed for the tunnel that led toward the cave's
entrance. The tunnel ran a long way up, and David passed a number of
other small rooms as he walked. A number of torches that hung from the
tunnel walls provided some dim light. David could still not see the cave's
entrance when he turned into an opening in the wall.

"Still water down there, I take it?" came a voice from the dark. David
looked in the direction of the voice and could just make out the prophet's
lanky frame crouched in the corner. Gad was about ten years older than
David, tall and lean with a shaggy beard and long hair.

"Still there," David replied. "Although we'll probably need to find
some more before long."

"We'll need to find some more food as well," said the prophet. "Our
bread is getting moldy."

"Hopefully my father will have brought some supplies with him."

"Yes, hopefully," answered Gad. David was about to say his father was
always prepared, and he'd be surprised to find the old man showing up
without provisions, when suddenly they heard a shout echoing through the
tunnels. It was indistinct at first, but then they heard it again. It sounded
to David like a man was calling his name, though the pair were alone in
the cave. Could it be David's family? Gad leapt to his feet, and the two
men held their breath and listened. Perhaps Saul had tracked them. There
was no way out of the cave, only back to the entrance. If it was the king,
he could sit and wait them out, or send a company of men in after them.
Horrible thoughts ran through David's mind.

The call came again, clearer this time.

"David!" He and Gad moved out through the tunnel, staying in the
shadows. They followed the tunnel until it turned upward toward the
entrance. A dark figure stood at the mouth of the cave, silhouetted against
the bright morning sky behind him. Once more the man called out, "Son
of Jesse!" This time David recognized the voice.

"Abishai!" A sliver of light passed the cave mouth and reached the tunnel in front of where David stood. He stepped forward so he could be seen.

"So here you are, you vagabond!" Abishai said with a laugh. "Don't kill me now, I've come here in peace."

David made his way hastily up the tunnel toward Abishai. The captain stepped down into the tunnel and the two men clasped hands and slapped each other's shoulders.

"What are you doing here?" David asked.

"Looking for you of course. Don't think you can run off on some wild adventure and leave me to rot back in Gibeah taking orders from my brother. I'll not have that." Abishai grinned.

"It does me good to see you, my friend. You are always welcome with me. Although," David laughed, "you'll get no fancy welcome here. Dirty water and two-week old bread, and a dusty floor to sleep on."

"You know me David, I don't stand on ceremony anyway."

"That's good, cause you'll not get it." Then David grew serious. "You know you'll be branded a traitor for this. If Saul catches you, you'll be killed."

"Saul won't catch me. He's not smart enough for that. Now come, step outside with me, you need to see this." The pair climbed out of the cave's mouth with Gad following behind. The sun was blindingly bright, and David had to shield his eyes with his hand. A short distance from the cave was an abrupt drop that went straight down about ten feet. They stepped up to it and looked down. David's mouth dropped open in surprise. Three hundred fully armed men stood assembled in three companies. With David in sight, a shout rang out among them. Abishai turned to face David and snapped to attention.

"My lord, here are all those most loyal to you, ready to commit our services to the true leader of Israel. We are at your disposal."

"How did you do this?" David asked in amazement.

"Easy. The hard part was not letting them all run off the first time we heard you were gone. We had to organize ourselves, or you would've had small groups of soldiers running around in the wilderness, some showing up and some getting lost."

"Thank you, Abishai. I am in your debt."

"I would've had more if I could have convinced Joab. The man is as stubborn as a mule."

"I know many of the men look up to him."

"He holds you in greater respect than he does Saul. But he thinks too highly of his reputation than for him to betray the king."

"I do not think the worse of him. He has a job to do." David turned toward the soldiers and raised his voice. "Men of Israel, I thank you. You have chosen to aide me in a dangerous adventure. I will not forget it." David looked up to the sky and held out his hands. "My God, Almighty Rock of Israel, I thank You. Help us, Your servants, to carry out Your will, that Your glory would be known in the earth." A shout went up among the soldiers. Gad moved forward and looked at David.

"The Lord shines on you, David. He will be your strong arm."

"May he be a strong arm for us all," said Abishai, "and we'll run Saul right off his throne."

"You cannot stay here any longer, David. There may be room here to shelter these men, but there is not food or water for them. Not to mention Saul will be out looking for these deserters. Let us go towards Hareth. The forest there will provide all we need."

"Hareth is nearer Gath than I would like to go," said David.

"The Philistines are of the sea peoples, and that forest is wild. They do not venture far into it, not without good reason," said Gad.

"I would agree with that," added Abishai.

"It is far enough from both Saul and the Philistines to allow time to prepare yourself for what the Lord will do next." Gad looked hard at David. "It is the only real choice. You cannot take this company through inhabited country and not be found out, and there are not enough men to fight against an army."

"We cannot leave without my family."

"Unless something ill has befallen them, they should arrive soon."

David thought very hard for a moment. "Let me pray on it tonight. Tomorrow, if my family is here, we will move if God wills. For now, Abishai, bring the men into the cave, and send out a few hunting parties."

The captain grunted in response and turned toward the soldiers, still assembled. "Alright ladies, file it off up through the cave mouth. Find yourselves a nice comfy rock to lay on."

The soldiers shouted again, and then in an orderly fashion one rank after another marched up a path into the cave. David stood by watching, thanking God in his heart.

Philcol wiped the dust out of his eyes and looked up. The late afternoon sun shined through the clouds, giving the land a hazy red appearance. The Philistine general stood in the bottom of a deep valley running north to south. In front of him, to the west, the walls of rock that sheltered the valley rose up several hundred feet. Sitting on top was the general's destination-a large city encircled entirely by high stone walls. Placed atop the walls at short intervals were turrets, each manned by archers. From below, it had the look of a fortress, rising impressively over the land. It was the city of Jebus, the capital of the Jebusites. Here Adonizedek reigned.

Philcol thought how fortunate he was to be coming in peace. Any attack on this place was surely doomed. Finding a winding path up the side of the valley, the general started to climb. Behind him followed a squad of ten other soldiers, his personal escort. Rarely did Philcol leave Gath without at least a company of one hundred, but this time he had not come out to fight. This mission needed speed and secrecy. The path was steep and covered in loose rocks, yet another obstacle for any attacker to overcome. More than one Philistine stumbled on the way up. When they finally reached the top, Philcol came into full view of the city gate. It was massive. It remained closed for most of the day, opening once in the morning and once in the evening. With a smaller fighting force than many of the other peoples of Canaan, the Jebusites found their security inside the city, protected by the terrain and their high walls. It was a good combination. Nearly three hundred years ago the Israelites had burned the city, but the forefathers of Adonizedek had recaptured it, built the walls and held it in their power ever since.

The gate was an enormous pair of double doors made of wood and iron. It was slowly being opened as the Philistine general strode up, allowing a squad of soldiers to march out of the city. The soldiers stamped their feet in cadence as they drew near to the Philistines. "Be ready!" shouted one of Philcol's guards. The Jebusite soldiers came to within a dozen feet of the general and came to a halt. The squad leader approached the Philistines and saluted.

"Greetings, general. I am Oman, and I am at your service. My lord is expecting you."

Philcol nodded. "Good."

"Follow me, general, and I'll see that you are all fed and watered." The Jebusite squad had split into two ranks facing each other. Their leader turned and walked between them, motioning for the general and his men to follow. The Philistines followed suit, giving uneasy glances to the soldiers that flanked them. After the last Philistine had passed between them, the soldiers turned and marched after them.

Oman led them through the huge gate and into the city. It was every bit as large as Gath, and nearly as prosperous. Tall buildings lined the streets, though few stood so high as the outer wall, which reached over twenty feet. It seemed less cluttered and noisy than Gath, which let thousands of people in and out throughout the day. Jebus was much more secure than any Philistine city.

Oman took them toward the center of the city, headed for what appeared to be a temple of sorts. It was a very wide, two-story building. The roof was open and full of people, busy preparing for a ceremony. Their guide took them inside the temple doors and into a hall. The Jebusite soldiers remained outside. The hall was wide and very dark, and Oman bade them sit down at the tables prepared.

"Help yourselves, my friends, this has been left here for you." Then Oman himself filled a cup from a pitcher of wine and drank deeply. Smiling, he looked at Philcol. "It is safe, general."

Philcol wasn't amused. "When am I to meet the king?"

"Soon, general. A sacrifice is to be held at sundown, and he will meet with you there. I will return and take you there myself shortly." With that, Oman trotted off, and the Philistines sat down to eat and rest. A jug of water had been provided for the men to wash, and there was plenty of food to go around for everyone. The open door they had come through faced east, and the shadows quickly grew long outside. It seemed a very short time when Oman returned with a grin on his face.

"It is time general. Your men may stay here and rest, but my lord is ready for you."

Several of his men started to grumble, but Philcol quieted them. "Stay here. I should not be long. None here has any reason to be hostile to me." He looked at Oman. "Let's go."

Oman led the general back the way he had come. Through several rooms they found a staircase and up they went. Oman took him all the way to top, popping out onto the roof. There were several dozen people standing in a circle. In the middle, a great fire burned brightly. Philcol could feel the searing heat. Next to the fire stood a large statue of something like a man, yet with the head like a bull. The arms were held out over the fire. Dusk was fast approaching. As the pair walked toward the circle, a tall man turned to face them. His beard and hair were both long and black, braided in long strands. He was lean with long arms, and even in the low light his eyes seemed dark and beady. A crown sat upon his head. He looked straight at Philcol.

"General," said Oman, " may I introduce King Adonizedek."

The king seemed to smile. "Welcome, general." Something about his voice made the general uneasy.

"I thank you for your hospitality, my lord."

"Yes, my hospitality. You have not come for my hospitality, though, have you?" The king's words were very drawn out, and his voice seemed very detached.

"No my lord," answered Philcol.

"You have come to ask me to help you destroy the Israelites."

"Yes, my lord. My lord Achish has sent me to ask for your assistance."

"Why should I aide you?" asked the king. "Neither you nor Israel can harm me here. No army north of Egypt has a chance at breaching my walls. Even a prolonged siege would not avail you, for you would not be able to stop my supply line."

"My lord, I am not here to threaten you with that," replied the general.

"What then? Give me a reason to aid you."

Philcol was getting slightly irritated. Who did this strange man think he was speaking with? "My lord, you have your own reasons to destroy Israel, I know well enough. I know your ancestors tried to and failed. I know you covet their fruitful land, as you look out in all directions and see territory belonging to them. You are completely surrounded by them, and soon enough they will overcome you if they are not stopped. And I know you hate Saul, whose sword has destroyed so many of your neighbors."

Adonizedek drew back somewhat, and cocked his head sideways as he looked at Philcol. However, his voice remained unchanged. "You know much, general. It is true, I hate Saul and all that he stands for. I hate only slightly less you Philistines, who seem to think it is your right to enforce their will on this region, though you are strangers. However, you are away on the other side of the highlands, while Saul parades on my doorstep." Philcol remained quiet. "Here's a deal for you, general. I will assist in destroying the Israelites. When they have been defeated, all land west of Zorah may belong to Achish. From Zorah to the sea of Arabah belongs to me. What say you?"

The Philistine general stood by in silence, thinking over the terms. However, despite his slow speech, Adonizedek was impatient. "Speak up, general. The time is passing."

"Very well. Let it be written down on a scroll, and have your seal put on it, and I will take it to my king."

Adonizedek suddenly gave a devilish smile. "Excellent general. A fine choice. I will ensure this is done so by the morning, and then you may depart. But for now, let us make a sacrifice to ensure my god's help." The king placed a hand on the shorter Philistine's shoulder, and led him toward the circle of men. "Molech desires the blood of the innocent. Do not fear, general, for you are not innocent. None are who have lived very long." From behind Philcol, back where the staircase came out on the roof, the general heard a noise, and it sent a shiver up his spine. He turned around to see a priest carrying a baby, walking toward the circle. The baby was crying loudly. The king leaned over and whispered in his ear. "By the blood of the innocent, we shall be victorious."

7

Saul's mind was clouded with anger. None of his men respected him. Likely, many of them plotted against him. He stood silently, his brow furrowed and mouth drawn tight. Twenty leaders from the families of Benjamin stood by him, as well as a group of soldiers, about thirty in all. None spoke. The king had called them here for counsel, yet none offered anything useful. They were gathered in the shade of a small grove of pomegranate trees, just south of his compound in Gibeah. The king's rule was unraveling. David was alive and on the run, and some of his former soldiers had left to join him. Even worse, his own son had helped him escape. At least some of the king's servants had to have known something, yet not a word of it had come to Saul until it was already done. Fools, all of them. Did they not know it was the king who provided all for them? Saul gripped his spear tightly, and broke the silence.

"Tell me, how many of you have conspired against me? Do you believe this son of Jesse, this boy from Judah, will reward you? Do you think he will give you lands and vineyards, or make you captains over his men? Do you?"

One man, called Abidan, spoke up. "My lord, we are all Benjamanites, of your own blood. None of us have helped David. What purpose would we have of betraying you?"

"My own son, to his shame, has helped David, and he is more my blood than any of you." The king's voice was loud and angry. "You tell me none of you have known his plans? None of you have known he would betray me?"

"No, my lord, we have not," answered Abidan.

"I am the one who shall reward you for your service, not David. I am the one who shall punish wrongdoing. Yet none of you aid me." Saul looked toward the compound, and saw two men approaching. "Only one has spoken to me of David's activities, and he is not even of Israel, much less of Benjamin. Perhaps it is to my own shame that I have relied upon my blood."

The two men drew nearer. One had a thick build and a dark, bushy beard. He had dark skin and the look of a man who labored outdoors. He wore a sword at his side. Next to him walked an older man, somewhat taller and leaner, with the bearing of a man in high position. They walked past the soldiers and into the inner circle, in front of the king.

"Thank you Doeg. You seem to be the only one who is deserving of thanks." Saul looked the other man in the eyes. "Tell me, Ahimelech son of Ahitub, why is it you have conspired against your king with this son of Jesse?"

The priest answered, "Is it conspiring against the king to aid David? He is your son-in-law, leads your soldiers, and fights your battles. Who else in your house has been so faithful to God and to you?" Ahimelech spoke clearly with no reservation. His lack of fear further irritated the king.

"You know much. You must have known David is against me, and seeks my life and my throne. His is now my enemy, yet you have helped him. Remind the priest, Doeg, in case he has forgotten."

The Edomite spoke up harshly. "The priest knew my lord was at odds with the son of Jesse, yet he inquired of the Lord for him, and gave him food and a sword. He is guilty of conspiring against my lord."

Ahimelech's voice remained steady. "The shepherd lies. I did not inquire of the Lord for him, for David did not ask me to do so. Though had he, I surely would have."

"You gave him food and a weapon," exclaimed Doeg. "You gave him Goliath's sword!"

"I did give him food, for he had none. And if anyone has a claim on the sword of Goliath, it is David." Ahimelech looked at the king. "He fought the giant when no one else would." Saul glared at him in anger, yet Ahimelech continued. "I did not know all that had transpired between you and David, though I knew it would happen someday. David is the anointed, and he will be king over you. Samuel has already warned you of this, though you will not believe him."

Saul looked at him with murder in his eyes. "You will die priest, you and all your house."

Ahimelech continued, his voice unwavering. "I knew this day would come, Saul. The Lord spoke of it to my father Eli, and the Lord's word is true. But His word is also against you, and you will soon go to your destruction."

"Kill him!" Saul looked to his soldiers, standing just beyond the leaders of Benjamin. "He is worthy of death!" Yet none of the soldiers moved. Several grabbed the hilt of their swords, but none were willing to come forward. "My lord," one shouted, "he is the high priest."

The king was furious. He looked at the shepherd. "Doeg, strike him down!"

The Edomite obliged. He drew his sword quickly and stepped back. The priest turned to face him, looking him in the eyes. With one swift move Doeg struck the head from his shoulders, and the priest's body crumpled to the ground. The king shouted.

"So to all who stand against Saul! Doeg, take what soldiers are true to me, and go to the city of Nob. Put all you find there to the sword!"

Doeg stood breathless, with a wild look in his eyes. "Very well my lord." He bowed his head to the king.

The king looked at the soldiers. "Let any man who wishes to prove his loyalty follow Doeg to Nob. And remember this lesson from today, for it is what will happen to all who are disloyal." He looked at the Edomite. "Go!"

Doeg bowed again, then turned and ran toward the compound. The soldiers followed after, hesitantly.

"David, the men are afraid." Abishai looked at David seriously. "They know we will be outnumbered, going into a walled town defended by Philistines. None of them are looking forward to this." The pair stood underneath the mighty trees of Hareth. It was late afternoon, and the tall forest blocked out much of the setting sun. They stood looking to the east, toward where the forest gave way to the rise of the central ridge line. A road ran out of the trees and up and over the ridge, headed toward the town of Keilah several miles away. That morning, word had come to David's camp that the town had been sacked by Philistine soldiers, at least five hundred of them. Keilah was a town of Judah. It was surrounded by high walls, but it had no military presence. The Philistines had spent two days threatening from outside the walls, until a squad of soldiers succeeded in climbing over during the night. The town surrendered to the Philistines shortly afterward, and the soldiers forced many people to leave. Several had made it to the forest, which was how David had heard the news.

David turned and looked at his captain in the eyes. "Neither am I. If only we had heard of this two days ago, we could have crept up on them while they slept outside the town. Now they will be strongly defended."

"Attacking a position reinforced with Philistines will be no easy task, David."

"I know. But how can we leave this alone?"

Abishai sighed. "We can't."

"How long until you expect Sibbechai and Elhanan to return?" The captain had sent the pair of soldiers to Keilah to see what they might be able to find out. It was only a few hours march at the most, and Abishai had sent them almost as soon as they had heard the news.

"If they didn't run into trouble, they should be back anytime now. If they did find some trouble, that pair is as likely to be able to deal with it as any. I'll give it to you, Sibbechai has turned out to be one of my best soldiers."

"I'm glad he decided to follow you here."

"So what about the troops? I'm not sure they'll all be as willing to go as Sibbechai, and we can't afford to leave any behind."

"Abiathar has enquired of the Lord, and the Lord said to go. So go we must. I'll talk to the men. Assemble them for me, while I talk again to the priest."

"Very well." The captain turned and walked away, while David remained. He looked again at the top of the ridge, hoping to see the two soldiers returning, but he did not. *Lord,* prayed David, *how great You are. You have said for me to go to Keilah, so I will go, for I trust You. Strengthen my men, that they may have trust in You. You are the Lord, strong in battle, mighty to save. Thank You, oh God, and may You carry us through.*

David turned and walked deeper into the forest. He could hear Abishai calling out the men. The trees were not overly thick, and he could see the camp and the soldiers as they were assembling. Abiathar the priest stood off by himself, in front of his tent. He had joined them only days ago, with a heart-breaking tale. Saul had ordered the execution of his father Ahimelech, and then the king had sent soldiers to Nob to destroy it. Abiathar had been outside the city examining sheep when it happened and had been able to escape. Very few had been that fortunate. The priest turned to look at David as he approached. Abiathar's face was long and somber.

"The men are in poor spirits, David. I'm afraid they have weaker faith then you."

"Perhaps." The priest wore a white linen robe, with a sackcloth covering his torso. Underneath the sackcloth was something very bulky, making Abiathar look somewhat lumpy and uncomfortable. "You have the ephod?"

"Yes. I will not separate it from myself until a safe place is found for it. There is no such place here." Abishai had the troops in formation now, and he turned to report to David.

"My lord," the captain shouted, "all present."

David walked toward the formation. "Thank you captain." He strode down the front rank, looking at his men. The constant strain of being on the move and knowing they were being hunted by the king was taking its toll. He had not seen them so discouraged before. "Men of Israel, I know you do not want to go to Keilah. It has a strong wall, no doubt, and it will be defended by Philistine soldiers, some of the best fighters in Canaan. It is no easy task that I ask you to perform. But I would not ask you to perform it if there were not a great need for it. These Philistines have come on to Israelite ground, and killed Israelite men, women, and children. Now they treat themselves to whatever they choose among their spoils. There are still Israelites who will be forced to serve them, and some will die if we do not act. I cannot bear to know this and do nothing. I know that you feel the same, despite your doubts."

David paused, and an archer in the front rank spoke up. "My lord, we know this is a great need. But we are ill-equipped to respond to this. Saul is still the king, and he should be bringing troops to retake the town, not us."

"I agree, Abiezer, the king should be the one to protect his people. But Saul is too preoccupied with finding us, and he will not care much about a small town of Judah. He will not respond, unless I am mistaken. But Israel's true King will respond. The Almighty has instructed us through Abiathar to go to Keilah, and if He sends us, He will fight for us."

Abiezer shifted uncomfortably on his feet, and cleared his throat. "Forgive me, my lord, but we have not seen that the Lord's hand is with you since you left Gibeah. You have done nothing but run-"

Abishai cut him off. "Abiezer, will you talk down to your commander? Maybe you and I need to take a walk alone so I can teach you some manners!"

"Let him finish, captain," said David. "Go ahead," he said to the archer.

Abiezer continued, not disrespectfully. "I do not mean to talk down to you, my lord. You have certainly had God's favor on you in the past. We are only uncertain of what you are choosing to do now. We have not seen God fight for you since you left Saul. We have been given no victories, only places to hide."

David nodded. "A fair question, Abiezer. True, we have not been given any victories. But we have also not been given any defeats. God has provided all we have needed, food, water, safe dwellings. He has not yet asked us to fight, until now. Now is the first opportunity for Him to give us a victory. Will you shy away from the chance?" David looked at the other troops. "Will any of you shy away from the chance? The Almighty has told us to fight, and He will fight for us, of that you can be sure." He turned toward the priest. "Abiathar, enquire again of the Lord. He will give you the same answer, and the men will know it."

"Yes, my lord." The priest removed the sackcloth from around his torso, revealing the breastplate of the high priest. The few rays of light still breaking through the trees caught the brightly colored stones and shined blindingly through the forest. Abiathar adjusted the golden chains around his shoulders and stepped into the tent.

The men remained quiet. Most had never seen the breastplate of the high priest before. David stood unmoving in front of them with his head up, eyeing his soldiers. After what seemed a long time, the priest re-emerged from his tent. "My lord," Abiathar proclaimed loudly, "the

Almighty says to go to Keilah, and He will deliver the Philistines into your hand."

David shouted. "Very well men. Now is the time to prove your trust in the Lord. Let Him use you to administer His justice. You have trusted Him before, I know. Trust Him now." David turned to Abishai. "Captain, break camp. We will not be returning to Hareth. We go to Keilah!"

Saul felt the crunch of rocky ground beneath his feet. His eyes ached from the glare of the sun, and his head was weary from the constant plodding sound of soldier's feet. The king marched at the head of nearly three thousand men, leading them along a stony cliff that overlooked the sea of Arabah. It spread out far and wide across the horizon, the hills on the other side barely visible off to the east. To the west the sparse terrain climbed higher, steadily rising as it reached toward the central highlands. This was the desert of En-gedi, a rugged country with few resources and less people.

Saul had been busy of late. For the better part of a year now, he had been in a near constant pursuit of his enemies. Shortly after the destruction of Nob, he had been told that the young warrior and his men were dwelling in Keilah. Apparently the town had fallen to the Philistines, but David's men had crept in during the night, scaled the wall and overtook the Philistines in their sleep. A man loyal to Saul had come and told the king, and Saul had immediately mustered his soldiers to attack the usurper. David had found out he was coming, however, and had escaped far to the south to the desert of Moan. The king had brought his entire army with him, following close behind David, when the Philistines raided the towns of Simeon in great numbers. Saul was forced to go and engage the Philistines to save Israelites. He had also had to deal with Jebusites attacking the territory of Benjamin, near Gibeah. Between the two, he had not been able to focus on finding David. Now, once again, Saul had received word of David's location, and the king was out to find him.

Abner's heavy feet stomped loudly behind the king. "We should be very close, my lord. David is said to be hiding in a group of caves, known as the crags of wild goats. If you look ahead, you will see the cave mouths jutting out from the side of the hill."

Looking ahead, Saul could see what the general was referring to. They were close, less than a mile away. "I see them," the king said flatly.

"It would be best if we hold the main body here, and you and I can go forward with a company or two and search. David can't send a large attack from the caves, it's too steep."

"Very well. Halt the men."

The general held up a fist as a signal, and the order passed along the columns to the rear. Then he called for his commanders, and stood impatiently waiting as they hurried to meet him. The king's son Ish-bosheth still commanded a third of the army; he was close to the front with the first division. Joab, the brother of Abishai, had taken command of what was left of David's division. Until recently, Jonathan had been the third commander, but he had chosen not to accompany the king on this mission. Elishama of Ephraim, who had served with Ish-bosheth, had been given the prince's command. It took several minutes for them to reach the front. The prince marched up first, just as tall but leaner than his brother Jonathan. Elishama arrived next, stout and gray-bearded, but still strong. Finally, coming up at a steady trot was Joab, taller than both and twice as strong with a bushy black beard. Standing next to the king's son, whose beard was light and thin, Joab looked like a bear.

The general gave strict instructions. "The king and I are moving forward to search those caves." Abner pointed to them. "You will all remain here. Ish-bosheth, give me two companies to come with us."

"I have two good ones for you sir," answered the prince.

"While you wait, I expect you to stay vigilant. Push some scouts up the hills to keep a watch. If they see anything out of place, I want to know about it."

"Yes sir," said the three in unison.

"Joab, you served under David a long time. Anything we should know?"

The big man stared at Abner blankly. "No," he answered.

"Very well. Go," said the general, and the men headed back to their places. Ish-bosheth quickly organized two companies to escort the king and sent them to the front. When they arrived, Abner had more specific instructions to give. Finally, they were ready to move. The general gave the order, and the detail marched toward the caves.

There must have been two dozen openings in the hillside. Most were small. Only a few seemed large enough to be able to accommodate a group of soldiers. Abner split the companies into squads, and they commenced to search the caves. "If David's here, we'll find him," the general assured Saul. The king did not reply. Saul was tired, and frustrated. This irritating boy was causing quite a disturbance in Saul's life. What was the king doing out here, searching through caves used by goat herders and the like? How he was ready to return to Gibeah and forget this nonsense. But first, he had to take care of David. Bit by bit, the squads returned, reporting no signs of anyone dwelling within the caves.

"My lord, he must not have been here, at least not recently. He certainly isn't here now." Abner's voice betrayed his confident manner. He was also tired and discouraged.

The king's temper suddenly flared. "Not here, you say. Then what have we been doing, wasting all this time running around in the desert? I ought to replace you with Joab. He at least might beat David's location out of someone, unlike you, who simply follows vague leads to whatever end."

The general was loyal and had a great sense of duty, but he had limits, and he was quickly reaching them. He gritted his teeth and stared at Saul, holding back his tongue. He turned to his company leaders. "Have your men climb up past the caves and look for any trace of a path they might have taken. The king and I will follow." Abner turned back to the king. "Ready, my lord?" he asked. Without waiting for a response, Abner started up the hillside. Saul fell in behind him in silence. The hill was steep and rocky, and it took the better part of an hour for the detail to get above the caves. There was a large flat piece of ground there, where several old sheep pens stood. As each man cleared the steep hillside, they gathered near the pens. When they had all done so, Abner called for a short rest.

The king needed more than a rest. "I'm going to step in here for a few minutes," said Saul, pointing toward the back of the flat area where the hill grew steep again. There stood a small opening in the rocks. It wasn't much more than a big hole, but it was just large enough for the king to fit if he stooped. "I won't be long." With that, Saul went into the cave, picking up the skirt of his robe as he stepped inside.

It seemed like hours had passed. David's limbs were getting sore from crouching on the hard ground. He and several other men were hunkered down inside a cave near the top of the hillside that ran along the sea of Arabah. Having received word that Saul was on the march toward him, he had ordered Abishai to take the majority of his men farther up the coastline in the direction of Nibshan, a small village to the north that might offer assistance. David wanted to stay behind and get a look at Saul and his men, however, so he hand-picked a squad of men to remain with him and wait. Earlier in the day, they had seen the main body of the Israelite army moving north along the cliffs, and they retreated into the caves to hide.

Unfortunately, that was turning out to be a bad decision. David had chosen not to cross the open hillside to keep from being seen, hoping the army would continue past without stopping. They hadn't. Abiezer had stayed near the opening to keep watch, and the archer had reported soldiers scouring the caves below. The cave was not deep, and any thorough search would certainly reveal them. As the soldiers came closer, Abiezer pulled back with the rest. Now the men huddled in the back, trying to keep quiet.

David could hear the low breathing of his men. It was hot in the cave, and they were all sweating, causing it to smell. It was very dark, except for a crack of brightness coming through the opening, but David's eyes had adjusted to the low light. He looked around from man to man. Aside from the archer, Sibbechai had also stayed, a loyal and trustworthy man. Next to him was Elhanan, another fine soldier. Those two were rarely separated anymore. Next to him was Eleazar the Ahohite, a relentless swordsman, and Shammah the Hararite, a big, strapping youth of great strength. Finally, there was a man named Uriah, a Hittite soldier of excellent combat skill and impeccable character. It was a good group of men, and David hoped he hadn't consigned them to death by his decisions.

A long time had passed since Abiezer had seen the soldiers looking in the caves. David and his men were just beginning to hope that they had moved on when the sound of voices carried into the cave. At first it sounded like only a few, but it quickly seemed to grow. Suddenly, David heard Abner's voice, loud and clear. It had been a long time since he had heard the general's deep voice, and for the slightest moment it made him glad. David had always looked up to the general. The moment passed quickly, however, and the seriousness of the situation sunk in. All the men in the cave held their breath and listened. If they were found, they would probably be executed immediately. They could hear Saul's soldiers moving around outside. Then David heard the voice that he had least wanted to hear. It sounded very close. The next moment, David felt a shiver run up his spine as the cave mouth suddenly became black. A dark form stepped inside, and David knew it was the king. Saul walked toward the back of the cave. His tall frame blocked most of the light from the opening, and he moved slowly. None of David's men even dared to breathe. David's heart beat rapidly, and every muscle in his body clenched tight. The king came to a stop directly in front of him, then pulled up the front of his robe and began to relieve himself. Sibbechai, who sat closest to David, nudged him suggestively in the back. David could feel the cold metal of the hilt of Sibbechai's sword. Then a dark thought came to David's mind. *Here's your chance, kill him! Kill him and you will be king!* David's mind raced. What better opportunity would he ever have to destroy Saul? This man was trying to kill him simply for jealousy. What had David ever done to him? Now he was in forced exile, living off the land. David quietly unsheathed a knife he kept around his belt. *No,* he thought. *This is the Lord's anointed. Saul has God to answer to, not me.* Quickly David cut a swath of material from the bottom of the king's robe. Just as he pulled back the knife, Saul finished and dropped the front of his robe. Then the king turned and slowly made his way back out of the cave. Saul stepped outside, and the light returned through the crack.

Collectively, David and his men breathed out. They kept quiet and listened as Abner shouted to the soldiers. After a moment, they could be heard marching away. Abiezer finally spoke to David in a hushed voice. "My lord, why didn't you kill him?"

"He is the Lord's anointed," answered David. "He will not die by my hand." David stood up and quickly walked out of the cave. Sibbechai jumped up and hurried after him, then the rest followed suit. Outside, Saul and his soldiers were already a ways off, marching west across the top of the barren hillside. David shouted out to him. "My lord the king!"

The entire formation of soldiers turned around. David waved both hands in the air, and called again. "My lord!" Saul stood frozen. Even Abner was too surprised to speak. David approached the group, hands raised in a submissive fashion. "My king," he said as he drew near. David's men came up behind him, wondering what he was doing. All of them stood watching, and David bowed down on one knee. He looked directly at Saul. "My king, why are you out here looking for a dog such as myself? I know people have said I mean to kill you, but I do not." David held up the piece of the robe. "See for yourself. I will not harm the Lord's anointed." David stood and handed the fabric to a soldier, who gave it to Saul. The king looked at it incredulously. "The Lord delivered you into my hands, my king. But I did not harm you. May He also deliver me from your own hand."

Everyone stood by silently. Saul looked at the fabric in his hands, then looked up at David. "You are more righteous than I, my son. May the Lord reward you for your kindness." Saul's speech began to stutter with emotion, but he continued. "I know the Lord will establish your kingdom in Israel. May you continue to show my house mercy when I am gone. Swear to me, David, that you will not destroy my family." Saul stared at David with solemn eyes.

"May the Lord do so to me, if I should destroy your house. God will judge between me and you. May He uphold my cause." David looked at Abner and gave the general an acknowledging nod. "My men will not seek out battle against the king's soldiers. You have my word."

"Understood, David," replied the general. "Neither will the king's soldiers actively seek you out by my orders." Saul remained quiet. "I will return with the king's army to Gibeah. You are free to move your men wherever you wish, so long as it is not toward Benjamin."

"Very well." David turned to his men. "Sheath your weapons. On the march. That way," he said, pointing northward. Without hesitating, David and his men quickly marched away. Saul and Abner watched them leave, then ordered their troops back to the king's army.

8

The wind blew strongly across the open fields, bending the tall grass. It came out of the north, with the rising cliffs along the sea of Arabah acting as a wind tunnel allowing it to pick up speed. By the time it hit the southern coast, it shot across the plains with force. Off to the east and west, higher land could be seen in the distance, but here were only wide plains that served well for sheep and cattle. Here stood the village of Carmel.

A woman strode through the fields, listening to the bleating of sheep. She was a beautiful woman, a little on the short side with long dark hair that she kept pulled back, so it didn't interfere with her work. Her husband owned this land, and her servants were busy shearing the sheep. She worked hard herself, making clothes and household items, preparing meals and overseeing family affairs. It was a full time job, and she performed it diligently. She walked out toward where a group of men were holding down a sheep. It was sheep shearing time, and this evening most of the inhabitants of the small village would be joining them for a feast. Seeing her approach, an older, portly man called out to her.

"Abigail, how come your preparations?"

"The house is ready, Nabal. Only waiting for the your men to bring the sheep for the meal."

"Good. They'll be along with them shortly." Nabal and his wife spoke curtly to one another. There was little affection between them. He was a cruel and surly man, who treated both his servants and his wife poorly. Yet she remained obedient, always trying to do as he bid her.

"Can I help with anything here while I'm waiting?" she asked.

"No, we're fine. You may return to the house."

Abigail turned around and began walking away. Though she was mostly ready for the feast, there was always plenty of work to keep her busy. She had been married to Nabal only a short time, and she had borne him no children, though there were children that lived with them. Extended family lived there, and some of the servants also had children, so the place was busy. When Abigail reached the house, she walked around to the opposite side, away from Nabal, and found two other women sitting on the porch there. An older woman, one of Nabal's aunts, and a younger servant girl sat and worked diligently weaving baskets from dried wheat stalks. Abigail picked up a handful of stalks and sat down on the ground beside them. "Jael," she asked, looking at the younger girl, "that looks like it will be very large. What is it for?"

The girl smiled, a little embarrassed, and she looked at the other woman. "Go on, tell her what you're making, she might as well know," said the old woman.

Jael looked back at Abigail. "I started this a few days ago, when you were telling me how you were looking forward to having a baby. I thought you could use it as a bed."

Abigail didn't respond at first. She and Nabal had tried for a baby, but the Lord had not blessed her with one yet. She had often felt that she was being punished, but she knew in her heart God was making her wait for the right time. Abigail looked back at Jael. She was a sweet girl, and was only trying to do something nice. The girl looked a little upset when Abigail didn't respond. "Thank you Jael. I know it will be safe for my baby with you working on it." Jael smiled.

Back in the field, Nabal stood up to stretch his back. He wasn't as young as he used to be, and he could feel it. Work was coming along well, and he was looking forward to this evening. There was little else he enjoyed anymore, other than a good meal and some strong drink.

"Nabal," said one of his shepherds suddenly, pointing to the west, "there are men approaching." Nabal looked across the fields. He had to squint, for they were a ways off, but sure enough a group of men were marching in his direction. "Who are they?" asked the shepherd.

"Why are you asking me? No one I know would be coming right now, not from that direction." All the servants had noticed them, and had started to walk over to Nabal. He had about a dozen men with him. "Pick up your staffs, all of you. Let's go and see who these visitors might be." The men obeyed, and the group started walking out toward the other men.

Despite the distance, it did not take long to get in view of the other men. The two groups drew near each other, and Nabal became more sure that they were strangers to him. In the front marched a tall, well-built man with long black hair, carrying a spear. Behind him in two columns came about twenty men, all armed and with the bearing of soldiers. Nabal felt a stab of fear in his stomach. The tall man hollered for the soldiers to stop, and Nabal and the shepherds stopped as well. Then the tall man stepped out toward the land owner.

"You are Nabal of the house of Caleb, are you not?" he asked in a respectful voice.

"I am. Who are you?" replied Nabal.

"Peace be unto you. I am Uriah, a servant of David, son of Jesse of Bethlehem. He has sent us to you, knowing that it is sheep shearing time, asking for any food you may be willing to provide us. We have a great deal of men in our camp, and there is little food out here in the desert. My lord wishes to remind you that we watched over your shepherds and their flocks while they pastured away from here, near the hill country. Your shepherds can testify to that. Now, if we have found favor with you, I pray you will provide us with whatever you feel." Uriah was well spoken and did not seem threatening. Though he had no soldiers, Nabal had many other men close by, and the fear in his stomach had somewhat subsided. It had been replaced with irritation.

"David asks this of me, does he? And who is David, that I should give him anything? Perhaps if he had not plotted against the king, he would not be leading a group of soldiers out in the desert with no supplies. Should I then also go against the king, by serving those who are his enemies?" The shepherds stood by without speaking, but they were obviously nervous about the way their master was addressing these men.

"You mean you will give us no hospitality?" asked Uriah, surprised.

"I will give you nothing. You would bring down the king's wrath on me as well as you! And I never asked for your services to keep watch of my herds. I have kept them a long time out here, and they have done well without soldiers to protect them. Now, unless you mean to take from me by force, go back to wherever you came from!"

The soldiers bristled and gripped their weapons tightly. Food had been scarce for David's men recently, and they had been expecting a much warmer reception. Uriah could sense the blood rising in his men. He turned to look at them. "Stay calm. We were given orders to remain peaceful, and peaceful we shall remain." He turned back to face Nabal. "You have made up your mind, it seems. Very well, we will leave." Uriah stepped closer to Nabal, giving the older man a stern look. "This is not a wise decision on your part. Remember this, should we meet again." The Hittite turned once again and started marching west. "Let's move!" he shouted, and the soldiers about-faced and headed back in the direction of the hills.

"Fool!" David said, angrily. "Does he think I am going to sit out here, idle, while my men go hungry and he insults me? How long did we watch over his flocks in Moan, and keep his servants safe, and he will not help us now that we are in need?" Uriah stood by quietly, having just delivered Nabal's answer. It was not often that David became visibly upset, but this was one of those times. As clear headed as he was, he was not immune to the stresses of leading such a large company through uncertain times. Worst of all, David had recently received news that Saul had given Michal, the king's daughter and David's wife, to another husband. That had hurt. David's heart burned within him. "Rouse the men, Abishai. Get them armed and ready to march. I will visit this man before the day ends, and see what answer he gives when there is a sword in his middle."

"Yes my lord." Abishai hurried off to muster the troops. David's small army had steadily grown since his stay in the forest of Hareth. More soldiers from David's former command had found their way to him. Many men of Judah had come to fight for him, out to serve one of their own. Others had also come to him, vagabonds and outlaws, looking for a fresh start. After David's overwhelming victory at Keilah, many sons of that city had joined him, looking for adventure and glory. His company had more than doubled since Abishai came to him at Adullam, with over six hundred men. The captain had trained them and sorted them into companies. Now they fell into formation with discipline.

"We will not abandon the camp, captain. Leave two companies to keep a watch of our stuff, and the rest will go with us to Carmel, " instructed David.

"Yes, my lord." Abishai turned to the formation. "Eliam! Zelek! Your men will remain here and keep a watch. The rest of you, we march to Carmel to claim our due of Nabal the Calebite's property." An approving grunt went up among the troops, and David and Abishai led them out from their camp. They had been staying south of the city of Ziph, dwelling in the lower hills that led from the highlands of Judah and Simeon down to the plains of Carmel. They were not far from Nabal's land, only about an hour's march, and there were several hours of daylight remaining. The men marched along steadily. David spoke little. His temper had subsided somewhat, but his resolve had not. He needed food for his men. Nabal had plenty of it, and his men were owed a portion. Before nightfall, the man would render their due, or he would pay the penalty.

After the better part of an hour, they reached a steep drop into a shallow ravine. At the bottom flowed the final part of a stream that reached back to the sea of Arabah. Though steep, David's men handled the climb down easily, and began to make their way across the knee deep water. Uriah, who led the squad that marched at the front, looked up the hill on the other side and saw a small group of people descending toward them. "My lord, civilians coming!" called out the Hittite soldier.

David looked up ahead and got a look at who Uriah was pointing at. "Bring them to me," he hollered back. It appeared to be a group of shepherds, maybe a dozen at the most, each leading a pair of donkeys laden with food. Behind them rode a woman. They all seemed very nervous. Abishai called for the formation to halt, and Uriah's men escorted the group to the edge of the stream as David came across. When he stepped up on the bank, the woman alighted off the donkey and bowed low to David with her face to the ground.

"My lord," she said in a lovely voice, "please allow your servant to speak with you. Do not heed the words of Nabal, I pray, for he is a wicked fool. I was not present when he sent your men away so rudely. I know your men are in need of food, and I have gathered here what I could. Several of these good men with me have told me of your graciousness, and how your soldiers kept them safe while in the wilderness. Please accept this gift, and let your anger be turned away from Nabal's house, for there are good and innocent people there."

David was surprised. "What is your name?"

"I am Abigail, wife of Nabal. I know who you are, my lord. The Lord of Israel will place you on the throne, for you fight the Lord's battles. Let my lord not shed blood needlessly and have this deed on his head." The woman continued to look at the ground, but it was obviously out of respect, not fear.

"Stand up, Abigail. If only I had a wife so wise and gracious. You deserve much better than your husband." She rose to her feet and looked at him as David continued. "Praise be to the God of Israel, who has sent you to me today. May you be blessed for your wisdom. I thank you for keeping me from coming down on Nabal and his house. It would have been a vengeful and unrighteous act." David smiled as he looked at her. She was beautiful. She returned his gaze with admiration. "Thank you for your gift. You may return to your husband. No harm shall come to him or your house."

"Thank you, my lord." Abigail bowed and smiled, then mounted her donkey. Her servants turned their charges over to the soldiers, and the group returned back up the hill they had come down. David stood for a moment, watching Abigail ride away. Abishai gave orders for the troops to turn back for camp, and David headed back across the stream. His heart no longer burned in anger. Now it ached with longing.

David stood at the edge of camp, pacing back and forth. From there, he had a clear view down from the hills to the plains that spread out below. He kept a close eye out, watching for any movement coming his direction. It had been nearly three weeks since he had met Abigail. She had consumed his thoughts ever since. He had never seen such a woman, so beautiful and wise and compassionate. Ten days after they had met, a messenger had come to camp with news of Nabal's death. It had not been a violent death. Apparently he had become sick after finding out what his wife had done, and then one day he simply did not wake up. David had decided immediately to ask her to marry him. However, there would be

seven days of mourning before he could officially propose. Yesterday had
been the seventh day, and David had sent several men to her last night, for
sundown would begin the new day. It was now late afternoon, and none of
them had returned. He should have had them come back as soon as they
had received an answer, for the waiting was killing him. David continued
pacing, looking intently at the fields below.

"I can see you're not at all worried about her response," said Abishai
as he walked up behind David. The young warrior looked at him and
grunted. "You seem to be making a nice path for yourself," said the
captain, looking at the footprints from David's incessant walking.

"Why haven't they returned by now? It only takes a few hours. It's
been an entire day."

"They haven't returned because you didn't tell them too. They're
probably not coming back until she's ready to come. You know how long
women take to do anything."

"What do you know about women?"

"I know enough not to be standing around pacing all day when I'm
waiting on one," the captain chuckled, "so I must know more than you."

"I'm going to have Sibbechai punch you in the mouth if you keep it
up," remarked David irritably. Abishai laughed again.

"Guess I ought to leave you be then. Don't worry, if you need some
more sandals after all that pacing, I've got spare ones." The captain walked
away, still chuckling to himself. He enjoyed giving David a hard time
about this. There was so little the man was anxious about, it was funny to
see him acting nervously.

David ignored the captain's ribbing. He knew it was all in fun. Still,
the waiting around for his men to return was getting unbearable. He
wasn't even sure of all the orders he had given them, he had been so
excited. If they didn't come soon, then it would be tomorrow before they
returned. He had already spent most of last night awake, and he didn't
want to have to do that again. David had almost given up hope when he
saw a group of people coming from the direction of Carmel. *Oh my Lord,*
he thought, *give me the grace to accept whatever her answer.* David stopped pacing
and stared intently at the group. As they came closer, David could make
out two columns of men, his men. Uriah marched at the front, followed
by his squad stretched out behind him. In between the two columns of

soldiers David could see six women riding on donkeys. Abigail rode at the head, her mount walking slowly behind Uriah. David's heart leaped within him. He turned and trotted excitedly back to the tent he shared with several of his leaders. Outside the tent stood Abishai and Eleazar the Ahohite. Abishai grinned as he saw David approach.

"I'm going to guess that she's here," the captain said to Eleazar.

"Where is Abiathar?" David said as he jogged up.

"Should be in his tent," answered Eleazar.

"Find him, and assemble the men," David said. "She's on her way up, and I want to give her a proper welcome."

"Yes, my lord," said the swordsman, immediately marching off to obey. Abishai looked at David and grinned. "So, do I need to tell you what you're supposed to do on your wedding night?"

"Not even your big mouth can bother me now, Abishai. And no, I'll be just fine without your advice."

"Ha!" laughed the captain, and he followed after Eleazar to assemble the men. David's troops were well disciplined, and it did not take long for them to all be in formation. David had put on a clean cloak and gone back to the hillside, where the priest came to meet him.

"Ready for this, David?" asked Abiathar.

"Yes, I am," he answered, still looking toward the group. Uriah's squad was getting close. David could see a big smile on the Hittite's face. Behind him on her donkey, Abigail looked breathtaking. She sat up tall and had her dark hair flowing in the wind. David smiled. *My Lord, you have been gracious to me. You have kept me from doing evil against Nabal, yet you have taken up my case against him. Now you have delivered unto me a wonderful woman, who has a heart for you. I do not deserve all this from you, my Lord. Thank You for Your love for me.* Uriah called a halt as they reached the edge of the camp. The troops stood at attention, and everyone was quiet.

"My lady," said Uriah as he extended his hand to Abigail. She took it and slipped off her donkey, then the pair walked over to David. Uriah let go her arm and stepped back.

Abigail bowed low before David. "My lord, please accept your handmaid into your house as your wife."

David reached down and pulled her up to him. "Abigail, I pray that I will make a good husband for you. Know that I will protect and provide for you all the days of my life."

Abiathar put his hands on each of their shoulders and prayed out loud. "Almighty God, we thank you that you have given us the covenant of marriage between man and woman. Bless this couple, that they may do good things for You. Let Abigail bear David many children, and let him be a good and loving husband to her. May all they do bring You glory. In Your great name we pray, amen."

David looked up at Abigail, then turned and looked at his soldiers. "I thank the God of Israel, for He has kept me from sin. Nabal thought to give me nothing, yet God has given me Nabal's best. He is trustworthy, and takes care of His children. Praise be to the Lord!"

The soldiers shouted in agreement, and Abishai called out over them, "Let us welcome my lord's new wife! We will feast with whatever we have tonight!"

The troops fell out to gather food and drink, and Uriah's men escorted Abigail's maids to settle them into camp. David pulled Abigail near him, put his arms around her waist, and spoke quietly to her. "May our God make us to be strong together," he said, and kissed her.

9

The king stood on his second story balcony overlooking Gibeah. The sun glared in his eyes as he squinted, looking out past the king's hall toward the main gate. Beyond the gate he could see the road that ran east, leading to the remains of Nob. Saul felt a pain in his stomach as he thought of the city of the priests. For that matter, many things brought a pain to his stomach these days. It had been months since he had returned with the army to his compound. After leaving David at En-gedi, he had been forced to march north toward Ashkelon in order to deal with a Philistine incursion into the territory of Ephraim. While still dealing with them, word came of several Jebusite parties raiding Israelite villages along the Kidron River east of Jebus. Abner had taken a company to handle them. Since the king had finally returned to Gibeah he had not left, though several times the general had dispatched soldiers to fight. Often now Saul had different armies fighting him. It seemed almost as if his enemies were ganging up against him. This never happened early in his reign. When Saul first came to the throne, he fought hard against the Philistines, and for a time subdued them. The Jebusites had never even had the courage to openly fight with Saul. It wasn't until David killed Goliath that the Philistines stepped up their efforts to overcome Israel. Now David ran free in the wilderness, enticing Saul's soldiers away and weakening his army, leaving the king to deal with the Philistine soldiers, Jebusite raiders and whoever else dared to raise a sword against Israel. The king's brow furrowed as he brooded on these thoughts.

The sound of knuckles rapping against wood came to his ears, and Josheb stepped out onto the balcony behind Saul. "My lord, there is a messenger for you."

"Who is it?" asked the king.

"Says his name is Jeshimon, a Ziphite," answered the guard. "He claims he has information about David."

"It was the Ziphites who last told me his location, when he was in Moan," muttered Saul, half to himself. " Bring him up to me." Josheb grunted and left the balcony, only to return a moment later. A short, thin man followed him. Immediately upon seeing him, the man bowed low to the ground.

"Jeshimon," said Saul.

"Yes, my lord," he answered.

"So you have news for me, do you?"

"Yes, my lord. I have news regarding the location of David and his men." He continued to bow low.

"Stand up, Jeshimon. Tell me what you know."

"My lord, may I praise you for all you have done in Israel. No other ruler has done so much for his people. You have fought the Lord's enemies and cared for His people-"

"Enough of that, man. I know all about myself. Tell me what you know of David."

"Yes, my lord. David is hiding in the hills of Hakilah, west of Ziph, in the desert. He has been ranging all across the southern highlands in this last year, since before my lord went to find him in En-gendi. He fights the Amorite tribes, stirring them up against us, and takes our livestock. His company is ever growing. It is no longer just his soldiers, but each man has his family with him. Soon there will be so many that all of the food in the land will be consumed by him." Jeshimon was nervous, and he spoke like a man who was saying what he thought the king wanted to hear.

"So you would turn him in to me because he is eating your food?"

"Yes, my lord, but not only that. He is a traitor, and seeks your throne. The king must not let him live." The Ziphite looked very serious.

"Very well, Jeshimon. What would you have me do?" asked the king dryly.

"Go after him, my lord. Disband his army and kill him."

"And give you a due reward for your service of finding him as well, correct?"

"I am not here for rewards, my king. But any kindness from my lord will be taken with appreciation."

Saul snorted. "I thought as much. Take him to Ziba, Josheb, and call Abner for me. I am tired of rotting in this place while Israel falls apart. I'll find David and finish this."

"Yes, my lord," replied Josheb with a nod. The big guard grabbed Jeshimon by the shoulder, pulling him roughly back in the direction they came. Saul stood for a moment thinking. If he could get rid of David, he would strengthen his hold on the throne and may be able to rebuild his army. Then he would be able to take care of the Philistines and the Jebusites. Saul left his balcony, went downstairs and walked quickly outside. He was headed for the training yard, knowing his general would be close by. It was midday, bright and hot outside, and the compound was full of people working and carting around goods and livestock. As he neared the training yard, Saul could hear the cracking sound of wooden swords and shouting. Abner always had his men training. A soldier could never be too prepared, according to the general. As the king came into view of the yard, he saw Abner standing off in front of the barracks as he was accustomed to do while training was going on. Meanwhile, a group of soldiers went through a series of physical conditioning exercises. A tall soldier paced in front of them, calling out cadence as they completed a set of push-ups.

"Down...up, down...up, down...up, down..." called the soldier, surveying the yard to make sure all the troops were using proper form. Spotting a transgressor, he stomped over to the man and stepped on his back. "Very well, Hanoch, stay down and rest. We will all continue until Hanoch here decides to keep form." A groan went out from the other men, and the tall soldier continued with his cadence. Saul looked back at Abner. He stood silent for a change, with his mouth drawn tight. The general turned his head to look as Saul approached.

"My lord," he said with a curt nod.

"The men train strenuously."

"They need it."

"Yes, they will. We have much work to do."

"You want to go after David." Abner cut right to the point. The king looked at him without answering. "I know the Ziphites sent a man to you again. You gave them so much grain and wine last time they were assured to come back."

"Yes, they have. And I'm glad they did. It is time we take care of David. Israel will be destroyed if we do not."

"What about En-gedi? David showed you mercy, when most men would not have. I gave David my word I would not send troops after him."

"Then I will send the troops. David showed me mercy, yes, but he is also tearing my kingdom apart. I won't let the one decent act he showed me blind me to what is happening. Prepare the men. All of them. We march in two days for Ziph. We will capture David and destroy his piddling army."

Abner looked at Saul coldly for a long moment. The king could tell he was thinking things over. Then the general turned his head back to the yard. "Very well my lord."

The king saw Josheb approaching, and he sauntered off to meet him. Abner stepped out toward the troops. "Elizur! Come here!" The tall soldier jogged over to the general and stood at attention.

"Yes sir."

"Good job today, but training is over. Have them fall out and clean up, then let them go eat. We will be moving out in force in two days, so tell them to start preparing themselves. Tomorrow I will give a more detailed plan to the commanders."

"Yes sir!" Elizur ran off to obey, and the general followed him with his eyes. He didn't like the king asking him to go back on his word. It would take a week at least before they encountered David, by the time the army was assembled and they had reached the deserts of Ziph. He may be able to think of something by then.

The night was dark and cloudy, with no stars to be seen in the sky. David crept along quietly, trying to make his way down the rocky path. He walked along an open hillside, down a gradually descending path that led down from the highlands toward the outskirts of Ziph. Behind him, Abishai, a man named Ahimelech, and a company of one hundred troops followed. Saul had taken up pursuit of David again, and the king and three thousand soldiers had spent the better part of the last week searching the desert for the young warrior and his men. They had made camp by the main road that ran west from Ziph through the mountains to Hebron. David had abandoned his camp west of Carmel in the hills several days ago after hearing that Saul was on the move. He had taken his men toward Hebron for two days. Then he had sent his main force farther north and doubled back with one company. He did not have enough men to challenge the king, not even with his main force, but that was not his aim. He had hoped Saul would follow the tracks of his men and he would be able to surprise the king somehow after coming back. Thus far, the plan had worked. Saul's army had fallen in trace of David's men, while the young warrior himself had been able to return without being noticed.

The path suddenly became more steep, and Abishai stepped up alongside David. "We are getting close. Can you see the road down there?'

"Yes," replied David. The path they were descending cut into the hillside, which rose abruptly on their right shielding them from view in that direction.

"It bends around the base of this hill to the right, and then spreads out straight for a long ways. If they're anywhere on the road, we'll be able to see them."

"Good." The pair marched at the front of the formation. Ahimelech, a cousin of Uriah, led the company behind them. They were moving slowly, trying not to make any noise. Surely Saul's men would have troops on watch, and David didn't want to alert any of them. After another few minutes, they had reached the main road. Abishai signaled for a halt, and the men came to a stop. On their right, the hillside remained as a wall to them, blocking their view. David, Abishai and Ahimelech stepped out around it to take a look down the road.

There was the army, camped on the road. They were stretched out so far down the road it must have been the entire force. David looked hard for any who may be awake and on watch, but he couldn't see any. That was strange. *My Lord,* he prayed, *how great You are. I thank you that You have kept us safe through this. I know You do not wish for me to kill Saul. I do not wish to shed any blood here. I pray, God that You will make them to sleep deeply, and make us swift and quiet.*

Ahimelech looked at David and whispered, "What's the plan my lord?"

"There are far too many to risk an attack," said Abishai. The captain knew David was no fool, but he couldn't imagine what he had in mind.

"We're not going to attack. I'm going down to their camp. Which of you will come with me?"

Ahimelech was a brave man, but he wasn't suicidal. He kept his mouth shut.

"I'll go with you," said Abishai. "But you owe me."

"Good. Ahimelech, take the men back up the path to where it started getting steep. You should be able to cross the top of the hill and keep a watch on us. If we're able, we may just climb up that way to you when we're done."

"Understood. But what are you going to do?" he asked.

'I'm not completely sure. Just keep a watch for us, we won't be long. If for some reason we are caught, go back to the main company and take them to Hareth."

Ahimelech nodded. David looked at Abishai. "Ready?"

"Ready as I'm going to be."

'Alright, let's go." Ahimelech turned to the men and ordered them back up the hill while David and Abishai crept out along the edge of the road. As they walked, David inspected the hillside to their right. Though it was dark, he thought it looked like a doable climb, which might be a quicker way out if need be. It didn't take long to reach the army, and David was amazed that no one was awake keeping watch. *Oh God, make haste to help me. Deliver me from my enemies.* The pair walked out into the sleeping soldiers, looking around for the king. After what seemed an eternity, David found him, sleeping in the middle of a large group of men. Next to him lay Abner, snoring away loudly. David found himself getting angry as he looked at the general. Abner had given him his word, and had broken it. David shook his head, and turned to Saul. The king's spear was stuck in the ground next to him. Abishai walked up behind David.

"David, this is your opportunity. God has delivered him into your hands! Let me kill him; I'll pin him to the ground with his own spear!" The captain spoke quietly, but he was obviously exited.

David fought the idea. *No, he is the Lord's anointed."* No Abishai. He is the Lord's anointed. Who can strike him and be guiltless? I will not lay my hands on him, nor will you. The Lord will take him when He wills. Now take his spear, and let us go."

The captain plucked the spear from the ground, and David grabbed a water jug that sat by the king's head. Then they quickly made their way off the road and started to climb the hill. It was not quite so easy a climb as David had hoped, and soon they were both breathing heavily. David had to constantly switch the water jug from hand to hand as his arms tired. Finally, he looked up and saw a familiar face looking down at him.

"Come on my lord, reach for me," said Sibbechai as he reached his hand down toward David. His grip tightened around David's forearm, and the big soldier dragged him easily up onto the hilltop. A moment later and Abishai was sitting next to him, catching his breath.

"Next time let's use the road," he said. David nodded.

Ahimelech had come up beside them, and looked confused. 'I don't get it, you stole his spear? Why not kill him?"

David stood up and brushed himself off. "None of you seem to understand this. I will not lay a hand on Saul. When the Lord is ready for me to be king, then He will place me on the throne." He looked around at the troops. "Have your men back away from the hillside and stay out of sight," he said to Ahimelech. The Hittite obliged, and David stepped to the edge and looked out at Saul's army. It was just before dawn, and the sky was beginning to lighten in the east. David took the spear from Abishai, then shouted out suddenly, surprising all of his men.

"Abner! Abner, son of Ner, wake up! Abner!" David's voice carried far down the road, and many of the soldiers began to stir. "Abner! Answer me!"

Down below, the general stood up. "Who calls for me?" he answered in his deep, booming voice. Abner scanned the hillside and saw a man at the top looking in his direction. "Who are you?"

"Is there any man like you in Israel, Abner? The commander of the king's army?" David yelled at the general. "Why then did you not protect your king?" The king's soldiers had almost all stood up by now, with some of the more disciplined leaders moving among them to get them into formation. The king had also risen and stood by without speaking. "Someone came to kill your king in the night, and you have not protected him. As the Lord lives, you and your men deserve to die."

"My king stands here by my side, alive," Abner shouted back.

"Look around you, general. Where is the king's spear, and his water jug?" David raised the spear high above his head. "I have the king's spear!"

Abner felt a chill run down his back from the sudden realization. How could he have let this happen? He turned to look at the king, but Saul was not looking at him.

"David, is that you, my son?" called the king.

"Yes, my lord." David took the spear and stuck it in the ground. "Why is my lord chasing after me? Did I not already prove to you that I am not against you? This is now the second time that the Lord has put you in my hands, and I have let you live. Yet you have pursued me without a cause."

Saul put his hand over his face in shame. When he removed it, his eyes were wet with tears. "I have sinned, David. No more will I seek your life. I know you will do mighty things, for the Lord is surely with you. Come back to Gibeah, and serve me again."

"No my lord, I cannot. Here is your spear. Let one of your men climb up and return it to you. As sure as I valued your life today, may the God of Israel so value my life." Without waiting for a reply, David turned and marched away, calling his troops to him as he moved. David's men swiftly fell into formation and they jogged quickly toward the path they had come down. David felt a sharp pain in his heart. The king had at one time been like a father to David, and Abner had been a teacher and friend. Now they were both out to kill him, and they would never stop. David knew this had been true for a long while, but for some reason it was finally hitting home with the young warrior. Perhaps it was time for him to move on.

10

The path was steep and rocky and hard to maneuver in the dark. It was early morning, and a large contingent of soldiers moved swiftly down the path in the pre-dawn light. Nearly a hundred men strong, this company had set out several weeks ago from the city of Jebus. Adonizedek had dispatched them to plunder any Israelite village that was undefended. The soldiers had moved due north from the Jebusite capital into Benjamin territory, raiding Hazor and Mizpah. Now they were preparing to launch an attack on the outlying village of Gilgal. Saul's army had recently been detained in the south pursuing David, and the Israelite king had not been able to organize a defense against the Jebusite raiders. Their king had strictly charged them to avoid combat against the Israelite force if possible. The Jebusite army was relatively small, and not built to handle an open fight against a large force. Instead, Adonizedek's plan was for his men to ruin as much of the Israelite country and kill as many civilians as possible, causing problems for the Israelite army and discontent for their king.

At the front of the formation marched a big, ruthless soldier. He stood head and shoulders above any other man there and he had a man with a bull's head tattooed on both sides of his face, images of the bloody-thirsty god Molech. His head was shaved clean, except for a long black braid of hair coming from the back. He carried a long spear that was pointed at both ends and wore a short sword on his hip. The big man picked his way carefully, trying not to make any noise. Ahead of him he could see a small village at the base of the hill they were descending. Inside, it appeared everyone was still asleep. That was how the big man worked. He was an excellent warrior, and could handle nearly any well-trained soldier in the region, but what he really enjoyed was the surprise of his prey. So even here, where no military force would oppose them, he chose to sneak up on them unaware.

As the men reached the base of the hill, the big man motioned for them to spread out into a line formation. There was no wall here, and the line of soldiers covered nearly all of one side of the village. Each man drew his weapon and held it at the ready. No one spoke. Even for the Jebusite soldiers, it was an eerie quiet. Finally, the big man held both his arms straight up in the air and roared.

"Attack!" His deep voice rang loud and clear in the still morning air. The Jebusites rushed forward into the village with weapons raised. "Pain! Bring them pain!" shouted the big man as he surged forward.

The villagers barely knew what was happening. It was still dark out, and many in the first buildings never even made it out of bed. The Jebusites crashed through openings and broke down walls, killing any living thing in their path. Loud smashes accompanied by shrieks of pain woke the rest of the village, but there was little they could do. Several men came out to face the marauders, armed with sticks and farming tools, trying to slow the Jebusites down enough for their families to escape. Those who were able ran with all their might, sprinting across the open fields to the north hoping to find refuge in the hills beyond. Few were that fortunate. Chaos ensued as people and livestock fled for their lives, being pursued mercilessly by these evil men. Most of the village had been destroyed when a Jebusite called out to the big man.

"Jozabad, come here. Look at this hero boy who fights for his god."

The big man stomped over to see, stopping to run his spear through a wounded old man along the way. He reached the soldier who had called for him and looked around. A teenage boy stood facing a circle of Jebusites. His leg was injured and his face bloody, but he stood holding an ox goad and refused to back down. Behind the boy were two smaller children, a boy slightly younger and a little girl. A woman, probably their mother, lay wounded and unconscious on the ground at their feet.

"Look at this. Will you save your family, boy?" laughed Jozabad.

The boy's voice was shaky, but he looked directly at the big man's eyes. "The God of Israel will save my family, for he is greater than you."

Jozabad laughed again. "Your god will not save you, boy. I will kill you myself. But first I will make you watch your family die." He shouted a command, and the closest Jebusite leapt on the boy and wrestled the ox goad away from him. Then the soldier put him in a headlock and turned him so he was facing his family. The big man raised his spear and stepped toward the younger children. They both screamed and hid their faces.

Out of nowhere, a trumpet rang out through the early morning air. Jozabad turned around, while all the Jebusites stayed their weapons and looked up. The sun was just rising, and coming toward the village out of the east charged a company of Israelite soldiers. The big man cursed, and barked orders at his men.

"Fall in! Reform the line! Now!" The trumpet sounded again as the Israelites came nearer. Without hesitating, they swept into the village and engaged the Jebusites. With their persecutors distracted, the few villagers still alive were able to escape into the fields. The teenage boy, injured but determined, picked his mother off the ground and ordered his siblings to follow him, leading them all safely away.

The battle was violent, and ended quickly. The Jebusites were outnumbered three to one. Jozabad was no coward, but he wasn't a fool either. Sensing his men were about to be exterminated, he set the village on fire, using the flames to help shield a retreat. The Jebusites returned up the path they had come with haste, shooting arrows in their wake to discourage any pursuit.

The Israelite commander turned his attention to the burning village and its inhabitants. "Jeremiah, take your men and sweep the village. Make sure no one is left inside. Obadiah, collect the wounded there," he pointed at a spot far from the flames, "and Eliel, have your men start digging a boundary around the perimeter. We need to make sure the fire is contained." His captains assented to their orders and set off to work. The commander walked out toward the fields to look for any of the survivors. He pulled his helmet off, revealing his short hair and brown beard. A young man armed with bow and arrows jogged up to him.

"My lord Jonathan, the Jebusites have crossed the top of the ridge and are moving south toward Timnath."

"Thank you, Ittai. Their force is cut in half. They will return to Jebus before they attempt any more raids. We will do what we can here before we move on."

"Yes my lord," the boy answered.

"Go back to the hilltop. Keep an eye out for any of the Jebusites, and the villagers if they haven't seen us."

"Yes my lord." Ittai jogged off toward the hills. Jonathan looked around him. He couldn't see any of the villagers. The fire was nearly finished, but it had destroyed everything. Few had been saved. The prince could feel himself getting angry. While his father kept the army busy chasing after David, Israel was under attack from real enemies. Jonathan would not follow his father after the son of Jesse regardless, but now his people were under constant threat from outsiders. He had more important matters to deal with. Every time Saul set out for David, the Philistines and the Jebusites would invade. It was almost as if they were working together. Jonathan seemed to think the Jebusites, who lived closer, were keeping an eye on the king's movements. When they sensed he was busy elsewhere, they would send word to the Philistines so they could launch an attack simultaneously. Abner must have thought the same. When Saul called out the army to march to the desert of Ziph in search of David, the general had given Jonathan three companies of troops with orders to patrol the central highlands, where the Jebusites had been raiding. It had been wise on the general's part. The prince had already come across half a dozen of their patrols and sent them running. The Jebusites were stepping up the number of men sent out; soon Jonathan's men would not be able to defend against them. Not only that, the Philistines seemed to be preparing a major operation. They were gradually moving their forces to the north end of their territory, where there was less of a presence of Israelite troops. With his father and David busy playing cat and mouse in the south, most of Israel lay unprotected. Jonathan couldn't shake the feeling that something of epic proportions would be happening soon. What the prince didn't know was who would be stepping up to his country's defense.

The noise of merchants and livestock, mixed with the yelling of soldiers, drifted up to David as he looked down on the city of Gath. He and Abishai stood on a low hill to the east of the main gate. Behind them stood all of David's men, six hundred strong, assembled in formation. A day earlier, David had sought out the commander of the Philistine outpost at Moresheth-gath. Frustrated and tired, he decided the only safety from Saul was to leave Israel for a time. He had taken all his men into Philistine territory and requested an audience with their king. The Philistine commander had been dumbfounded when David marched his troops right up to the outpost and called him out. He had immediately sent to Achish, who gave instructions for David to come to him at Gath. Now they stood outside the city, awaiting an escort to the king.

"Of all the ways I thought I'd be going into Gath, this wasn't one of them." Abishai stood watching the Philistines guarding the gate. "I'd say none of them were expecting this either."

"No, probably not," answered David. For several days now he had been trying to remember all that had transpired at his last visit to this city. Achish had not been so impressed with him then, but this time he had a small army with which to offer service. As they stood watching, a small detail of soldiers marched outside the gate. There were about two dozen, bearing spears and looking like professional warriors. At their head was a stocky man with a dark beard. David recognized him as the detail drew nearer. He had an irritated look on his face, and he stared at David with loathing. The detail marched up the hill and came to a halt a short distance away.

"Greetings, general," David said as Philcol walked up.

"Save your subtleties for another," sneered Philcol. "I've been ordered to bring you to the king. Your men will remain here until Achish tells me otherwise."

"Very well sir. May my commander accompany me?"

"Only him," replied the Philistine shortly. Abishai turned around to face the troops and pointed to Eleazar, who nodded and stepped out in front of the Israelite formation. Then David and his captain fell in with the Philistine detail, and the group marched back down the hill and in through the gate. As they entered, the guards stared at the two Israelites with mistrust.

Philcol led the group into the middle of the city, taking them through the marketplace that was packed with people. As they walked, a Philistine soldier in formation next to the general shouted for everyone to clear a path. This they did eagerly, not wanting to invoke the wrath of the hard-nosed general. They marched quickly, and it didn't take long for the detail to reach the king's great hall. The guards outside the doors came to attention and saluted as Philcol came up, then held the doors open as they went inside. As David's eyes adjusted from the bright sunlight to the much dimmer hall, he could see the throne at the far end set between the statues of Dagon and Baal. The king sat upon the throne, looking at the group as they approached. When David had first met the king, he had been surrounded by counselors and servants. This time he was alone. The Israelite warrior wasn't sure if that was a good sign or a bad one.

"General, I see you have brought me Saul's defector," said Achish loudly. He sounded in good spirits. Philcol bowed his head as he addressed his king.

"Yes, my lord. Here is David the Israelite, as you requested." The general barely concealed the disdain in his voice. Achish looked at David. The king thought he looked somewhat different than the last time he had seen him. David had appeared before him the first time as a young man on the run for his life, alone and in need of help. Now he stood before the throne confidently. He had an army with him and a loyal commander at his side. It had been several years since then, and the experience David had gained leading his men through difficult times was obvious. The king looked down at him and grinned.

"So David, we meet again. It seems you are much better off than the last time."

"Yes, my lord. I have been fortunate, for my God has provided for me." David bowed his head as he spoke to the king.

"Yes, your God does seem to be on your side. You have gained an army and become a formidable opponent to not only Saul but also my own soldiers. Even Philistine troops tell of some of your accomplishments. Your state of mind has also improved, helped by your situation, no doubt." Achish smirked. "Now, tell me why you have come to me."

"My lord, King Saul has chased me from his house. He has taken my wife from me and seeks my life. I owe him no allegiance. Many men from my former command have chosen to follow me rather than serve him. I have no wish to keep them in Israelite lands where we are constantly threatened by both the king's army and subjects loyal to him. Allow me to live in your territory, and I will give you my service."

"Your service. Yes, your service will be required, should you remain in my lands." Achish looked at Abishai. "I take it you have more than one man at your disposal. How many?" he asked.

"I have six hundred men, well-armed and trained for battle."

"That is not so many as I have heard. Have you lost significant men?"

"No, my lord. You may have heard I have more because my men have defeated some of your units that had greater numbers. My men fight well."

Philcol growled. "My lord, this man openly insults my troops. His presence here will cause trouble, I can promise you. There is not a soldier in Gath that does not want him dead."

The king laughed. "They are my troops, not yours, general. And my troops should not be threatened by this man if they are as good as you always say." Achish looked back at David. "However, my general does have a point. Your presence in Gath could very well lead to problems."

"My lord, there is no need that my men and I remain in Gath with you. If I have found favor with you, let us be given a place in one of your small towns outside the city."

The king thought for a moment. "There is a town south of here, called Ziklag. It is large enough to hold all your men and their families. There are no soldiers there, so you would avoid any problems of that nature and provide me with an armed force in the area."

Philcol spoke up. "My lord, will you not consult your counsel before agreeing to this? At least listen to them, if you won't listen to me."

"I'll not take advice from men with no backbone. That is all I have on the counsel. I know you have backbone, general, and I respect your opinion. But we disagree on this, and I overrule you." Philcol grimaced in anger. The king continued. "David, know that you will surely march out to battle with me should the occasion arise. Even if that happens to be against Israel, I expect your loyalty to me."

David looked straight at the king. "Then you will see for yourself what your servant can do, my lord."

"Ha!" The king slammed his fist down on the arm of his throne. "I hope to see what you can do, David. Don't make me regret this, my friend." Achish leaned forward toward the Israelite. "If I regret it, so will you."

11

The sound of soldiers marching in unison drowned out all other noise. The ground seemed almost to shake with the thunder of many footsteps. The noise of horses stamping their feet and men barking cadence added to the excitement. Philcol smiled. There were few things in life he enjoyed so much as watching his troops in formation, preparing for a battle. When the fighting began, he would be busy devising strategies and giving orders. But right now he simply stood and watched, taking in the scene. The Philistine king had called out the entire fighting force, from every major city of his territory. Askelon, Ashdod, Gaza, and Ekron had all answered the call, and Philcol had brought his men up from Gath. Now thousands of Philistine soldiers marched across the plains, preparing a major offensive into Israelite lands. They had moved far to the north, beyond Philistine borders to the city of Aphek. It sat near the coast on the wide plains of Megiddo. And the plains were indeed wide. Far to the south, Mount Carmel stood tall on the horizon. To the east, one could scarcely make out the hills of Zebulun. Aside from that, there was nothing to be seen but open plains, plenty of space for an army to maneuver. If they could entice the Israelites to fight here, it would give the advantage to the Philistines, with their greater numbers and iron chariots. It was so big, the general thought all the armies of the world could line up and do battle here.

Philcol stood on a small rise accompanied by the other generals and governors of the Philistines. Achish, their king, sat behind them on a portable throne. All of them were dressed in their best armor and looking sharp. The massive Philistine army was conducting a pass-in-review for their rulers, with each unit marching by the small group to be observed. It was an impressive sight to look upon.

As the army of Ekron marched past, Philcol turned to its general. "You have nearly as many men as I have, Abimelech. It may be best to have Ekron line up alongside Gath on the main front."

"You have more men, general, and yours are better equipped thanks to being based in the capital city. But my men will perform excellently, you have my word. Perhaps even better than yours," Ekron's general said, only half joking.

Philcol guffawed. "You are a braggart, Abimelech. You always have been. I can remember how you sang your own praises when you helped capture the ark of Israel at Ebenezer so many years ago."

"I'm only a braggart when I have something to brag about."

"Do you remember how you begged like a woman for the ark not to be brought to Ekron after it had destroyed Gath? Maybe you wouldn't have such a high view of yourself if you thought about that more often."

"Don't fault me for being smart enough not to let that cursed thing in my city," Abimelech answered.

"You had nothing to do with it. No one took orders from you back then."

"They do now. And my orders will kill more Israelites than yours."

Philcol didn't respond. He had no interest in foolish arguments with the man. In truth, Abimelech was his subordinate here. Though they each led the army for their respective city, Philcol had been assigned the command of the entire force. The general continued to watch the soldiers pass by. They were nearing the end of the formation now. Once it was over, the soldiers would set in to camp for the remainder of the day while he and the other commanders worked on battle plans. Their scouts had told him just this morning that King Saul had started moving his men north to meet them. It would be nearly a week before the Israelites were close enough to engage with them. As Philcol saw the final unit approaching, he became startled. The commander of the final group was David the Israelite, followed by his own men. All the men standing before the king seemed to notice at once, and a collective grunt went up.

"My lord, what is this? Why is David here to fight with us?" Philcol was about to lose his temper. All the men turned to look at the king.

Achish looked down on them from his throne. "This is David the Israelite. He has defected to me, and served me for over a year. All that time, he has done no wrong in my sight. He is no longer loyal to Saul, and will be a strong opponent of his former master."

"No, my lord!" All the men were openly against this. Abimelech spoke up to the king, "My lord, do you not remember how a group of Israelites numbered themselves with us at Micmash? When the battle turned against us, they fell in with their own people. That is surely what these men will do."

Ahuzzath had followed the army along with the other advisors. The sight of David had stricken him with fear. He pleaded with the king. "My lord, is this not David, about whom they sang that he has slain his tens of thousands? What better way for him to get back in Saul's good graces than by taking him our heads?"

Achish was growing angry. "You are always against me. What need do I have of counselors anyway. Look, all of you!" The king pointed to David's men. "He has been joined by Ittai the Gittite and many of that man's soldiers. General," Achish looked down at Philcol, "Ittai has lived in Gath all his life, and is a proven fighter. He has taken his men and now fights with the Israelites." As the king said, David's men had nearly doubled, as many of the Gittite companies had chosen to follow him. "David could not return to his old master. He has spent nearly a year raiding Israelite towns and killing their people! He cannot return to Saul."

"My lord, he plays you for a fool." Philcol was enraged. "He has spent the year killing off Canaanites living in Israelite territory! Ittai has simply bought into all David's nonsense about the Israelite god, and he has betrayed us! If you would only listen to those who have been assigned to help you, you would know this! David cannot fight with us! Send him back!"

Now Achish had lost his temper. "You forget your place, general. I am the king here, and I make the decisions, not you! Perhaps I'll have you whipped for disrespect!"

By now, the last of David's men had passed by, and all the soldiers had marched off to make camp. The other men had grown quiet. Philcol, still angry, realized he was treading on thin ice. The king may be wrong, but he was still the king. The general spoke again, with restraint this time. "My lord, you are not a fool. But David is being deceptive. He will turn against us if you allow him to fight." He paused for a moment before going on. "If David stays, I will pull my men and return to Gath." Philcol turned to the other generals. "Who's with me?"

It was just before mid-day, and the sun was growing hot. The heavy stamping of feet and the creaking of leather and weapons caused a steady ache in David's ears. The young warrior led his men across the low hills and rolling plains south of Gath and west of Israelite territory, headed back to the town of Ziklag. Recently, they had mustered with the Philistine armies near Aphek in the north. Three days ago, however, the Philistine king had ordered David to take his men and return to their home. Apparently, the Philistine generals had disapproved of their presence, fearing that David would turn against them on the battlefield. Now they marched home to wait out the fighting.

David had not been idle since he had come to Ziklag. He had dwelt there more than a year, and his men had spent that time training and improving their weapons and armor. Often they had gone out raiding the Canaanite tribes along the borderlands of Israel, cleansing the land of its heathenism. David felt a burden to finish Joshua's work, and he intended to act on it. Not only that, he had been convinced to take another wife, a woman named Ahinoam of Jezreel. She was a good woman, humble and attractive, but it had been done mostly to strengthen David's claim as a ruler. He also struck up a friendship with a Philistine commander named Ittai. He was quite the soldier himself, in charge of nearly six hundred men of Gath. With permission from his king, he had put them in David's service. Ittai had been ordered to remain in the north, and the Gittite companies had not returned with David's men.

David was weary from the journey. His head hung low and he looked at the path before him, watching his steps. He wore a heavy pack on his back, full of food and clothing, as well as spare armor, which added to his weariness. Next to him, Abishai plodded along in step. The soldiers behind them were all the same. Each man walked quietly, trying to avoid thinking of the ache in their legs. David was ready to be off of his feet. He was also hungry, but he knew they too close to break for a meal.

David looked ahead of him, hoping to see his home. Instead, something dark could be seen rising over the land. At first, he didn't realize what it was.

"What is that?" David said out loud. Abishai looked up and stared. For a moment he didn't answer.

"Smoke."

David knew he was right. It was thick and black, and it rose high in the air, standing out sharply against the bright blue sky.

"Something's burning," said the captain ominously. Every muscle in David's body tensed. From behind, he could hear the anxious murmuring of his troops. The whole formation began to walk faster. David looked out across the plains to see where it was coming from, but he didn't want it to be true.

"It's Ziklag," Abishai said what David didn't want to. "It's not far. We can make it at a run," he remarked quietly.

David called out the order himself. "Forward! Double-time!" The tired men instantly found a well of energy. While staying in formation, the entire group took off at a run. With David and Abishai in the lead, they covered the distance quickly, driven on by the fear of what they might find. As they grew closer, they could see that the whole town was aflame. The outside of the town had been settled with tents, and they were completely burned through. The small buildings in the center were made of mud and brick, and stood somewhat undamaged. But every window had flames reaching out as the interior of the buildings went up. With loud cries, the men broke ranks and rushed onward, looking desperately for their families. David fought his way through smoke and fire to reach his own house. He could feel panic setting in. Everyone kicked through broken doors and stamped out smaller flames, searching for their loved ones, but no one could be found. No women, no children, not even any livestock were there. The men smothered what fire they could, and Abishai ran around directing others to separate the fuel from the fires that were too big to be smothered. Some of the flames began to die out, but the ring of tents would have to be left to burn out on it's own. The men moved away from the town to avoid the smoke. Then they began to break down.

Many just sat on the ground. Others walked in circles, not knowing what to do. Everyone wept.

David stood by himself away from the others, trying to decide what to do. All their families had been taken captive, and their town had been burned. Who could have done this? How could they find them? He didn't know, and his mind raced as he tried not to think of what may be happening to Abigail and Ahinoam. He had been quiet for some time when several of his men began arguing with one another. David watched, and very quickly the argument turned physical. Several others jumped in to intervene, but that only caused more fighting. David rushed over to stop it.

"Men, this is no way to act. Will fighting each other save your wives and children? We must not turn on each other now."

One of the soldiers involved sneered at David. "How wise of you to say so, David. You have no children that were taken, only a pair of women you sleep with. Who are you to tell us how to act?"

David looked at the soldier, angry. "You think because I have no children that I am not upset for my wives? I would hunt these men down to the ends of the earth for them."

More men started in on David. "You're the reason our families are gone. If we had not followed you, they would be safe with us, back home in Israel."

Another man yelled, "Instead they are likely dead, while we follow a vagabond who thinks he should be king!" Many of them agreed, and shouted against him. Suddenly, one yelled, "Stone him!" They all stood in a large group just away from the burning town. David stood in the center of the group, and most of his men were beginning to crowd around. They were very upset, and were looking to take their disappointment out on him. The men were loud and acting rashly, and David was afraid. *Oh my God, protect me. Deliver my life from their hands. Do not let them shed blood in their anger.* As he prayed, David looked at the men around him, hoping to find an ally.

And he did. Sibbechai barreled his way through the crowd and stood up next to David. Then he shouted out to the men. "Any man who wishes to kill David has to go through me." The big man drew his sword and held it between David and the crowd. Elhanan stepped up as well, followed by Shammah and Eleazar. The four formed a circle around David, each with a weapon in hand. Uriah the Hittite called out to his company to separate from the crowd.

Abishai walked through the mass of soldiers, shouting at the men. "For shame, Israel! For shame! Who has done more for you than David? Who is anointed by a prophet of the Almighty? David has led you righteously, and you respond like this? For shame!" The captain started grabbing troop leaders, strictly ordering them to separate their units. As they complied, some of the tension began to go down. David walked away from the men to find a spot alone. He walked back into the town and found his home, which was near the center. It was made of brick and still stood upright, but the inside was nothing but ash. He was beaten in spirit. His family was gone and his men wanted him dead. David fell to his knees.

Hear me speedily, oh my God, for my spirit fails me. Do not hide Your face from me, or I will be like those who go down into the pit of death. My spirit is overwhelmed and my heart is desolate. Cause me to hear Your loving heart. Lift up my soul, oh my God.

As David prayed, the gloom and pain in his heart began to melt away. The Lord was good; that he did not question. The Lord loved him; that he also did not question. David stood up. The God of Israel was Almighty, none could overcome Him. He was a Shield, and Protector, and Deliverer to those who trusted in Him. Suddenly David knew what to do. He left his home and walked quickly back to his men. Most had scattered again, trying to deal with their grief. "Abiathar! Where is the priest?" David yelled.

"Here, my lord!" called out Abiathar. He came up to David quickly.

"Inquire of the Lord. If He wills, we will go after these men and bring back our families."

"Yes, my lord." The priest shuffled off.

"Abishai!" called David.

"Yes, my lord?" answered the captain.

"Have some men look for tracks, or any other evidence of who may have done this. Look for where they may have gone. Let me know what you find."

"Yes, my lord." The captain went off, shouting to the men to obey. David stood where he was, watching as Abishai started rounding the men up and getting them back to the right state of mind. It did not take long before Abiathar returned, wearing his priestly garments with the ephod strapped to his torso. He looked grave, but purposeful.

"My lord," he said as he walked up, "the Lord says to pursue, for he has given them into your hand, and you will recover your families."

Just as the priest delivered the message, Uriah ran up to David. "My lord, we have found their tracks, heading south. It looks like there are many of them."

"Abishai!" called David immediately, without responding to either. "Have the men prepare to march. We are going to rescue our families. Let us be off!"

Their pace was fast. The slow, laborious trek of the last few days had been forgotten, and the men jogged almost without stopping, driven on by fear and anger. It had been just past noon when they set off from the remains of Ziklag. For several hours now they had followed a road running south, which showed signs of a great deal of traffic recently. David had six hundred warriors with him, men of courage and skill, but it appeared they were following a group many times that. Their track was not consistent, but David and his men seemed to be running along it well. The young warrior jogged at their head, a fire raging in his heart.

The terrain was rough. There were no large hills, but the land was rolling and it was tough ground, covered with rocks and rough vegetation. The men still carried their packs they had borne out from Aphek, and they would soon be slowing the men down, no matter their anger. The sun continued to move across the sky and their pace began to slow. By mid-afternoon, they came to a deep ravine with a shallow river at the bottom. Looking down at it, Abishai groaned.

"We must have lost the path somewhere. No way they crossed this, not with women and children to deal with," said the captain.

"Not to mention livestock. Is this the Besor?" asked David?

"Must be."

David looked up and down the ravine. He could see nothing in either direction. "No, they definitely didn't cross here. But there's only one town they could be heading for this way, called Sharuhen. They'll have to go there, there's no way to feed all those mouths out here in the open, at least not for long. The quickest way to the town is directly across the Besor. If we cross, we may have a better chance of overtaking them."

"So, you want to climb down this?" asked Abishai doubtfully.

"Yes. It's doable, and this may be the only way we catch them."

"Whatever you say." The captain turned to the men. "Listen up, ladies. I hope no one is afraid of heights. If you are, you're going to get over it today. We're crossing this ravine. Eleazar!"

The soldier stepped up. "Yes sir?"

"Your men are first. Spread them out and let half your company go at once. Get them ready."

"Yes sir!" Eleazar turned to his men. "Let's go! First and second platoon, you're up!" he said, pointing the men out. Several of them seemed nervous. One soldier spoke up.

"Sir, I can't make this climb carrying a pack, at least not right now." Several others said the same. Eleazar grunted his dissatisfaction. He didn't like hearing his men talk like this.

The captain stepped in. "Very well. My lord, with your permission, we will leave the packs here and set a guard on them. We won't be needing them if we catch up today." David nodded. "All of you, ground your packs back away from the ravine," continued Abishai. "Eleazar, take those who say they aren't strong enough and make them a guard. If they won't climb, they won't fight."

"Yes sir," he answered. All the men took off their packs and staged them together. David stepped up so all the men could hear him.

"Listen up men. If you are afraid of the climb, or feel you are not strong enough, then you will stay here. The Lord fights for us, and He will see our victory. If you wish to stay, then stay." At first, a few men walked over and stood by the packs. Then more. Then more, until David thought all of them would go. Finally, it seemed that about two companies worth had elected to stay.

Abishai couldn't believe how many had given up. "What a lot of women! All of you are choosing to stay?"

"Let them stay, captain," said David. "The Lord makes one man as a thousand. We have plenty." He looked at the men who were going to stay. "Very well. You men will remain here with the packs until we return. Now, the rest of you, let's go! Eleazar, take them over."

Eleazar stepped up to the edge and flopped on the ground, sliding himself down without hesitating. He grabbed at jutting rocks and holes in the cliff face and quickly moved downward. His men followed. It was deep, but not so steep that one would drop straight down, except for a few places. It was a grueling climb. Several times men lost their grip and slid downward, only to stop themselves farther down. David and Abishai climbed down with the first company. As they reached the bottom, each man waded across the river and climbed out on the other side, which was much lower. Then the next company followed. Before long, four hundred men had crossed the river and stood ready to resume the chase.

They set off again at once, heading across the land. The vegetation grew thicker, full of high grass and tall bushes, and it became harder to see far ahead. After they had gone a ways, Eleazar, who was just behind and off to the side of David, stumbled and fell face down on the ground. Abishai halted the formation and turned back to his leader. Eleazar stood up, unhurt, and walked back a few steps. There in the grass lay a man, groaning from being run over.

"Look at this!" said Eleazar, surprised. He looked at the soldier beside him. "Help me out." The two reached down and sat the man up. He was obviously dazed, but not from being stepped on.

David walked up to them. "Give him some food and water. It looks like he hasn't had any in a while." Several men pulled out skins of water, and one a hunk of bread he had kept with him.

The captain looked at David. "The sun is starting to get low. We don't have much time for this."

"Do not withhold good while it is in your power, Abishai. This man will die without help." The captain didn't respond. The man ate and drank, and after a few minutes he seemed a little better. "Who are you?" David asked him.

The man looked up at David quizzically, as if wondering who this man was who spoke to him. "I am an Egyptian, the slave of an Amalekite. I became sick a few days ago, and my master abandoned me."

"What was your master doing out here?"

"He is a soldier, and belongs to a large company. They have been raiding villages throughout the Negev."

"Have they been to Ziklag?" asked David.

"They burned Ziklag," the man said quietly. Several of David's men who could hear began to mumble angrily. David could sense the blood rising in them again.

"Can you lead us to these men?" he asked.

"I will lead you, if you swear you will not kill me or return me to my master. He is an evil man."

"By the God of Israel, I will not. Take me to them."

They picked the man off the ground. Eleazar ordered two of his men to help him walk, as he was still shaky on his feet. As they went, his walking improved, and in a short time he was supporting himself. The man seemed to think they were very close, and Abishai had all the men stay quiet. He guided them back away from the trail they had been following, moving more in a western direction. As they went, the land began to rise. It wasn't long before they began to hear the voices of many people, as well as the sounds of sheep and cattle. Abishai had the Egyptian taken to the rear of the formation, then spread the troops out in a sort of modified line. They continued to walk up the slope as they fought the thick vegetation. David and Abishai were pushed out slightly in front, and soon came to a thick row of bushes that marked the top of the incline. Looking over, they could see the ground slope away downward into a wide open space. They could also see the source of the noises. A great company of men nearly twice the number of David's troops were scattered abroad across the field. They were eating and drinking, without a care in the least. Women and children were mixed in among them. Most of them sat quietly or served the men, looking very nervous. Finally, there were large herds of livestock roaming about. David motioned to Abishai, and the captain sent a message down through the ranks. All the men, still on line with each other, crawled up even with David and the captain. Every man quietly drew his weapon and held it ready, each of them looking earnestly for his family.

Oh my Lord, David prayed, *thank You for bringing us here. Now, Lord, be my strength. Teach my hands to war, and make my men stronger than a bow of steel, that we might destroy the Lord's enemies and take back our families. You are our Shield and our Protector, oh Mighty God.*

He whispered to Abishai. "On my command." David drew his sword and gripped it tight. Leaping to his feet, he shouted, "Forward Israel! The

Lord fights for you!" David rushed downhill, and every man with him jumped up and followed suit, shouting as they went. The Amalekites, completely off guard, looked up in surprise. Some did not have a weapon in hand, and many were drunk. None were ready to fight. The women among them all threw up their hands and grabbed their children, running as far from their captors as possible and huddling together. As the Israelites bore down on them, the Amalekites turned to face them as best they could. It was in vain. David's men slashed and hammered their way through the unfortunate group. A large portion of the Amalekites made a hasty retreat, some mounting camels and riding away with as much speed as possible. Abishai ordered Uriah and his men to collect the families, then sent Eleazar and Shammah to lead their men after the fleeing heathen, slaughtering all in their path. Few of them escaped. None who fled on foot survived the chase, only a handful that had been able to outpace the Israelites on a camel.

Everything that had been taken was recovered. Every man's wife and children were alive and mostly unhurt. All the livestock had been rounded up. As they gathered everyone together and prepared for the march back home, David thanked the Lord for His graciousness. How great was this God, who brought families back together and protected His children?

12

The rain fell in sheets, soaking the men as they walked. There were three of them, all hooded and cloaked to withstand the rain and conceal the armor they wore. They walked all in a row. The one in front was big and strong. Behind him walked a younger man, not quite so heavy but well-built with a bushy beard. In the rear marched a very tall man, though he walked with his head hanging low to see through the rain. They were just south of the town of Endor, a small town in Issachar's territory. The townspeople had directed them here.

The ground was wet and muddy. The big man led them down a path that ran from the top of a hill into a deep draw. The sides were very steep and it was dark at the bottom, giving it the look of a pit. The place had an ominous feeling about it. The men walked carefully, trying not to slip as they made their way down. When they reached the bottom, the draw spread out on both sides of them for quite a ways. They could not see the end in either direction. Not knowing which way to choose, the tall man pointed down one side and they resumed walking. It was not very wide between the walls of the hill, and the big man had to turn sideways in several places to get through. The rain was a little better than on the hilltop, but the mud was worse, as all the water was slowly making its way into the bottom of the draw. After walking for several minutes, they reached a dead end. The tall man shook his head and they went back in the other direction. With him in the lead now, the men continued on past the point they had descended in search of their destination.

This direction was longer. After walking for almost three times the distance, the draw began to open up. It led into a wide flat area on the edge of slope. To the right the wall receded, but to the left in ran straight on until the men could see the opening of a cave. Seeing it, the tall man stopped and let the other two pass on in front of him. As they walked up to it, they could see a fire burning within. There were several young goats and a sheep laying down in some hay near it keeping warm, and a few chickens wandering around. There were also several blankets laid out and a handful of old bones in a pile on the ground. It did not appear that any people were there.

The big man stepped inside and threw back his hood. "Avishag!" he called out. The sound echoed of the cave walls, spooking the animals. They stood up and trotted to the back of the cave. The big man waited for an answer, but got none. He called out again, this time louder. "Avishag!"

This time there was an answer. "Who are you?" The voice was soft and cold. The big man could see no one.

"I am here to enlist your services," he said, looking around. Still he could not see anyone.

"What services do you seek?" It was a woman's voice, not loud but very clear. It seemed to bounce off the cave walls, making it hard to tell which direction it came from.

"You are a witch," he said bluntly. "I would have you call up the dead."

"A witch, you say. Do you not know that the king has banished all those with a familiar spirit from the land? They say none of them remain."

"You are a witch, woman. Do not waste my time. I have payment for you." The big man tossed a small sack into the hay. For a moment there was no answer.

The tall man in the rear stepped forward without removing his hood. "You may have our word. We are not after your life. I am in need of your help."

From a shadow behind the fire a figure stepped out. She was shorter than the men, and slender with long black hair that reached almost to her waist. She was much younger than any of them expected. She walked slowly over to the hay and picked up the sack to examine it. Inside were several small gems, very brightly colored. The fire reflected off them, making them shine in the dark cave. Then she looked at the men. "Come, sit down and dry yourselves off." The men obliged, sitting on the blankets and wiping the rain off their faces. The tall man still did not remove his hood. The woman replaced the gems inside the bag and tucked them into her waist band. She looked hard at the tall man. "What may I do for you?"

"Call up a spirit for me, for I need his counsel," he replied.

"Whom shall I bring up for you?"

The tall man took a deep breath. "Samuel."

The woman was taken aback. "The great prophet?" she asked hesitantly.

"The same," the tall man replied.

The woman was quiet for a moment before answering. "I will call him, but I promise nothing."

"Call him," said the tall man.

"As you wish." The woman walked over next to the fire, closed her eyes and held out her hands. She began to move her lips as if speaking, though no words came out. She also started swaying her body rhythmically, to some unheard music. The men all remained quiet, watching. All of them, but especially the tall one, began to feel very uneasy. There was something unsettling, yet unseen going on in the cave.

With a suddenness that surprised even the woman, the small fire blazed up with incredible heat, growing to three times its size. The woman shrieked and fell backward, stumbling over her livestock and scattering them. The men all jumped to their feet in fear, the big one drawing his sword without knowing why. All three watched the fire, expecting something terrible to leap out at them.

"Who are you!?" cried the woman, speaking to the tall man. "Why have you come to me?"

The tall man stood tense and afraid. "What do you see?" he asked anxiously.

"You have deceived me! You are the king! No prophet of God comes at the bidding of a witch!" She was terrified, crawling backwards on the floor to get away from the fire.

The tall man through his hood back, revealing the face of Saul. He stepped forward towards the woman and bent down near her face. "I am the king," he said calmly. "Now tell me, what do you see?"

The woman could not take her eyes off the fire. "I see an old man, with a mantle and a staff. He is surrounded by a strange power, though it is not his own."

Saul stood up and looked at the fire. He could not see the prophet, but he could sense that Samuel was there. He stepped closer to the fire, feeling it's searing heat, and bowed low to the ground. As he did so, a noise came from the fire. To the other three, it sounded like a great crackling of wood. But Saul could hear the prophet's voice.

"Why have you disturbed me, Saul, son of Kish?" The voice was unmistakably Samuel's, yet it was younger and stronger than it had been at his death. Saul quivered in fear.

"My kingdom is in great danger," said the king. "Israel has lost faith in me, and the Philistines have come up to destroy me. I cannot overcome my enemies. The Lord has departed from me, so I have called for you. Please, Samuel, tell me what I must do, and I will do it."

"I cannot help you," came the prophet's voice, gravely. "The Almighty will do what He has sworn. He will rend the kingdom from your hand and give it to your servant David, because you have not obeyed the word of the Lord." Saul began to weep as the prophet continued. "Your time is over, Saul. Tomorrow, the Lord will deliver Israel to the Philistines, and you and your sons will go down to the grave."

As suddenly as it had flamed up, the fire went out, leaving nothing but ashes and smoke. The room immediately felt cold. Saul fell forward on his face, weeping silently, his body heaving in anguish. The big man rushed to the king's side and knelt next to him.

"My lord, what happened?" asked Josheb, his head guardsman. The others had heard no words, and did not know what the king had heard. The big man turned to his partner. "Doeg, start the fire again, we need to warm him up." Josheb looked at the woman. "You, prepare him a meal."

"No," groaned the king. "I will not eat." He sat up and wiped his face. Saul's face was covered with grief.

The woman stood up and brushed herself off before coming near to the king. "My lord, this man is right. You are very weak, and need to eat." Saul just shook his head. "Please, my lord. I have obeyed your voice, so listen to mine. Allow me to set a meal before you, that you may recover your strength."

The king remained silent for a long time, staring directly at the wall behind where the fire had been. What did it matter if she made him a meal? It didn't matter. Nothing mattered.

Finally, the king nodded his head. "Very well."

The general watched the ground sweep by as his chariot raced across the plain. Philcol squinted from the wind as he looked forward, trying to keep the Israelite army in view. His driver whipped the horses onward. Behind him spread out nearly three thousand chariots, followed by five thousand footmen. They had come from all over Philistia for one purpose: to destroy the Israelite army.

The Philistine unit commanders blew horns and shouted, trying to keep their men in the correct formations. The Israelites were assembled in the valley of Jezreel, which lay under the shadow of Mount Gilboa, one of the highest points in northern Israel. Philcol knew that the Israelites would try and lure his soldiers up away from the valley into the hills. With no chariots and only half as many troops, they had little other choice. The general could see them, lining up for battle as the Philistine chariots drove hard in their direction. He could hear the thunder of hooves on the hard ground, and see the lather building on the horses' mouth and chest. Philcol's blood was pumping fast. He was ready to engage.

As the chariots drew near, the general heard the Israelite trumpets sounding for battle. They did as he was expecting: the Israelite formation fell back and moved to higher ground. They knew they had no chance of standing up to a charge of iron chariots. Now he had to beat them to their next move.

"Archers!" he yelled, waving his arms to signal the command. Those chariots in the front had been outfitted with bowmen, and at the general's command, they loosed their arrows into the retreating Israelite soldiers. Philcol must have announced it at the same time as the Israelites, for a return volley came even as the Philistines fired. The Israelites had bowmen set in position further up the mountain, and many of their arrows found their targets. More than a few chariots became disabled as their drivers or horses went down with an arrow in them. Philcol had expected as much. Waving his arms again, he redirected the charge to move right under the Israelite retreat. As the formation moved, the Israelite soldiers found themselves in between the Philistines and their own archers, forcing the archers to hold. The chariots came to a halt, and the Philistine bowmen continued to fire, inflicting many casualties.

Another Israelite trumpet sounded. Suddenly the Philistine chariots found themselves under fire from their rear. A company of archers had been hidden on the far side of the valley, and when the chariots had turned toward the mountain, they had rushed out to take advantage. Then the trumpet sounded again, and the Israelite soldiers who had retreated up the hillside now rushed headlong toward the stalled chariots. For a moment, Philcol thought they might be overcome. "Dismount!" he shouted, and his men drew their weapons and leapt to the ground to face the assault. The general blew his own horn, calling for the footmen to move forward. Still standing on his chariot, he looked around to take stock of the situation. All along the line, the Israelite soldiers were pushing forward. They had the better position, and until the footmen arrived, they had more troops. Philcol needed to take out one of their leaders. He tried to find Abner, but couldn't see him in the confusion. Looking higher up the mountain, the general saw something better. The king's standard flew above a company of soldiers. That's what he needed, the head of Saul. The general turned to look for his footmen. They were closing in. With his driver on the ground fighting, Philcol grabbed the reins and swung his chariot around, circling wide to avoid the mass of horses and men that had piled up on the ground. He whipped his horses into a gallop, their strides swallowing up the ground as they raced toward the oncoming Philistine soldiers. The general pulled them to a stop as they reached the front line.

A big Philistine marched at the front, towering over the other soldiers. "General," he bellowed, "what are our orders?"

"Anchises, look there!" Philcol pointed high up the mountainside. "That's the standard of the king. Take your men straight up there and kill him!"

"Yes, general." Anchises carried a giant war axe. He lifted it high and shouted to his men. "Follow me, you lazy women! Philistines are dying! Follow me!" The big soldier rushed forward followed by several companies under his command. Philcol raced his chariot up and down the line, giving the other commanders their orders. The advantage had turned now. Philcol sent a division across the valley to take care of the Israelites who had attacked their rear. Then he sent a huge contingent straight ahead at the main line of battle. The Israelites had nearly decimated the grounded chariotmen, but with the massive wave of foot soldiers advancing, they broke off the attack and retreated up the mountain. Philcol drove his chariot at the rear of the formation, watching the advance develop.

Up on the mountainside, Anchises led the way as his men climbed toward the king. The big Philistine smashed through the Israelite defenders, swinging his mighty axe with fury. As they came closer to the king, a tall Israelite shouted against them. He called for archers, and a volley of arrows flew at Anchises' men, dropping quite a number of them. Then the tall Israelite drew his sword and led a large group of soldiers downhill to meet the oncoming Philistines. He was a skilled warrior. The two lines met, and he dropped two Philistines with one stroke. Anchises moved toward him. The big Philistine brought his axe down on the head of an unfortunate soldier, splitting his skull. The tall Israelite took down another Philistine, then engaged another. After that soldier fell at his feet, Anchises stepped up to take his place, recognizing the prince of Israel.

"Ahhhhh!" yelled the Philistine, swinging his axe hard at Jonathan's head. The prince ducked and slashed with his sword, clanging across the Philistine's chest armor. Anchises swung again, and Jonathan blocked it with his blade. The pair exchanged blows, each blocking the others' attack. Suddenly, with a quick move, Jonathan stepped in low and sliced his blade across an unprotected spot of the Philistine's waist, spilling blood and causing Anchises to bend forward and hold his middle. Jonathan stepped back, reared up to his full height and raised his sword overhead, preparing to swipe the man's head clean off. But before he could bring his sword down, Anchises let go of his belly and struck Jonathan with a powerful blow, landing the back of his fist and forearm on the prince's face and knocking him flat on his back. Standing tall, the big Philistine stomped on Jonathan's chest with one foot and kicked his sword away with the other. He gripped his war axe with both hands, raising it over his head. With a roar, Anchises brought the blade down on the prince with all his might. Jonathan's body went limp.

Saul looked down from the mountainside, watching the chaos unfold. He stood about halfway up Mount Gilboa, surrounded by ten of his personal guards and a company of soldiers. From his position, he could see his army breaking down. Abner had come up with an excellent strategy, and for a time it had looked as if it was going to work. The general's aim was to draw the Philistine chariots into range of the archers, then cut them down with the infantry before the Philistine footmen could arrive. Then they would have retreated into the hills to force the fighting onto ground that was more in their favor. However, the Philistine soldiers had arrived much sooner than Abner had hoped, and they were beginning to overwhelm the Israelites. The general was down in the thick of the battle, trying his best to turn the tide somehow. The king could see the Philistines pushing the main body of the Israelites back into the mountainside, where there was little room for retreat.

Several Philistine companies had gone around the flank of the two armies and were attacking straight uphill, going after the king. His son Jonathan, deciding to join the king in his defense of Israel, had been with him on the mountain, and had taken a group of soldiers down to meet the advancing Philistines. Saul had lost sight of him in the melee, but he had no time to wonder what may have happened to him. Another Philistine company was marching up in his direction. The king would have to lead this charge himself.

"Josheb, have the guards fall in behind me. Captain," Saul called to the company leader, "set your men in formation! We will move on these Philistines!"

"Yes my lord!" he answered, and shouted orders to his troops. Josheb and Doeg the Edomite lined up next to Saul. The king had a sword sheathed at his side, and carried his spear in hand. He raised his spear up over his head and shouted. The soldiers shouted a response.

"Forward men!" yelled the king, and he took off at a run followed by his men. The Philistines drew their weapons and charged, and the two lines crashed together. Saul fought like a madman, smashing men with his spear and then running them through. Josheb fought by the king's side, cleaving his sword into any Philistine who came near. One who made it past the big guard managed to break Saul's spear in two with his sword, but the man paid dearly for it when the king deftly drew his own sword and brought it to bear on the Philistines neck. The two groups were evenly matched, but the Israelites had a better position and soon got the better of their opponents. As the last Philistine fell, Saul looked around to see how his men had fared. More than half lay dead on the ground.

A volley of arrows began to fall around them. As the Israelites at the base of the mountain were being decimated and looking for a path of retreat, more Philistine companies were marching uphill. Saul did not have enough men left to effectively engage them.

"My lord, more are coming," shouted Josheb, pointing at them. "Surround the king, shield's up!" he called to the king's other guards. All of them moved to protect the king, and the remaining soldiers fell in around them. "Back up the hill, move!" ordered Josheb, trying to get the king away from danger. The mountainside was rocky and uneven, and the group was still being pelted with arrows. Several of the guards fell as they were hit. Doeg was standing right next to Saul, when an arrow pierced his neck, dropping him to the ground. The Edomite left a gaping hole in the king's protection as he fell. Josheb stretched to cover the king with his shield, but it was too late. An arrow flew past the shield and sunk deep in Saul's back.

"Uuunngghh!" moaned the king as he stumbled, barely keeping himself on his feet. Josheb grabbed him and stood him up. The point of the arrow was sticking out the right side of Saul's chest, and blood was flowing freely from the wound.

"My lord!" cried the big guard, terrified. The remaining men were able to surround the pair and provide some temporary cover. The Philistines had ceased to fire their arrows but continued to pursue the group. Saul looked at the oncoming Philistines with a blank look in his eyes. Then he turned to Josheb.

"Draw your sword, Josheb, and kill me," the king said softly, as blood ran out of his mouth. "Or else these uncircumcised men will abuse me."

Josheb shook his head. Never had the big man been so afraid. "Please," stammered the king. The guard shook his head again. Saul looked down. Somehow, he had managed to hold on to his sword. The king looked at the Philistines once more, then back at Josheb. The big man was shaking in fear. Saul grabbed the sword at mid-blade and turned the point toward his stomach. Then he fell on it, crying out in anguish as he hit the ground.

Josheb screamed. The other men, seeing their king dead, dropped their shields and ran. The big guard looked and saw the Philistines closing in. With a wail, he turned his own sword point to his belly and fell on it, crying out in agony. As he lay there bleeding out, the big man forced himself to roll over on his back. Above him appeared a man carrying a sword. Josheb watched the sword coming down toward him, and then he could see no more.

The Philistines overran the small group. None of Saul's men survived. The pagan soldiers swarmed the bodies of the Israelites looking for spoil. Anchises marched up toward the body of the king. He raised his hand in the air, holding up the severed head of the Jonathan. "Take his head! We will bring it to Dagon!"

13

The hot afternoon sun beat down on the rolling plains. A lone man walked slowly along the rocky path, heading southward, farther away from Israelite territory. He was an Amalekite, and he was very tired. Three days ago he had fought as a hired sword for a Philistine company against King Saul's army far to the north. The Philistines had overpowered the Israelites, killing the king and his son and destroying much of the army. The Israelite soldiers had scattered, every man fleeing to his home as they were left without a ruler. Meanwhile, the Philistine king had established his presence in the land that had been Israel's, and began fortifying military posts there to secure it. Achish's soldiers had plundered the area, taking Israelite weapons and supplies and raiding the defenseless villages nearby. A foreigner to both sides, the Amalekite had deserted in the night and headed south.

He looked ahead of him down the path. A ways off, he could see what looked like a group of tents rising from the land. There was something else beyond the tents, but he was too far away to see. He continued to march along, optimistic with the plan he had formed for himself. He was dirty and disheveled from his hasty journey, and was looking forward to a meal and a wash. He picked up his pace, expecting to be well received. As he came closer to the tents, he could see there were a group of buildings that lay to the rear. They all looked black and in disarray. The tents all looked to be recently put up, and there were many of them. The place looked busy, full of people going about their daily business. As he watched the town, he could see children running to and fro in play and women singing as they worked by the tents. He could see a large group of men working around the buildings, seemingly repairing the mess. He also noticed several armed men set at along the perimeter, keeping watch. One of them must have noticed him as well, for the soldier had motioned to his comrades, and another soldier came and stood beside him. The pair watched him intently as he walked up the path toward them.

The Amalekite was of average size and build, and had a small sword sheathed at his side. He also carried a sack on his back. His tunic had been torn in two and hung raggedly from his chest. His head was covered in dirt, as if in mourning.

"Who might you be?" asked one of the soldiers, a tall and lean youth holding a spear.

"I am called Eliphaz, an Amalekite," the man answered. "Is this Ziklag?"

"What's left of it," said the tall youth, somewhat irritated. "Why are you clothes rent? What has happened?"

"I have come from the battle at Mount Gilboa, in Jezreel. I have come with news from Israel."

The other soldier, who was shorter and thicker, looked at the man with suspicion. "What's an Amalekite have to do with Israel, that he would bring us news?"

"I know you are led by David, son-in-law to the king. I have great respect for the man, for I have heard of his deeds. I have word he needs to hear."

The tall youth looked at the other soldier. "Let's take him in. David would want him fed at least before sending him away, even if he is lying."

"We'll take him to David first." The shorter man looked at Eliphaz. "Give me your sword."

Eliphaz obliged, and the two men led him into the town. As they walked, many of the women and children stared at him in wonder. The Amalekite noticed that most of the tents were still being put up, and they still had the appearance of being settled into. There was a broad space between the tents and the older buildings, and it was littered with burnt remains of metal spikes and other tent materials. The buildings were obviously burnt. What could have happened here? Eliphaz began to question his strategy, hoping nothing had taken place that might thwart him. As he came, the men who were busy repairing the buildings paused from their work and looked in curiosity. It didn't take long before they had reached the center of town, where a large building stood. From inside could be heard several men talking and going about their work.

"Keep him here," said the shorter man, walking ahead into the burnt home. After a moment, he reemerged followed by a man with a short, very dark beard and scraggly black hair. He was not overly tall or broad of shoulder, but he looked strong and well-conditioned, and he carried himself with authority. He was dirty and sweating from work, as everyone here seemed to be. Eliphaz could tell he must be the man he was looking for.

"Welcome to Ziklag. Tell me who you are," said the man, in a tone that suggested obedience. Others started to gather around, sensing something of note may be happening.

"I am Eliphaz, an Amalekite. I have come seeking David, the son-in-law of King Saul, for I have news for him."

"I am he," said the man. "What news do you bring?"

The Amalekite fell on his face and looked at the ground. Without raising his head, he said, "I have important word for the king of Israel." Abishai and Shammah came out of the house behind David and stood beside him. Neither spoke as they took in the scene.

"Stand up, and tell me what your message is," said David after a moment. The comment about the king had given him pause.

The Amalekite stood up and looked at David. "Yes, my lord. I have been at the battle at Mount Gilboa, in Jezreel. The Philistines have routed Israel, and the Israelites have all scattered to their homes."

The captain didn't trust Eliphaz, and it was obvious. "What were you doing there?" he asked. "Where you in the battle?"

"Yes. I was in Israel's camp, fighting against the Philistines. They had far too many men, and they overcame us. Many soldiers have fled, and Saul and his son Jonathan have been killed."

Though David almost never lost his bearing, his men could tell he was deeply moved. He stood silent, staring at this man who had come to him. No one else spoke. Eliphaz watched David nervously. This was not the reaction he had expected. Finally David spoke to him.

"How do you know that the king and his son are dead?"

"As Israel retreated from the mountain, Jonathan mounted a final defense and was killed by a Philistine warrior." The Amalekite spoke gravely. "Then I saw the king fall on his spear. He lay mortally wounded, and called out to me, for there was no one else near him. The king pleaded with me to give him mercy, before the Philistines could abuse him. I knew he would die from his wounds, so I took my sword and did what he asked."

Everyone was quiet. This man did not appear trustworthy, and David was hoping it was a lie. "You killed him?" David asked.

"Yes, my lord." Eliphaz took the sack from his back and pulled out a pair of bright golden objects. David's heart almost stopped, but the Amalekite continued. "I have brought these here to you, my lord. The king's crown and royal bracelet. They are meant for the new king of Israel." He stepped forward and went down on one knee, holding them out toward David.

David groaned loudly. He grabbed his clothes and tore them, pulling them almost completely apart. Then he stepped forward and snatched the crown and the bracelet out of Eliphaz's hands. "Tell me, how is it you were not afraid to reach out and strike the Lord's anointed?" he said harshly. "Is it for you to take the life of the man God has appointed to rule?" The Amalekite was stunned, and couldn't answer. "Your blood be on your own head," said David. He looked at Shammah. "Take his life, quickly."

Shammah stood right beside David. Even bigger than Sibbechai, he had extraordinary strength. Though he carried a huge sword and a long spear in battle, he had neither of them now. What he did have was a mallet, as he had been working in the houses. Quick as a cat, the big man stepped forward and grabbed the Amalekite by the neck, slamming him to the ground. Two powerful swings of his tool and the job was done. Shammah stood up, not even breathing heavily. He turned to David. "My lord, shall I take him out of the camp and bury him?"

David nodded. "Thank you Shammah. You have brought judgment on the man who has slain the Lord's anointed. Do with him as you have said."

Shammah picked up the lifeless body as if he were picking up a small child. "Fetch me a shovel," he called to one of his men nearby as he walked away.

David turned to the rest of his men. "No more work today. We will fast and mourn, for the king of Israel is dead. Each man go to his family and tell them the same." As the men started to leave he looked at Abishai. "Where is the priest?"

"I haven't seen Abiathar, but he's probably working on his house," answered the captain.

David handed the crown and bracelet to Abishai. "Give these to him, and make sure he has a guard for them."

Abishai took them and looked at David seriously. "It may soon be time for you to wear them."

"I'll not put them on until I'm sure the Lord has told me to."

The sun was just breaking the horizon, sending its rays through the darkness. The sky began to lighten, and the fluttering of birds broke the early morning stillness. David stood alone on the outskirts of Ziklag. For seven days now, they had been in mourning. David had cared deeply for Jonathan, and even Saul had at one time been like a father to him. Their deaths had greatly saddened him. He had believed for several years now that Saul would come to an untimely end. How else would the Lord bring him to the throne? However, David had not suspected that Jonathan would also fall. He and his men had been far removed from his own country, living in Philistine lands, but he could only imagine the fear and chaos in Israel now that the king had been killed and the army scattered. David was sure Achish would be gearing up to take more land from Israel now that it would not be defended. Someone needed to stand up and protect God's people. Was that someone him? David had spent much of the last week remembering the day Samuel had come to Bethlehem. David had been watching his father's flock when his brother Ozem had come to fetch him to the sacrifice. When he arrived, the old prophet had looked at him with wonder. David could still remember the cool feel of the oil running down his head and neck as Samuel emptied the horn on him. Then the old man had told him that 'you are the one'. Over and over David revisited the events in his mind, trying to make sure he was certain of what had happened. After he had begun serving the king, David would often speak about it with Abiathar's father Ahimelech. The high priest had gone over the scrolls of the law with him, pointing out what Moses had written. Judah was blessed by his father Jacob, and told that his brothers would bow down to him. Judah was also given the scepter, and the ruler's staff, to be used by his descendants until one came who would require the obedience of the nations. David was in the line of Judah. Was he really one who would rule over his brothers in Israel, and have them bow to him? Though Saul was dead, and the prophesy appeared to becoming a reality, David was very unsure. Who was he to rule God's people? David now had his own scroll of the law, written in his own hand. Years ago, Samuel had shown him that Moses had commanded the king of Israel to write out the law himself, that he know it well. David had started writing it with the aid of Ahimelech, and finished it with the help of his son. He read it often. He carried it with him now, though it was still too dark for him to read.

David dropped to his knees and set the scroll on the ground. Then he leaned forward with his face near the dirt and began to pray. *Oh Lord God, merciful and gracious, mighty and just, holy and pure, hear my prayer. My God, I wish only to be a vessel for You, to do Your will here on the earth. If I have found favor with You, my God, lead me down the path You have planned for me. Saul is dead, and Samuel has anointed me to be his successor. If it is in Your plan for me, Lord, lead me in how I should go forward from here. Your people are scattered on the mountains, and Your name is blasphemed among the heathen of the land. For Your sake, allow Your people Israel to be led by a true servant of Yours, who will protect Your people and bring glory to Your name. Not for my sake, Lord, but for Your sake, lead me down the path You have prepared for me.*

David continued to pray as the sun rose higher in the sky. Before long, the darkness had completely disappeared. David remained bowed close to the ground. His skin seemed to tingle as he poured out his heart to the Lord, asking for clarity. If he was to claim the throne, he needed to be sure it was God's purpose for him. David kept on for some time, until his knees and back ached and his stomach growled. Finally he stood up and dusted himself off. Picking up his scroll, David walked back toward the town. Work had ceased since the Amalekite had brought the news of Saul and Jonathan, so they had not finished repairing the buildings and most of his men were still in tents. David made his way to the priest's tent, set off by itself on the outskirts of the camp. Outside stood the priest, finishing his own morning prayers. Already he wore the ephod of the high priest, the gems bright and shining in the sun. As David approached, he heard Abiathar singing a hymn of praise. He finished the hymn and turned to see David walk up.

"You wear the ephod this morning. Have you spoken to the Lord?"

"He has spoken to me, though I have not inquired of Him." The priest had a strange look in his eyes this morning. "You have spoken to the Lord this morning?"

"Yes," David answered, thinking he was asking about his regular morning prayers. "I have just finished."

"Did He speak to you today?" The priest looked at him intensely. David wasn't sure what to say to him.

"I have come to you to for an answer to that. My heart is sure, but not my mind."

The priest had a slow manner of speaking, but today it was even more drawn out, almost as if he was trying to emphasize something. "David, the Lord has spoken to me this morning. You have a question to ask of Him. It's time to ask it."

For a moment David didn't reply. Once the question was out, he knew Abiathar would inquire of the Lord, and the Lord would answer. Then David would have to obey. Finally he answered, "Should I go up to Judah to become king?"

"I will inquire of the Lord for you," said the priest with the same strange look on his face. He turned and entered his tent while David stood outside. David was sweating and nervous. He hit his knees in prayer. *Oh my God, forgive me of my lack of faith. Forgive us that we come to You here from this place, and not the Tabernacle You had made for Your Presence. But I know You do not dwell there, for not even all of heaven can contain You. Please hear your priest, and answer him that he may show me Your will. Not for my glory, Lord, but for Your own.*

Several minutes went by as David continued to pray. His body quivered as he pleaded with God to give him the strength to carry out His will. Suddenly, the tent flap flew open and Abiathar stepped out. David jumped to his feet and looked at the priest expectantly. Abiathar grabbed David by both his shoulders and leaned in close to his face.

"This is the Lord's answer to you, David. Go to Hebron, and accept the scepter of Judah. You will carry the ruler's staff, and in time your brothers in Israel will bow down to you."

David felt as if a weight had been lifted from his shoulders. It would be a long hard struggle, of that he was certain. But now he was sure in both heart and mind. "The Lord has spoken. I will obey."

Gad the prophet stood overlooking the scene. A large field spread out in front of him, green and well-watered. It was an important field, and had been taken care of. Beyond it, level ground stretched out for miles, gradually sloping downhill away to the east. Far off, the dark waters of the Arabah could barely be seen. Behind him stood a mass of rock that jutted up out of the landscape and merged into the hillside that rose abruptly to become the central ridgeline of Israel. At the base of the rock, the mouth of a great cave yawned open, leading deep underground. It was a high as two men and wide enough for ten men abreast to walk inside. This was a place of great importance in Israel. This was the cave of Machpelah.

It was very noisy. Thousands of people had gathered in the field. All the elders of Judah had come to meet David, and many families from the tribe had come to witness the event. David's men and their families had accompanied him to Hebron, and now they also stood among the crowd. The people shifted uncomfortably on their feet as they waited a long time in the hot morning sun. Many had chosen to sit on the ground. Without warning, a series of short trumpet blasts rang out. A company of David's men wearing full armor marched in from behind the crowd, clearing a path through the mass of people and heading toward the cave. The troops set themselves into two columns, one on each side of the path. Coming on their heels, another twenty-four soldiers passed between the columns. They marched up to the prophet and set themselves into a line facing the crowd, with twelve men on each side of him. Six men on each side bore a trumpet in one hand, and all wore a sword on their hip. Gad raised his hand, and the trumpeters each blew a blast in unison. Up the path came Abiathar the priest, wearing the breastplate and the ephod and carrying the crown and the bracelet of Saul. Many in the crowd covered their eyes as the sunlight reflected brightly off the gems and the crown. The priest fell in beside the prophet and turned to face the people. Again, Gad raised his hand, and the trumpets blew, this time longer. All the people were on their feet, looking down the path. From behind the crowd, David came forward followed by Ahinoam and Abigail. The two women walked side by side, each wearing flowing gowns of white. David wore his leather armor over a clean white tunic and waist coat. Slung on his back he carried the huge sword of Goliath. His head was bare, showing off his dark hair and beard. His face had the bearing of a ruler. David walked up and stood in front of the prophet and the priest and came to a halt. His wives stopped behind him.

Gad looked at the young man. "Kneel," he said. David bowed to one knee. The prophet held up a horn of oil and spoke out to the crowd. "Lord, You have chosen whom You shall anoint as king. Let Your Spirit be on David as he rules in Your great name." Gad poured out the oil slowly, letting it run through David's hair and down the back of his neck.

Abiathar reached out and placed the crown on David's head. "Lord, may You give David wisdom and power to lead Your people." Then the priest placed his hand on David's shoulder. "Rise, David." The trumpeters blew in unison, and the other soldiers drew their swords and held them high overhead. David stood up, and Abiathar slid the bracelet on his left arm. "May you wear these with honor."

David turned around to face the crowd. His two wives stepped up next to him. Gad held up a scroll and spoke out again. "The Lord is your true King. May His word guide the steps of His servant." The prophet handed the scroll to David, and shouted, "Judah, I give you King David! Long live the king!"

"Long live the king! Long live the king!" roared the crowd. Soldiers held their swords in the air, and the people clapped and shouted. The trumpets sounded and many cheers went up. The remainder of David's men, assembled together on the outside of the crowd, shouted for joy. Abishai stood in the front, soaking up the moment. It had been a long road to this day, and he was happy that it was finally here. Maybe now there would be some stability for them. Maybe now they would be able to rest from their many labors. The captain certainly felt that they had earned it.

Eleazar grabbed the captain's arm and pulled him away from the troops. Next to him stood a younger man, breathing heavily as if he had just run a long way. "Asahel? What are you doing here?" asked Abishai, incredulous.

"Joab sent me. He is coming this way with troops who are going to pledge loyalty to David."

"Good. Let them all come and swear loyalty to him."

"They're not all coming. Joab sent me with a message."

Eleazar clapped the runner hard on the back. "Go on, tell him," he said impatiently.

The young man looked the captain in the eyes. "Abner has made Ish-bosheth king over Israel."

14

"So, the cowards have decided to come back across the river, have they?" said Asahel. He was the youngest of the three brothers, as tall as Abishai yet leaner and swifter in build. Joab was the tallest, and thicker and stronger than his two younger brothers. They all wore dark hair and black beards.

Abishai stood next to Asahel, and answered without looking. "Of course Abner came back. He only retreated east of the Jordan to regroup. Now that his master's son is crowned, he'll be trying to place him on the throne in Gibeah." They stood in Gibeon, an easy day's march north of Saul's old compound. The pair stood at the front of David's army, which had grown quite considerably in the past months. Many from Judah had come to serve him since his coronation. Including the Gittites and the soldiers brought by Joab, David had nearly two thousand men. David had taken several companies under the command of Uriah and gone straight to Gibeah. He had sent the remainder under Joab to cut off Abner, who was bringing his own army south to the secure the old king's compound.

They stood assembled outside the town, in front of a deep natural pool used by the Gibeonites as a well. On the opposite side of the water stood the soldiers of Ish-bosheth. They were slightly fewer in number, mostly Benjamites. A great number of Saul's soldiers had deserted, some even following Joab to join David. At the moment, Joab had gone to meet with Abner, possibly to agree on terms to keep from bloodshed.

"You think he will try to avoid battle?" asked Asahel, referring to their older brother.

Abishai continued to look forward. "You've been with him more than me. What say you?"

"He's never been in command of the entire army before. Does he have more experience? Is that why he was put over you?" Although he was fully grown, around his brothers, Asahel still played the role of the naïve youngster.

"No. Not running the entire command. He's fought longer, just because he's older." Abishai was a little sore on the subject. He had led David's men for years, ever since the cave of Adullam, but David had named Joab captain of the host. "When it comes to leading the entire command, I am more experienced."

"And smaller," boomed a deep voice. Abishai turned to his right to see Joab standing next to him. The big man had a serious look on his face. He looked at Abishai intensely without speaking. Asahel became quiet, but Abishai wasn't intimidated.

"What's the plan?" he asked.

"Representative combat," boomed Joab. "Twelve men of ours against twelve of theirs."

"You have twelve men picked out?"

"That's your job. You know them better than me. No captains."

"Very well." Abishai turned toward the troops. "Company commanders! On me!" The soldiers closest to the front echoed the call, and in only a minute or two all the company leaders made their way to the front. Abishai looked at each one as they circled around him. "We will pit twelve men of ours against twelve of theirs. All of you, give me a fighter, and he had better be worth his salt." The captain counted the leaders. They had fifteen. "Since we'll have more than twelve, I'll make the decision when they all report as to who will sit out. Understood?" The men all voiced agreement. "Very well. Do it quickly." The commanders all hustled back to their troops. Joab had walked out in front of the formation by himself, probably to assess the fighters coming from the other side. Abishai returned to Asahel and waited.

"I've never seen this done before," said Asahel.

"That's because you didn't start fighting until Saul was only chasing after David," answered his brother. "The only battles Saul engaged in with you around were defensive moves against invaders, when the Philistines or the Jebusites had to be chased away."

"Have you seen it before?"

"Only once, when I was much younger. It worked well that day." The soldiers selected to fight began to arrive up front, and Abishai ordered them to fall into a line. Once they had all assembled, the captain stood in front of them. "Who wants to fight?" he shouted at them. All the men shouted and raised their hands. Abishai started walking down the line, trying to decide who would sit out. They all seemed capable, but he picked three who seemed slightly less so and sent them back to their companies.

Joab had sauntered up to check out his fighters. "These are your men?" he asked Abishai.

"Yes," came the answer.

"Listen to me," Joab boomed at the twelve men. "You have the chance to save many of your brothers. I don't want you to die for me, I want you to kill for me. Understood?" All the soldiers shouted again. "Go then, and fight." The hulking captain turned around to see Abner's fighters standing next to the general at the front of Ishbosheth's army. He shouted so loud every man on the field heard him clearly. "Send your men, Abner!" Joab waved David's soldiers forward, and the twelve men drew their weapons and walked toward the middle of the open ground between the two armies. Abner's selected men did the same. Each man lined himself up in front of another from the opposite side. All of the soldiers from both armies shouted in anticipation. Abner and Joab each followed their respective men out onto the battlefield. When everyone was set, Joab nodded to the general.

Abner gave a great shout, and the fighting commenced. Both armies shouted and banged weapons in excitement. Joab and Abner stalked up and down behind their men, calling out advice to them. The two groups appeared pretty evenly matched. Within a few minutes, half from both sides lay wounded or dead on the ground. A short man from Abner's men, fighting on one end, had taken out his opponent and now turned to another. He wielded a short sword with particular skill. Most of the other's, larger than he was, began to noticeably tire out as the fighting went on. As the line diminished, so did some of the shouting from the two armies. However, from Abner's men came shouts of, "Hezron!" calling out the name of the short man who was now on his third opponent. He was in excellent shape, and still fought as he had at the first. Finally, only one man of David's remained, mostly unhurt, to face him. He was much larger than Hezron, and carried a spear. The shorter Israelite approached him, dancing in and out as he slashed with his sword. The bigger man made two or three successful blocks with the staff of his spear, until Hezron swiftly ducked low and drove his sword into his opponent's belly. Israel cheered, and the bigger man roared in pain. But he wasn't done. He dropped his spear and grabbed Hezron by the arms, pulling the short man into his chest. The big man wrapped one arm around him to keep him there, then pulled a small dagger out of his belt. He sunk the dagger deep into Hezron's side and held onto him tightly as the pair fell to the ground.

The shouting subsided. Joab looked to Abner and drew the great sword he carried from his back. "General," he boomed, "we must settle this the normal way. Fall back to your men." Abner turned and headed back to his formation as Joab turned and jogged back to his. Joab had eight companies on line, with seven in the rear. He pointed to his brothers. "Abishai, take the four right companies. Asahel, fall to the rear and send reinforcements where they are needed. I will lead the four on the left. Judah!" he shouted out to his men, "stand by to attack!" The entire army shouted with vigor.

Across the field, Abner ran along his front line, ordering his commanders. Seeing Joab preparing to go on the offensive, he decided to try and beat him to the punch. "Forward Israel!" called out the general as he raised his sword high. Abner's men lunged forward, sprinting across the open field.

Joab shouted to his own men. "Forward, Judah!" Following their brutish leader, Joab's men rushed forward to meet their attackers. The two lines converged with a loud crash as metal shields and weapons slammed together. Chaos ensued at the front as men tried to hack and slash their way through each other. The ranks to the rear of the front line on both sides held their discipline, moving into position as their leaders ordered them. As with the representative combat, the two armies were closely matched. However, Joab had more men in reserve, and as the fighting in the front began to stagnate, he called for Asahel to bring them forward. Though normally at the front, today Abner observed from the rear, trying to time the placing of his own reserves just right. Unfortunately, he did not have enough to stem the tide. Slowly the soldiers of Judah pushed the Israelites back, dropping more of Abner's soldiers than he could replace.

At the rear, Asahel had yet to engage in the battle. He had sent all of his men into position, though not all were actually fighting yet. The young man's blood was up. Asahel was ready to fight. His brothers were both proven men, fighters and leaders, but his career as a soldier had only begun recently. He had not yet shown himself to be a worthy fighter, and he was waiting for that chance. Asahel kept his head up and looked around. Though he was tall, he could not see over the mass of bodies in front of him.

"You, come here," he hollered, tapping a soldier on the back. "Take a knee and give me a boost." The soldier dropped to one knee and Asahel stepped up on the other, holding on to the man's head and shoulders to keep steady. That was just the advantage he needed. Asahel stepped down. "Fall back in," he said, and the soldier complied. His men would be fine without him. They were mostly seasoned men and knew what to do.

Asahel could run like a deer. He took off at a sprint, his long legs swallowing up the ground, and raced wide around the right flank of the battle. He ran completely around the front lines and came to bear on the rear of Israel's formation. Their reserves were already engaged, and they had no archers, so Asahel was unimpeded as he ran toward the center of the line. He could see Abner in the center, shouting orders and encouraging his men not to give up. Standing around him stood two men, likely the command guards. Amazingly, none of them saw him coming. Asahel raised his sword and plunged it into the nearest soldier, dropping him immediately. The other turned just in time to watch Asahel's sword slicing through the air as it closed in on his neck. With his sword bloodied, Asahel turned to Abner.

"Come on general," he shouted as he aimed a strike at Abner.

Abner raised his spear and blocked the sword, then landed a blow with a blunt part of the staff. "Asahel!?" he shouted. "Go and fight another!"

"No! Fight me!" shouted Asahel. The younger man continued to swing his sword again and again, only to be blocked each time by the more experienced fighter.

Once again Abner shouted at him, "Go!"

"No!"

Finally, the general went on the offensive. Catching Asahel's blade on his spear, he shoved the young man backwards, making Asahel's arms swing out to his sides to steady himself. Without hesitating, Abner stepped forward and drove the point of his spear through Asahel's chest. The young man shouted in pain. Abner pulled his spear back out and Asahel crumpled to the ground in a heap.

The general turned back to his duties. Israel was being overrun. It was time for an exit strategy, or they would all be done in. Abner moved forward toward the front, looking for his commanders. Calling out to them, the general disengaged one company at a time, moving them back and setting up to hold off the assault while another company displaced. Israel continued to leap frog backwards until a solid group of Benjamites were able to temporarily get the upper hand on the Joab's men, forcing them to break contact. Fortunately for Abner, by that time Israel had reached the base of a defensible hill. The general called all his men to assemble on him, and he led Israel up to the hilltop and set them into position.

The men of Judah were worn down. To this point they had certainly held the upper hand, but looking at the uphill attack they were going to have to mount was discouraging. Joab stalked back and forth in front of his men, shouting. "Drink, and adjust your gear! Be ready to move on their position!"

Abner looked around him. His force was down by a quarter of its strength, while Judah had taken only a handful of casualties. His men were tired and discouraged. Now was not the time to fight. The general walked just past the front of his lines. "Joab, Joab!" he shouted. The big man turned and looked up at him. "Will the sword devour forever?"

"As long as it needs to," shouted Joab.

"Do you not know that Israel and Judah are brothers? You may destroy us on this hill, but many of you will pay with it for your lives."

"What do you want?"

"Give me the road, and I will not go to Gibeah. I will go north, for now."

Joab snorted and stomped his feet. He stalked back and forth in front of his lines, considering the offer. He had Abner pinned down, but the general was right. Much of David's army would likely be spent taking them out. For now, they had lost few men. He wanted to keep it that way. "As the Lord lives, if you had not spoken, all of us would have died today. Go your way, I will not stop you." Then he added, "For now." Joab turned to his men. "Fall back, and assemble at the pool! We will seek out our dead and tend the wounded!" Judah did as they were ordered, while Abner sent men to tend to the fallen.

For some time, both sides made themselves busy rendering aid and fixing weapons and armor. As the night began to fall, Abishai approached Joab. "Have you found Asahel?" asked the big man.

"Yes," answered Abishai in a strained voice.

"Where is he?"

"Dead."

"Where's Rizpah?" asked Ish-bosheth, looking at the young women. The Israelite king stood inside a common room in the building next door to his own house. David had abandoned Gibeah shortly after Abner's initial retreat, leaving the traditionally Benjamite town to its tribal owners and pulling his own men south into Judah. With Saul's compound unguarded, Ish-bosheth had brought in the entire Israelite force, housing his soldiers in the barracks and taking up residence in his father's former home. For nearly two years, he had resided here, enduring a futile struggle with the rising strength of David's army as well as more internal strife than he had expected. Ish-bosheth was ill-equipped to deal with such things. He was neither an exceptional leader nor a man of great courage. Whatever their faults, both his father and older brother had been more suited for the crown than he was.

There were four women in the room, all young and beautiful, selected specially for the king. He was very tall, and towered over them. They all stood quietly with their heads bowed. "Where is she?" the king asked again.

A girl with dark skin and long hair spoke up softly. "We have not seen her recently, my lord." She continued to look at the ground.

"When did you last see her, Hadassah?" asked Ish-bosheth calmly.

The dark-skinned girl looked up slightly at her name. "My lord, I have not seen her since before sundown."

Another girl, obviously older and fairer of skin, stepped up forward toward the king, placing her hand gently on his arm. "May I be of assistance this evening, my lord?" she asked, the hint of a smile on her lips.

Ish-bosheth was in no mood for that this evening. "No," he said quickly, brushing her hand away. The king looked up and stretched his neck, irritated. Behind him, he heard feet clamping on the ground as someone approached. Turning around, the king saw Ziba enter the room with a smile on his face.

"Looking for company this evening my lord?" asked the steward humorously. The short old man stepped lightly around the room, as if looking to tidy the place up. Seeing the expression on the king's face, his smile faded. "Something wrong, my lord?"

"I am looking for Rizpah. Have you seen her?"

"No my lord," answered the steward quickly. "I have not."

"Think carefully," said the king, eyeing the old man. "You have not seen Rizpah today?"

Ziba stood with a cautious look on his face for a moment, as if unsure how to answer. Speaking slowly, he said, "I have not seen her since before sunset."

"Where was she before sunset?" Ish-bosheth was becoming noticeably angry. Ziba looked thoughtful, as if trying to remember something. "You are not so old as that Ziba. Don't play the forgetful trick with me."

"No my lord, I've just had a busy evening and am trying to think of where I was when I saw her."

"Come with me, steward." Ish-bosheth grabbed Ziba by the arm and the pair walked outside. The night was pitch black, with clouds covering the stars. It was late, and no other people were out. Everything was quiet. They stood on the steps of the house, a tall young man and a short old one. The king leaned down close to the steward's face, squeezing his arm tightly. "Tell me what you know."

Ziba looked up at the young king. He was not a very capable leader, but he did have a temper, and could easily kill the old man if he chose to. "As you say," said the steward. "I have heard that Abner has been calling her to him in the evening."

Rizpah was a member of the king's harem, as were the other women in the house. For any other man to sleep with one of the king's women was to attack the king's right to rule. For a man with so much authority as Abner to do so may very well be an attempt to gain the throne. Abner had done an incredible job holding the army together, despite the circumstances, and the king owed him much. But many had whispered to him of the general's secret ambitions, and Abner had certainly seemed to be acting strange of late. Ish-bosheth had to uncover this or risk his very life. The young man let go of the steward and stood up tall. "Call for my guard. Have them meet me at the general's home." The king leaped off the steps and marched hurriedly across the open yard, headed for Abner's quarters next to the barracks. Ziba scurried off to alert the king's guards.

Ish-bosheth was seething with anger. His long strides covered the distance to the barracks in no time. The general's home stood off by itself, away from the training yard. As the king approached, the soft light of a candle could be seen through a window. Otherwise it was dark and quiet inside. The king stepped up to Abner's door and banged loudly. At first there was no response. He banged again, louder this time. A noise of shuffling could be heard coming from inside, and then a pair of feet padded their way toward the door. It gave a creak as it was slowly pulled open, and the general was standing on the other side, fully clothed.

"My lord?" said Abner, with a puzzled look on his face. "Is something wrong?"

Ish-bosheth was to upset for pretenses. "Where is she?"

"Who?" Abner's face grew even more questioning.

The king shrugged his way past the stocky man and began to look around. "Rizpah," he said as he continued through the room into the next. Abner shut the door and followed after him. The general was uncomprehending of the problem, not even sure who the king was talking about. Ish-bosheth stalked from room to room. It was only a small house, and it didn't take long to realize the general was alone. Finally he stopped in front of Abner. "What have you done with her?"

"Who?"

"Rizpah. Don't play me as the fool." Still the general was unsure of the problem, but the king was obviously angry with him. "She is one of mine."

The puzzled look on Abner's face started to fade, being replaced with a frown. "One of yours," he said slowly. "If she's one of yours, what would she be doing here?"

"Tell me you haven't brought her here for yourself," said the king, looking intently at Abner. Before the general could respond, there was another banging at the door. Without waiting for a reply, several soldiers stepped in, fully armed and somewhat out of breath. The man in the front looked to the king.

"What are our orders, my lord?" he asked. He was tall, though not so tall as Ish-bosheth, and well-built with dark hair and skin.

"The general has something to tell us, Rechab." The king looked back at Abner. The frown had grown, and was now accompanied by furrowed brows. "Why have you slept with my concubine?"

Abner gritted his teeth, silent for a moment. He stood tensely, his fists closed tight and his face turning red. "You foolish boy," he said in a low voice. "Who has been telling you these lies?" As he spoke, his voice grew louder. "Am I a dog, that you come to accuse me of such a thing? Have I ever shown anything but loyalty to your father's house? Even when Saul was nearly mad, consumed by his hate for David, did I ever once falter in my service of him?" He continued, his voice almost at a shout. "And now, though you are a weak and fearful boy, leading us all into ruin, have I ever shown you disloyalty?" The general strode to the side of the room and grabbed his spear standing against the wall, then spun to look at the soldiers in the doorway. "I was killing men before any of you even split your mother's legs," he said, looking intensely at Rechab. "Go now, or I will bury you all."

Rechab could feel the general's anger, and knew he was likely to try it. The man was an excellent fighter, and though there were four of them, Rechab was likely to go down, being the closest to the general. The soldier also knew that Abner had the loyalty of the army, not the king. Nothing about this situation seemed good to him. "Let's go," he said to his men, and the small group slowly backed out of the house. Abner stepped over to the door and slammed it shut, leaving the soldiers standing outside. The general stepped back over to Ish-bosheth. The king's anger had gone, replaced with uncertainty and fear. He gripped his sword hilt tightly as it rested in its sheath.

Abner looked at the king. "You have trusted in cowards and liars," he said in a low voice. "From now on, you may follow their advice. This day I am against Saul's house. May God do so to me, unless I give the kingdom over to David, as the Lord has sworn to him." Abner picked up his sword belt and girded it around his waist. As he turned to leave the room, he looked back at the king. "Look to yourself now, boy."

"Open the gate!" shouted David. The ruler of Judah stood in the middle of a courtyard of brick and stone, surrounded by a high wall that protected a cluster of houses that had been built into the steep hills of Hebron. It was not a large or extravagant place, but it served well enough as David's capital. It sat near the peak of a group of hills, surrounded on all sides by villages inhabited by the king's soldiers and their families. The heavy double gate that barred the entrance slowly began to swing open as the soldiers on duty pushed hard against its doors. On the other side stood a squad of twenty Israelite soldiers, armed and looking uneasy. In their center stood Abner in full battle armor, and a beautiful young woman, tall and slender with long flowing hair. She too wore a look of uneasiness. The doors of the gate clanged loudly as they came to the extent of their reach.

"Abner! Come here!" called out David to the general. Abner complied. He took the woman by the arm and came forward, looking around as he approached. David stood in the center of several other soldiers, two of which Abner recognized. Sibbechai and Elhanan stood on either side of the king, weapons at their side. The Israelite soldiers fell in behind the general, keeping several steps behind. Abner came to within a few paces from David and stopped.

"My lord," said the general, "here is your wife, as you have requested."

"Michal." David stood looking at Saul's daughter, the one whom he had once cared for so deeply. It had been years since they had seen each other, not since David had first ran from Gibeah to escape Saul. The former king had given her a new husband shortly thereafter. Now Abner had run the man off and brought her back to David. She looked at him with soft eyes, sad and uncertain.

"David." Her quivering voice betrayed the calmness in her manner. She had once loved David greatly. Yet he had never been able to return to her as he had promised, and over the better part of a decade, she had grown to love another man. Now he too had been taken from her. She knew David had taken other wives. How could she not be heartbroken?

"It does me good to see you again," said David after a long silence. Michal continued to look at him with her sad eyes.

"As it does me," she replied quietly.

"My lord," broke in Abner, "I have brought her to you so that you may believe my words. I have spoken to the elders of Israel. They are prepared to accept you as their ruler over Ish-bosheth."

"So you have brought her to me to strengthen my claim to his throne?" asked David.

"In part, yes. The Lord of Israel has anointed you king, has He not? It is time for you to take the throne. Ish-bosheth cannot defend the people, and civil war is ruining the land."

"What would you have me do?" David looked at Abner sternly. "You know better than most I have tried to avoid shedding Israelite blood, yet your master fights me tooth and nail at every turn."

Abner grimaced. "He is no longer my master. Allow me to gather the elders to you. They will accept you as king. The army will follow me to your service. Ish-bosheth will then have little choice."

David stood quietly for a moment. Was this the way God would place him on Israel's throne? He needed to be sure. "I will pray on the matter tonight, and inquire of the Lord. In the morning I will give you an answer."

"Very well. My men and I will lodge with you tonight, if that is acceptable."

"Of course." David's face brightened, as if he had shrugged off his worries. "My friend, I am glad to see you. Come, let us feast today. Sibbechai, see that Michal is taken to the chambers prepared for her. Elhanan, make sure Abner's men are given a place to rest." His men obeyed, and the servants hurried about to prepare a meal. David slipped off by himself to pray as the commotion went on.

"I will assemble all Israel for you, my lord. God has granted for you to rule all Israel, and so you shall." The night had passed quickly. Abner looked at his men outside the gate as he prepared to leave. The Israelite soldiers waited in formation for the general to order them on.

David stood in the darkened gateway underneath the wall next to the general. "I will not move on any Israelite position until you have sent word to me."

Abner reached out and clasped David's right arm, leaning in close to the king. "I will go with haste. I am proud of you, David."

"I am in your debt, Abner." The men let go of each other and Abner marched away, calling out to his men to move. The Israelites headed down the road, which wound its way northeast through the hills toward Mamre. They moved swiftly, and soon were out of sight to those watching from the gate. David remained where he was. Due east from the compound was a wide opening in the hills through which the rising sun could be seen. The first rays had broken the horizon some time ago, and now most of it was visible, chasing away the darkness. For some time, the king just stood and watched it's beauty in silence.

Praise be to You, Lord, prayed David. *Yours is greatness, and power, and glory, and majesty, and splendor. Everything in heaven and earth is Yours. We give You thanks in Your glorious name.*

David almost jumped in surprise when the soldier on the wall above called out to him. "Troops coming in my lord!" The king turned to look toward another pathway that ran up through the hills to the gate. Up from the steep road came Joab, with a company of men following in trace. They had been out for several days, searching for Philistines in the area. David watched as the big man led the way toward him, calling a halt as they drew near the gate.

"My lord," called out Joab, nodding his head in greeting.

"Joab," returned David, nodding back. "How was your patrol?"

"Uneventful. I think we have done well scaring any raiders away from Judah. There are none within our borders."

"Good. Release your men, then get yourself some food and rest. Within a few days I expect to be assembling the entire army." David looked at the incoming soldiers. They certainly looked ready for some rest.

"Why?" asked the captain. "Have you any news?"

David looked up at the much taller man. "Abner has been here. He will be assembling the elders of Israel to bring to me. He says they will name me to rule."

Joab's face became tight. "Abner has been here?"

"Yes," replied the king. "He arrived yesterday and left just before you returned."

The big man turned and looked down the road. He walked back and forth for a moment, then grunted. "You let him go?"

"Yes. Abner is not my enemy."

"No, my lord. Abner wants the throne himself. He must have come to spy on you." Joab was clearly irritated, and trying to maintain a respectful tone with David. "He must not be allowed to return to his army, or he will attack us here."

"Abner is not trying to take the throne." David was surprised at Joab's reaction. He had never shown any dislike for the Israelite general before. "He brought Michal back to me. He came to help me take Ish-bosheth's throne."

"A ruse, don't be…," Joab stammered, struggling to hold his tongue. "My lord, Abner is not to be trusted."

"Joab, Abner is as good a man as I know," said David sternly. "Release your men and clean yourself up. If you wish to make plans for an Israelite attack, then do so. I will be eating breakfast. When I am done, I want a briefing on your patrol." With that the king turned and headed inside the gate.

Joab was fuming. The big man stomped back toward his men. "Return to your homes. Eat and get some rest, and clean up your equipment. Ezri, come see me. The rest of you, fall out!" he boomed. The men all began heading home, some toward the main gate but most walking off toward one of the nearby villages. A young, lean soldier with short hair and a scruffy beard walked up to Joab and stopped in front of him.

"Yes sir?"

The big man stepped close to Ezri's face and lowered his voice. "Run after the Israelites, they can't be very far," he said, pointing down the road that ran to Mamre. "Tell Abner David needs him to return, and quickly. Go now."

"Yes sir." The young man took off at a run down the road. Joab watched him go until he was out of sight. Then the big man walked over to a large rock outside the wall and sat down to wait. He took his spear and planted it firmly in the ground, leaned back and wiped the sweat from his face. Though he was tired from the patrol, he was also angry, and soon found himself on his feet again pacing back and forth. He didn't have long to wait. Ezri was fast, and the Israelites were well rested. Soon he could hear the steady marching of soldiers' feet. Joab looked up to see Abner at the head of the Israelite formation, with Ezri next to him.

"Troops coming in!" shouted the soldier on the wall. Joab knew he needed to act fast. The big man plucked his spear from the ground and walked over in front of the Israelites as they marched up.

"Abner, your lord needs you," said Joab as they came to a halt. The general looked around, then locked eyes with Joab.

"Where is he?" he asked.

"Come, I will take you to him." Joab looked at his runner. "Ezri, you may return home." The young man nodded and left the formation. Abner instructed his troops to wait and walked over to the bigger commander. "Follow me." Joab led the way as they walked through the gateway. He stopped as they reached the dark shadow below the top of the gate. The big man turned to the general, grabbing his arm and nudging him further into the shadow. "Listen closely Abner," said Joab as he reached down to his waistband. The general stood looking at the big man, trying to make out his face in the dark. Something seemed very wrong. Abner began to step backwards, only to find Joab's grip tightening around his arm. Then he felt as if he was punched in the stomach.

"Oommph!" bellowed the general, pain searing through his middle. The spear Abner held dropped to the ground as he wrapped both hands around his stomach. Joab's broad hand was pressed up to him, the hilt of a knife sticking out of a bloody hole in his midsection. Groaning, the general looked up at Joab. The big man's face was close enough now, and Abner could see two dark eyes looking into his.

"Die," whispered Joab softly.

15

The joyful sounds of a child's laughter carried through the house. Aiah went from room to room, cleaning and picking things up. It was almost midday, and soon she would be preparing a meal. She could hear her grandson laughing as he played with his uncle. Reaching the boy's room, she opened the door and stepped inside. A boy of about ten lay on a bed, with a tall man stooped low over him, tickling the boy's stomach. The boy laughed hysterically, almost to the point of not being able to breathe.

"My lord," said the woman in a somewhat chiding tone, "you will wear the child out. He cannot be handled roughly." The tall man continued for a moment, then stood up and looked at the woman.

"Ahiah, do not worry so. The boy is strong despite his ailments." As the boy calmed, his uncle turned back to him. "Alright Mephibosheth, we must listen to the woman." Quickly his hand darted back to the boy's stomach for one more tickle, and the boy shrieked in laughter.

"My lord," implored Aiah as she stood in the doorway.

"Very well, I'm leaving." The tall man patted the boy's head and left the room. After he had left, the woman came over to the bed and sat next to the boy.

"My boy," she said as she caressed his head. "Are you ready to eat?"

"Yes, mother," said the boy, still wearing a big smile on his face.

"I will bring you some food, dear one." Aiah kissed the boy's head and stood up to leave. She reached down and gave him just the slightest tickle as she walked out, and the boy chuckled. Shutting the door, the woman headed for the kitchen to prepare the meal. Though it was a large house, the king's house in Gibeah, there were few people here today. Only she, the child, and the king needed to be fed. She went to a storage room and took out a small loaf of bread, just enough for the three of them and continued for the kitchen. Reaching it, she found the king already there, munching on some fruit that had been left out.

"May I make you some food, my lord?"

"No," replied Ish-bosheth. "I am going to lay down awhile. I've been with Mephibosheth all morning. I think playing with my nephew is more tiring on me than on him."

"That's true of all children, lame or not." Aiah walked over next to the king and picked up the rest of the fruit. "If you don't want to eat, then leave these alone. I've a use for them other than your snacking."

Ish-bosheth smiled, snatching one more piece out of her hands. "That's it, I'll eat no more." The king turned away and headed toward the stairs to go to his chambers. "I'll be resting if anyone calls."

Aiah cut up the fruit and tore off some bread, set it on a platter and took it back to the boy's room. He dove into it hungrily and she went back to help herself. Just as she began to eat, a soft knocking came from the front door. The woman stood up and went to answer it. Opening the door, she found a pair of soldiers, wearing swords and armor. The first was tall and well-built, very dark in hair and complexion. This one she recognized.

"What do you need, Rechab?" Aiah did not like him, though he had been chosen to guard the king. Something about his manner made her nervous.

"I have a message to give the king, if he is available." Rechab smiled, giving the woman something of a chill in her spine. "May we come in?"

"Who is your companion? I've not met him before," she said, eyeing the second man. He was of nearly the same height and build, with similar features.

"This is my brother Baanah. He has recently been made a guard of the king." The second man nodded and smiled at the woman.

"Has he? I've not heard of any change." Aiah was suspicious. Normally she was well acquainted with Ish-bosheth's guards.

Rechab smiled again. "It just happened. Likely the king forgot to mention it."

Aiah grudgingly stepped back and pulled the door wide, motioning them inside. "He is in his chambers. If you will wait here, I will get him for you." The kitchen could be seen from the doorway, Aiah's meal sitting out on a table. Rechab noticed the food and spoke up.

"Dear woman, it seems we have interrupted your meal. We will gladly let you finish eating and go get the king ourselves." Something about the way he spoke was very unnerving. Aiah didn't like it.

"Might there be food for us available?" Baanah was not at all bashful. "We have not had time to eat ourselves yet."

Aiah wished these two would leave, but she did not want to pass on her duty to provide hospitality. "I will prepare you both some food while you speak to the king."

"A good woman," said Rechab. "If the king is in his chambers, why don't we let him rest? We will speak with him after we have eaten."

Aiah was growing very irritated. "Very well. Wait here, I will go fetch some bread from the storeroom." The woman turned around and quickly made her way to the storeroom in the back, out of sight of the front door. As she looked for another loaf, she could hear footsteps on the stairs. The king must have heard them come in and decided to come down. Grabbing some bread, she went back to the kitchen, expecting to see the three men talking. To her surprise, no one was there. She went to the front door and looked out, but no one was there either. The message had not seemed to be urgent, but perhaps they had needed Ish-bosheth elsewhere.

Upstairs, the door to the king's bedchamber creaked as it slowly opened. There lay the king, dozing on his bed. Quietly, Rechab and Baanah slipped into the room. The sound of a sword being drawn from its sheath caught the king's ear, and he opened his eyes and looked around. Still groggy, the sight of his guardsman standing in his room did not at first alarm him. "Rechab?" said the king sleepily.

Before Ish-bosheth could cry out, the soldier raised his sword and brought the blade down on the swiftly king's neck. "Go back to sleep, my lord."

David swung his sword hard to left, blocking the thrust coming at him. Moving quickly, he stepped out with his left foot and brought his weapon around in a circle, aiming a strike at his opponent's right side. It landed with a loud thud, and the other man groaned. David lowered his sword and stepped back. "Moving a little slow this morning, are you?" he said through heavy breaths.

Sibbechai grinned and looked back at his king. "I'm just letting you feel good about yourself, my lord." The pair lifted their wooden swords and came at each other again, circling and striking at each other as they moved about the open courtyard in Hebron. David made sure his soldiers trained often, and he held himself to the same standard. Though it was just after sunrise and the air was still cool, the two men were sweating heavily as they labored against each other in full armor. Back and forth they went for nearly an hour, one gaining the upper hand and then the other. David was the better swordsman and nimbler on his feet, but Sibbechai was much stronger, able to endure David's strikes and wear the king down with his own. Finally, they broke apart, blowing heavily. Nearby, a servant brought out two skins of water, one for each man.

"Another two skins of water, please, then you may prepare breakfast," said David to the young man. He nodded and walked off to obey. David and Sibbechai each pulled off their helmets and stood drinking their water as they caught their breath. "Good work, Sibbechai. Any bruises?"

The big man nodded. "Many, I'm sure," he said, smiling. "But nothing that will keep me out of the next battle."

Before the young man had returned with more water, a soldier from the wall above the gate called out to David. "Men coming in, my lord!" David wiped his brow and looked at Sibbechai.

"Do we have anyone out?" he asked. The big soldier shook his head, and David looked up at the watchman. "Who is it, and how many?"

"Only two, my lord, both armed," came the reply. "One calls himself Rechab, son of Rimmon. They say they have a message for you."

Sibbechai tossed his wooden sword on a table close by and picked up his real one, sliding it into the sheath on his hip. David did the same, and the king motioned to several other soldiers on duty near the gate to draw near. "Let them in," he called out, and the soldiers at the gate began to pull it open, straining against the heavy doors. As they were pulled wide, the two men came into view. Both looked like seasoned soldiers. One carried a bag in his hand, filled with something heavy. Two of the soldiers at the gate stepped forward, ordering the men to give up their weapons. They obliged, each giving a sword and a long knife over to the soldiers. David stood in the center of the courtyard with Sibbechai on his right. The other soldiers made a semi-circle around the king. As the two men approached, they each went down on one knee and bowed their heads to the ground.

"Who are you?" asked David.

Only the man without the bag looked up at first. "My lord, I am Rechab, son of Rimmon a Beerothite. This man is my brother, Baanah. We have come hastily to you from Gibeah with an important message."

"Why have you been in Gibeah?" asked the king. The man had a haughty attitude, it seemed, and something about him rubbed David the wrong way.

"We have been in the service of the Israelite army, my lord," answered Rechab. Neither man had been nervous at their arrival, but the king's demeanor was not very encouraging. "My brother has something of great importance to you, my lord. May he show it to you?"

"Does your brother speak?" asked David, looking hard at the man. Baanah looked up at the king with an uncertain look on his face.

"Yes, my lord."

"Your name is what?"

"Baanah, son of Rimmon my lord."

"Very well, Baanah, show me what you have." David stared at the man so hard, that for a moment Baanah didn't react. Then, realizing he was supposed to do something, Baanah picked up the bag and poured out its contents. With a thud, a man's head hit the ground and rolled toward David, stopping near his feet. The king bent over and turned it upright so he could see the face. The skin was tight and the face was discolored, but it was without a doubt the face of Ish-bosheth, king of Israel. David stood up and looked at the men without speaking.

Rechab spoke instead. "My lord, this is the head of the Ish-bosheth, son of Saul, your enemy and the seeker of your life. The God of Israel has avenged my lord the king this day of Saul and of his seed." As he finished speaking, Rechab bowed his head again. Seeing his brother, Baanah did the same.

David's face was stern. "Tell me," he said, "does the God of Israel look with favor on those who slay the innocent?" Rechab looked up quickly, the haughty look gone from his face. "A man came to me once, saying that Saul was dead by his own hand, fallen in battle. He came thinking I would be pleased, and would give him a reward. But I was not pleased. I had him killed for slaying the Lord's anointed." Baanah looked up now. Both men's faces were full of fear. "How much more should I do to you, you wicked men, for slaying an innocent man, a king to whom you have declared service, no less." David looked at his soldiers standing by. Each had a hand on their sword hilt. "Kill them."

A young man stuck his head inside the door to the bedchamber. "The elders have arrived my lord. They are being escorted in now." David sat up on his bed and nodded, dismissing the servant with a wave of his hand. He stood up and walked over to a table that had a bowl of water sitting on it, from which he drank a little and then washed his face. He had spent most of the last several days in prayer and fasting, trying to determine the Lord's will. It was clear to him now. It had been clear for several years now, yet David had not wished to act; he had been waiting for the Lord to do so. Now He had, and it was time for David to step up into the role God had prepared for him. David was to carry the scepter, and the ruler's staff, until it was passed on to whom it belonged. Not just for Judah, but for all Israel. He found a clean tunic and put it on, cinching the sash tightly around his midsection. Then David bowed low to the ground and prayed.

Oh Lord my God, You are my strength and my song. I have waited patiently for You, and You have turned to me and heard my cry. I desire to do Your will, oh my God, Your law is written on my heart. Instruct me, Lord, teach me in the ways that I should go. Counsel me and watch over me that I might serve Your people. Praise be to You Lord, my God and my Rock, glory and honor and praise forever.

David stood up and breathed deeply. This was the day that he had looked forward to with excitement and fear ever since that fateful day with Samuel on the hill outside of Bethlehem. More than twenty years had passed since that day. David stepped over to the table to splash his face with water once more. As he bent over the bowl, he caught a glimpse of his reflection in the water. It had been a young, innocent and optimistic boy who had been anointed by the prophet that day. David had loved the Lord then, but he had been so naïve. It was not that boy who looked back at him now, but a hardened warrior, whose face bore the stress of battle and rule. His heart was marred by loss and betrayal, and it carried the weight of the lives of his men. Yet through the turbulent years he had endured, his eyes had been opened to the incredible love and faithfulness of his God. His faith was not the fresh and blissfully joyful faith of a teenager, but the deep and wholly trustworthy faith of a man who had been carried by the Lord through a life of trials. In a way, it was so much sweeter now.

David splashed his face once more, the water dripping through his thick beard. He ran his hands through his shaggy dark hair, then picked up a towel and patted down his face. There came a knock at the door. "Come in," answered the king, and the young man re-entered. The servant walked over and began to set out the king's armor, which had been cleaned and dried, then proceeded to help him strap it on. Sitting on the table was his crown, which he set on David's head, and his royal bracelet, which he slipped on his arm. His sword lay in its sheath, that great sword, the sword of Goliath. David picked it up and buckled the belt, slung it across his body over one shoulder and tightened it around him. Then he stood up tall, straightened the tunic under his armor, and walked out the door into the hall followed by the young man.

Abishai stood by the door waiting for him. He had a very somber look on his face. "My lord," he said. The captain was not often at a loss for words, but it seemed this was one of those times. Abishai put his hand on David's shoulder and gripped it tightly.

David looked at the captain. "Ready?" The captain nodded and they all headed off through the maze of rooms and hallways that led out to the courtyard of David's compound at Hebron. Though there were walls separating them, it was essentially one big house, built right into the rock wall of the mountain. The rooms were empty, as all the inhabitants had gathered outside. Finally they reached the double doors that would put them out into the courtyard. The trio stopped before going through, and Abishai turned to David.

"My lord, if I know any man worthy of this, it is you."

"I would not have seen this day without you Abishai," answered David. "I thank the Lord for you." The pair turned back to the doorway and walked through. The mid-morning sun was bright and warm, and it shined straight into their eyes as they came out into the open. The courtyard was full of people. Several hundred soldiers had managed to pack themselves both on top and around the outer walls. Inside of them, the families who lived in Hebron had also found space to stand. The gates stood wide open, and outside of them and in any other available space, the local citizens of Judah had squeezed themselves in. Finally, in the center of the courtyard stood the elders of all the tribes of Israel, one hundred and forty four of them, twelve men from each tribe.

As David came forward, Abishai and the king's servant fell back near the wall of the building where many of David's captains and his wives stood. The king continued until he came within a few feet of the Israelite elders, where a small platform had been raised for David to stand on. Stepping up on it, he looked out over the crowd, which had become very quiet. "Why have you come to me, Israel?" he called out with a loud voice.

An older man near the front of the elders walked down to an empty space in front of David's platform. "My lord," he said as loudly as he could, "I am Zadok, son of Ahitub, a priest of the Lord. The rule of the house of Saul has ended, and Israel is without a king. In the past, you were the man who led Israel in battle. The Almighty God of Israel has said you will be the one to be our shepherd, and our ruler. We are of your own flesh and blood. Make a covenant with us, and we will submit to your rule."

"Hear me, Israel," answered David. "My brothers of the house of Judah have made me their king. But you are also my brothers. The Lord has anointed me to shepherd and protect you, His people. Submit not to me, but to the Lord. He has placed me over you, and He will protect you, as He has protected me. Anoint me your king, and I will lead you in obedience to the Lord's will."

The elders of Israel all began to call out in agreement. Hearing them, all the soldiers and the families, and everyone else, began to shout in excitement. Zadok stepped up next to David and slipped off the horn that had been slung around his shoulder. Gad the prophet approached from behind the king and joined the pair on the platform, making it seem crowded. The priest was slightly shorter than the king, and the gray-headed man instructed David to take a knee. He obliged, and Gad removed the crown from his dark head. Zadok lifted the horn above the king and poured out the oil inside, letting it run down David's hair, onto the back of his neck, and over his face into his beard. Cheers went up from the crowd as Gad replaced the crown on David's head. The prophet held up his arms to call for quiet, and in a few moments all the shouting had ceased.

"Rise up, David, son of Jesse," shouted Zadok. "Rise as king of all Israel! Long live the king!"

"David has been made king of all Israel." Achish looked hard at his general. "I want to crush that man." The Philistine king stood surrounded by his top military leaders and several of his counselors. The group was outside the walls of Gath to the west, standing in a wide open field watching several hundred soldiers conducting training maneuvers. Earlier that day, word had come of David's coronation, and the king had not taken the news well. Philcol had to hide a smirk.

"What do you suggest my lord?" asked the general. He wanted to point out to Achish that if he had listened to his advice when David had feigned madness, or even years later when the Israelite had come with his small army, that they would not be in this position. With David as king, they would likely find Israel a much stiffer opponent than they had been recently. Though Saul had been a competent military leader in his early years, he had never been as good as David. For that matter, had they continued to push through Israel after Saul's death instead of allowing the Jebusites to increase their territory, they may have contained David in the south and limited the strength of his army. Now he would have all Israel to draw from.

"David has but a small fraction of the manpower that we have. I want to assemble the entire force, as we did at Jezreel, and march against him." David on the throne of Israel was an insult to the Philistine king, who had not only let him live but given him territory and spoke his praises as an ally to the Philistine lords. It burned Achish that he had done so.

"You want to march on Hebron, my lord?" asked Philcol. "Our numbers and chariots will not work in our favor in the mountains of Judah."

"David is not in Hebron," said the king. "Oman," he said, turning to face a man on his right, "tell them what you know." A man slightly taller and much leaner than the king stepped forward. He was obviously not a Philistine, and seemed somewhat uncomfortable addressing them.

"David has left Hebron," he said as he looked around at the group. "He has started moving north with his men. He is on his way to Gibeah to unite with the rest of the Israelite army. Gibeah is much less defensible than Hebron. If David remains there for any length of time, an offensive may be able to be mounted against him."

"Who are you?" asked a Philistine commander.

"I am Oman, a servant of Adonizedek. The king of Jebus fears that if David is left to himself, he will reclaim all the territory that Israel lost when Saul died. Not only what we have taken, but what you have as well."

"We will assemble at the plain outside of Sorek," said the king. "If David stays in Gibeah, we can move east through the valley to the north side of the city. The Jebusites," he said as he turned to Oman, "can move north from Jebus and attack from the south. The Israelite army will be stuck in the middle with no path of escape."

The general spoke up. "My lord, we will need to send word immediately. It may take a week to muster our entire force. If David gets word of our movements, he will move and we will be forced to attack with less men, or fight in a worse location." Philcol enjoyed seeing the king irritated by David, but he was definitely in favor of destroying the Israelites. If Achish would commit to it, they had a good chance of being successful.

"As you say. Send riders at once to the other cities. Prepare your own army, and march as soon as possible," said the king. "Oman, make haste back to Jebus. Tell Adonizedek the Philistine forces will be ready to move in less than a week. Have him send me messengers to Sorek to keep in contact with him. And if there is any new word about David, we need to know about it."

"Very good, my lord," answered the Jebusite.

"Everyone clear? Anything to add?" asked Achish, looking around at his men. From the back, Ahuzzath, the disgraced soldier-turned-counselor, raised his hand. "Do I want to hear this, Ahuzzath?" said the king.

"My lord, would it not be best to leave Israel alone? David has evaded any serious harm attempted against him for more than a decade. At each turn he has become stronger, and gained more of a following. It seems obvious that he has the support of Israel's god. If we attack him in his own land, we will incur his god's wrath."

The king's thick face grew red with anger. "I am so sick of your false tongue. Never do you speak in favor of your own people. I'll listen to you no more." Achish looked at his general. "Pick out a squad of men. Have Ahuzzath escorted out of the city. Anywhere, I care not." Looking back at Ahuzzath, he said, "If I ever see you in Gath again, I'll have you executed for treason."

"Yes, that sounds like an acceptable plan," said Adonizedek in his drawn out voice. The tall king of the Jebusites stood off to one side of the main road in the center of his city, near the front gate. Next to him was a large building, with two broad doors swung open wide. A train of workmen were slowly making their way out into the road, each carrying a heavy bag of grain or a barrel of wine. As they reached the road, they all followed the man in front of them farther into the city to store their load. The king watched each man as they walked by. "How many days until they are ready?"

"It shouldn't be more than four or five until they are assembled at Sorek. Achish asks that we send men to meet him there, to assist in communicating with you." Oman had just now returned from Gath, finding the king immediately after coming through the gate. He was tired and dirty from the journey. The soldiers that had accompanied him, about a dozen, stood at ease a few feet away.

"Very well." The king looked over at Jozabad, who stood near the doorway keeping a close eye on the traffic coming out of the building, which seemed to be unending. Several of the men started as they came out at the sight of a big soldier with a tattooed face glaring at them. "Jozabad," the king said louder, "how soon can you have your troops assembled?"

"How many, my lord?" he asked.

"All of them," came the answer.

"Two days. Assembled and ready to fight."

The king nodded slowly. "You will meet Achish at Sorek," he said, again speaking to Oman. "Take thirty men. Make sure they are runners. You will march with the Philistines from there, sending men back and forth to me, so that I will know how things are progressing. I will not leave the city until well after the Philistines march from Sorek, for we are much closer. Once we have reached Gibeah, you will rejoin me with the army."

Oman nodded. "Yes, my lord. Have you any news on David? Has he reached Gibeah?"

"No, he has not. A small group of his men were seen moving past here, probably to prepare Gibeah for his arrival. But I believe David is still far to the south."

"But you do think he will go there?"

The king's face was without expression, and he continued to look away from Oman in the direction of the workmen. "It is likely, but I do not know. Even if he does not, we may be able to draw the Philistines in after them. Achish hates David, for David has made him look a fool. If we can convince him to fight David in the mountains, both sides will suffer heavy losses. I will pray to Molech that the blood runs thick for both Israel and the Philistines." Finally, Adonizedek turned and looked at Oman. "You must be tired. Go and rest my friend," said the king with an unnerving smile.

16

T he light was fading rapidly as the Jebusite soldier crept along. It had been four days since Oman had returned to Jebus. He had already reached the wide plains north of Sorek and met with Philcol. Four of the five Philistine armies had already assembled there; only Gaza's soldiers had yet to arrive, and they were on the march. That morning, Oman had ordered the man back to the city to update Adonizedek and return with any new word of David. Now the young soldier walked softly along the bottom of the Kidron valley, which ran along the east side of Jebus. Nearly four hundred feet above him to his right towered the city, dark and imposing with the sun setting behind it. On his left ran a small brook, coming out of the north and running the length of the valley. Across the brook, even higher than the city stood a great mountain, the peak still bright with the last rays of the sun.

He traveled a well-worn path along the valley floor. Though the main gate of the city was high above it, the Jebusites often used this road for troop movements and for supplying the city with food from nearby fields and water from the brook. The man continued down the path until he was below the center of the city and then made a sharp right, walking almost directly into the rock wall of the valley. There, almost invisible in the low light, was a break in the rocks, just wide enough for a man to fit through, that ran deep into the side of the valley. Out of it came a stream of water that flowed into the brook. Feeling more secure, the man stomped through the water and made his way into the tunnel, chanting a song to himself. He had gone only about a hundred feet or so when he heard the sound of running feet on the rocks behind him. The soldier turned just in time to see the blunt end of a spear whipping towards his face. It landed with a sharp crack and the man crumpled to the ground in a heap.

"Got him," said Elhanan grinning as Sibbechai and Abishai came running up behind him.

"Good," replied the captain. "Tie him up, quick, and we'll get out of here." Sibbechai helped his friend bind the soldier's hands and feet, then picked up the Jebusite and slung him over his shoulder.

"Take the weapons. We'll leave no trace," said Abishai. Elhanan picked up the sword that the man had dropped.

"Let's go." The captain led the way as the three men made a hasty retreat back out of the tunnel. Exiting out the crack, they ran along the west side of the brook, so as to stay in the shadow of the city.

"David was right," said Elhanan quietly as they jogged along. "How could he have known about the tunnel?"

"He didn't, not exactly," answered Abishai. "David once heard the Philistine general Philcol speaking about a secret path into the city. The general had never seen it either, but Adonizedek had said something of it to him once. Anyway, David guessed it must be somewhere along the brook, as a way to get water."

The men continued on without speaking, trying to save their breath. By the time they had reached the south end of Jebus, it was completely dark. Here another valley running east and west converged with the Kidron. The men crossed the brook, which was no more than knee deep at most, and headed south along the other side. It was very dark, but Abishai knew the land well, and soon had found a path that ran eastward through the rolling landscape. After about five minutes, they heard a voice in the dark ahead of them.

"The Lord fights," it said loudly.

"He fights for Israel," answered Abishai. "Uriah, we have a captive. Give me some men to help carry him. I think Sibbechai is done."

"Almost," said the big man, blowing. Uriah the Hittite stood at the head of a hundred men, all spread out tactically along the pathway. He called the men to assemble on the road, and pulled several to take over Sibbechai's burden. The Jebusite was somewhat conscious, but only speaking in groans at the moment. His nose was broken and his face was covered in dried blood.

"Make sure to pass him often, so you are not worn down. When he seems awake enough to walk, cut the cords around his feet and let him. If he won't comply, let me know, and I'll make sure he does." Abishai spoke loudly for all to hear. "We've a long way to go and a short time to do it. Make sure to move quickly and watch your step. The last thing I need is men with sprained ankles from carelessness." The company all marched off with the captain in the lead, continuing east away from the Jebusite capital. They kept at it for several hours. As they walked, the ground began to slope gradually downhill, and the hills fell away into open fields. Before the moon had reached its peak, Abishai heard another voice ahead of him in the dark.

"The Lord fights," came the challenge.

"He fights for Israel," replied the captain, seeing a squad of fully armed Israelites guarding the road. The moon had come out, and the night had brightened just enough for Abishai to make out what was beyond them. Many hundreds of men lay encamped in the open fields. All of Israel and Judah had moved under darkness, in small companies over several days to avoid detection by the Jebusites. Now David's entire army was assembled only a few hours march from Jebus. Past the camps, unable to be seen in the darkness, stood the remains of the city of Nob. No one inhabited the place now, and few men from any of the peoples of Canaan had reason to go there. It was the perfect place for an army to hide.

Abishai turned command over to Uriah with orders to settle the men into camp to get some rest. As the men filed in, Sibbechai and Elhanan strode up with the captured Jebusite, who was now walking with his hands bound in front of him. Finally waking up due to the jarring ride, he had agreed to walk under the threat of a painful death.

"How is he?" asked Abishai.

"I don't think he is very pleased," said Elhanan, "but no serious injuries."

"Not yet, anyway," quipped the captain, looking at the captive. "Take him to my tent. I'm going to report to David, then I'll come have a talk with our new friend."

David looked at all of his chief men. Almost fifty of them, all his company commanders and another dozen or so of his best warriors, stood in front of him in a tight group. Behind them, his entire army, more than three thousand men, stood in formation outside the ruins of Nob. The camps had been broken, and every man was fully armed and ready to march. It was mid-afternoon, just past the hottest part of the day. Thanks to Abishai's skillful interrogation the night before, the Israelite king knew the Philistines were probably at least two days from being ready to fight. He had also found the weakness in the Jebusites' defense. Now was the time to march, to begin cleansing the land for the Lord. Long ago, the Almighty had instructed His servant Joshua to rid the land of the pagan Canaanites, lest they cause the Israelites to stumble. David took that order very seriously.

"The Lord willing, tonight we will attack the fortress city of Jebus," said the king to his group of warriors. "As you have been instructed by Abishai, there is a small tunnel that runs from the valley up inside the walls of the city. A company of men will attack up the tunnel into the city and open the gates from the inside. With the gates open, the army will invade the city and destroy any who oppose us." David looked around at the men. All of them were brave and strong, battle-hardened leaders who could be trusted. "To lead this attack up the tunnel will be a great honor. The man who goes up first I will make my chief captain, over the entire army. Who wishes to take on this honor?"

"I will lead," came a booming voice. Pushing his way through the group came Joab, tall and broad and strong. Several of the men thought the mere sight of him coming through the tunnel could scare the Jebusites into submission. The big man strode up to David and took a knee before the king, bowing his head. "My lord, I pray that you will give me this honor."

David looked down on Joab. He had not held a command since the death of Abner. The loss of that great man had been tragic. Joab had been horribly wrong to commit such a sin. But the king knew how the death of his brother Asahel had affected the big man, and he had shown willing submission in his duties since then. Joab was also an incredible fighter, almost certainly the right man for this task. "Very well Joab. You will lead the attack. Succeed, and you will be reinstated to your command."

"You will not regret it, my lord." Joab remained bowed before the king.

"Sibbechai and Elhanan will go with you, for they know the way to the tunnel. You may pick the remainder of the men to follow you. It cannot be many, for you will need to move without being seen to the entrance of the tunnel."

Joab looked up at the king. "Yes my lord."

"Decide who will go with you, and you may gather them at our last rest before we reach the city. Now, rise up. We must be on the march." The big man stood and bowed his head once more gratefully to the king. As Joab stepped back, David continued. "Abishai, you will order the movement and be in command outside the city walls. All of you fall into your formations, and ready your men to move."

"Yes my lord," came many voices at once. The company commanders all returned to their men, and the other mighty soldiers fell into a formation behind the king. Abishai walked out at a distance from the army, looking up and down as he waited for everyone to be ready. Every soldier had his hands down at his side at attention. When each company was ready, the bannerman next to the commander raised his standard as a signal. Abishai counted the banners. Thirty of them stood high above the formation. All was quiet as everyone waited for the command.

"Ready!" shouted Abishai. More shouts could be heard as each commander echoed his order. "March Israel!" Again his command was echoed, and the entire army stepped off at once, headed by the king and his group of soldiers.

David led his men out of the flat land outside Nob and into the rolling hills. It was hot, but the temperature was slowly dropping as the sun became lower in the sky. They followed the same road that Abishai and Uriah's men had come down the night before. Another road farther to the south led to Gibeah, but this one ran northwest straight through to Jebus. Though they were going uphill, it was daylight, so their pace was slightly faster than Abishai's had been. As they went, Joab moved back and forth down the lines, calling out the men who would follow him in the attack. After only about two hours, the peak of the mountain east of Jebus could be seen over the hilltops. David continued until he came within view of the place where the two valleys met. He could only just see the small brook as it flowed south. Wanting to make as little noise as possible, the king held up his fist to signal a halt. The sign was passed all the way through the ranks, and the entire force stopped for a short rest. Soldiers adjusted their gear and passed around water and food. David called Abishai and Joab over to him, and the three of them walked a short distance away from the formation.

"Are your men ready?" David asked Joab.

"Yes my lord. I have thirty, already assembled before the first company," he answered. The king looked over to see Joab's group. Most of them he recognized, stout warriors all. Shammah stood near the head of the group, along with a big Ruebenite named Elizur. There was Ahimelech the Hittite, who had followed Uriah to serve David; a young man named Benaiah, who fought like a lion; and a tall, long limbed fighter called Adino. Sibbechai and Elhanan had fallen in with Joab's men, ready to lead them to the tunnel.

"You seem to have made good choices. I hate to think of who will not return." David looked at Joab. "Make no mistake, I am sending you into a very difficult situation. You will be alone inside the city, surrounded by Adonizedek's army. Your only task is to open that gate, by whatever means."

"I understand, my lord," said Joab in a low voice.

David reached out and gripped the big man's massive arm. "Take heart. The Lord is on our side. If I know nothing else, I know that."

"You will succeed, brother," said Abishai. "Those cowards will wet themselves when they see you coming." Joab grunted.

"We will let the sun go down a little more, then we will march out to face the city from the south, blowing trumpets and making as much noise as possible," explained the king. "Then you will take your men up the valley on the east, staying as close to the rock wall as possible. Sibbechai will lead you to the tunnel. You only have a short time to get inside, because we will need to bring the army around to face the main gate on the east side. Once you're in, you're on your own. Open the gate, and we'll meet you on the inside."

"Understood, my lord," said Joab.

"Now, I am going to pray. Prepare yourselves as you see fit." With that, David walked a little further out and found a smooth place to kneel.

Dropping down to his hands and knees, he bowed his face near the ground.

Give an ear to my prayer, oh Lord. Let my words come forth into Your Presence. Save me by Your right hand, for I have trusted in You. Deliver me from my enemies, from the wicked that oppress me. They have spoken proudly against You. They are like a lion that is greedy of his prey, lurking in secret places. Deliver me from these wicked men, oh Lord, that Your name be made great among the heathen.

Behind him, almost all of the soldiers close to the front had noticed the king kneeling to pray. He remained there for some time, fervently asking the Lord for help. When he finished, he stood up and turned around to see the army watching him closely. David walked back over to rejoin the brothers.

"It's time," he said, looking up at the sun. "Get them ready."

Abishai walked back down the line, holding up his spear to signal the imminent departure. The sign was passed down the line, and the captain stood and waited for the standards to be raised. They were raised from the back forward, so no banner was raised before the one behind it. After a few minutes, the final banner stood high in the air. Abishai turned to look at David and nodded.

The king had not yet taken his place at the front, but remained out where most of the troops could see him. He pulled his great sword from its sheath and held it high. "Israel!" he shouted. "The Lord fights for you!" A great shout went up from the army, loud and strong, and it could be heard echoing across the valley to the city walls. David pointed his sword at Abishai and quickly fell into formation at the front.

"Forward, Israel!" called out the captain, and the army stepped off toward its destination. There was no turning back now.

"How have they come this close without my knowing?" Adonizedek bent his tall frame near the face of the young servant standing before him. The king's usual drawn out monotone had become quick and angry, almost fearful. "I will execute my scouts for this when we are finished with Israel." The king had been reclining after a hearty supper, enjoying the early evening air on a balcony of his personal quarters when the peaceful sounds of the city were suddenly interrupted by a great shouting and the noise of trumpets. Before he had been able to make it off his balcony, a soldier had come running with the news that Jebus was under attack. Only a few minutes later had the king learned it was David who stood outside his southern wall, with the entire Israelite army behind him.

The alarm had been sounded throughout the city, and every available fighting man had reported for duty. The city walls were thick with soldiers and growing thicker every minute. As the king approached the southern wall, men continued to stream from their homes to find a post to stand. Atop the wall standing on a turret, Jozabad shouted orders to the soldiers scampering about, calling for his best archers to report to that side. Adonizedek hastily climbed the steps up to join him, wanting to get a look at his attackers. Reaching the top, he stepped to the wall and looked out. The king's mouth dropped open in awe. Spread out in formation across the Hinnom valley, in fact almost completely filling the valley, stood the Israelite army. More than three thousand fully-armed men, each clashing his weapons together and stomping in unison. In the front, several men walked the line, shouting at the troops and seemingly working them into a fit. This was no political bluff. Israel meant to tear his city down.

"Have they offered terms?" asked the king. Adonizedek trusted in his city's defensive position, it's high walls and difficult terrain. But David had a knack for being successful in tough situations, and the king wasn't looking forward to having to fight him off.

"No," said Jozabad. "They've not given any word." For another moment, they stood and watched as the Israelites continued their posturing. Then a soldier came running up the steps behind them.

"My lord," he called out to the king, "all posts have been filled, with men to spare on every side."

Jozabad snorted and looked over at his king. "They cannot come in here. What do they think they will do? Climb the walls? We'll cut down every Israelite who tries, and won't lose a man doing it." In the last few days, Jozabad had been mustering all the Jebusite troops he could find, so the city was brimming with fighters. Even so, they had only half of what David had, for the Israelite people were far more numerous. "Bring me a company of men to stand in reserve along this wall," Jozabad ordered the soldier, "and take another company to stand in reserve at the main gate." The soldier assented and hurried off to obey.

"Wind the horn, Jozabad. It's time to get his attention." Adonizedek was a cruel man, but he was not a warrior. This whole ordeal was turning his stomach. The sooner he could get out of it, the better. Jozabad lifted a large bull's horn to his lips and blew. It was not the short, clear blasts of the Israelite trumpeters as they called for battle formations. This was a long, deep sound meant to get David's attention. Jozabad held it until he could see the Israelites coming to attention and their leaders looking up at the city. He lowered the big horn, chest heaving to catch his breath.

A lone soldier carrying a small white flag came running up the steep incline toward the city wall. It was not an easy climb, and it took him several minutes. By the time he reached the wall he was breathing heavily. After catching his breath, the soldier looked up at the king and shouted. "King Adonizedek, my lord David, king of Israel, sends this message to you. Open your gates, and flee every one of you from this land, and you will be spared. Remain inside, and all of you will die. This land belongs to Israel, given to us by Almighty God, and you have no claim to it."

Adonizedek felt a pang of fear run through his heart. But he was too prideful than to give in to a message such as that. "My gates will remain closed. You can give David a message for me. Turn around, and go back to Hebron, and we will not shoot an arrow in the back of all your soldiers."

Without considering the king's offer, the Israelite shouted again. "A second and final offer, King Adonizedek. Gather your house and your people, and flee this city, and you will be spared. Do not trust in your high walls, for Almighty God fights for Israel."

Before the king could respond, Jozabad yelled down at the soldier. "You have heard the king's answer, fool. Come on if you dare. Your god cannot get in here. The blind and the lame could fight you off. Come if you dare, and die on the wall. I will give all your bodies to Molech." Jozabad motioned to an archer by his side, and an arrow flew into the dirt at the Israelite's feet.

Joab stopped for a second to look behind him. Shammah stood a few feet below him, and Sibbechai a few more. Beyond them, another twenty-eight men were spread out in single file. The bottom of the staircase could not even be seen anymore. The stairs were steep and uneven, covered in mud from the bottom of the tunnel and very slick. It was dark and Joab could not see the top, but he sensed he still had a long way to go. The big man was moving as quickly as he could, but he could not risk slipping and bringing down the entire group behind him. So far, it had gone as planned. The main army had made so much commotion that no one in the Jebusite city had been able to take their eyes off of them. Joab and his men had quietly slipped into the growing shadow on the east side of Jebus and hastily made their way to the entrance of the tunnel. Joab and Shammah had barely fit through the crack, as it was so small. Joab had thought it likely that they would encounter some resistance, a guard at least, but there had been none. A quick jog through the wet ground and they had reached the long, winding staircase, which they were now climbing.

The big man was starting to feel short of breath. Just when he thought he would need a break, Joab looked up and saw the last of the steps, and a flat, wide cave-like area with a wooden door built into a low ceiling. Joab bounded up the last few steps and bent forward to avoid bumping his head. He ambled over to the door and stood there panting, trying to listen for anyone on the other side. Shammah joined him, also crouching over. About ten others managed to crowd themselves in before they ran out of space. Joab motioned for them to drink and catch their breath, and everyone reached for his skin of water and readjusted his gear. After a minute or so, Joab looked up at the door and found a latch with a handle. He pulled it down and the door opened. When he stood up, his head was almost completely level with the floor above him. The room looked dark and empty. After taking a good look around, Joab jumped and pulled himself up through the doorway. Hopping up to his feet, he found himself in a large room, completely dark except for the dim sunlight that streamed through the cracks in what looked like a large doorway. Joab stalked around the room as his men each pulled themselves up. It was completely empty. Outside, the sounds of soldiers marching and men shouting could be heard. Joab guessed that by now David had begun moving the army toward the east side to get near the gate, which would mean the Jebusites were already shooting at them. Time was running short.

This room was plenty large enough for all of Joab's men, and it did not take long for them all to climb through the trap door. The big captain went and stood by the doorway leading outside and looked through the cracks. He couldn't see much. He was pretty certain the gate was to the right, but all he could see were men running back and forth. The plan was to make a dash for the gate, killing any in their way. He had five men assigned to open each side of the gate, and twenty assigned to protect their rear. Joab walked back through the dark. He knew it was time to go. "Be ready," he whispered to all his men. Shammah and Sibbechai, as well as his other big soldiers such as Benaiah and Elizur, all stood at the front.

"Now!" boomed Joab, and the big man kicked the doors open wide. The sunlight flooded their eyes, momentarily blinding them all, but not enough to slow their advance. The whole group rushed forward shouting with weapons raised. Several squads of Jebusite soldiers stood facing away from them, watching the action on the walls. Hundreds of archers leaned over their turrets, shooting arrow after arrow into the invading army. The main gate stood only a short ways away, and it was swarming with Jebusites ready to defend it. Almost before their enemies could react, Joab came swinging his mighty sword through the air, followed by his men. The Jebusites were so surprised, that many fled from the initial shock, and those that remained were hacked to pieces. In seconds the Israelites had reached the gate.

The advantage would not last for long. Even as Joab's men braced themselves against the gate, Jebusites were rallying to face them. Joab positioned himself in the center of his twenty rearguard, all of them facing outward to fight off their attackers. Shammah, Sibbechai and the other big men went to work on the gate. A huge wooden crossbeam lay across the gate holding it shut, which was about chest high. Together the big men all squatted and put their shoulders under it, trying to lift it off.

Over the din of shouts and the noise of battle came an angry roar. "Kill them all! They cannot take the gate!" Jozabad came sprinting toward the Israelites' left side, his spear raised high. The big Jebusite plunged it deeply into one of Joab's men, then ripped it out and engaged another. Behind their leader, scores of Jebusites rushed into the fray, anxious to defend their home. Joab and his men were hard pressed, and were slowly pushed back toward the gate. Arrows flew through the line of Israelites, and several found a mark on the men striving to open the gate. Others defending their friends also started to fall.

"Fight Israel! Fight to the last man!" called Joab. Jozabad noticed the big man laying waste to his soldiers and started working his way toward him. When he was only a few steps away, the Jebusite hurled his spear at Joab, who was just turning to face him. It grazed the big man's left shoulder, causing him to drop his shield and leaving a gash that spewed blood. Joab grunted in pain. Jozabad drew his sword and rushed him, swinging his blade at Joab's head. The big Israelite blocked it with his own sword as the weapons clanged together. Again and again Jozabad swung at Joab, only to be blocked. Then Joab got the other man off balance and reared up to his full height, even taller than the Jebusite. Joab swung his sword with both hands with such force that it snapped the other weapon in half. With his opponent on his heels, the big man lunged forward, sinking the blade of his sword into Jozabad's side. The Jebusite doubled over in pain. Joab deftly pulled out the sword and brought it down on Jozabad's neck, sending his head rolling across the ground.

The sight of their leader dead shocked the Jebusite soldiers who were close enough to see it happen, causing many to hesitate with fear. With renewed vigor, the Israelites pushed forward, driving the Jebusites back. Joab rushed over to the gate and dropped his sword. The big captain squatted down and drove his right shoulder into the bottom of the crossbeam. "On me!" he called to the other men. "Ready, push!" With one motion they pressed against the heavy wooden beam. Joab could see the veins popping out of Shammah's neck as he strained with all his might. With that last great effort the crossbeam was off the gate. The men tossed it off their backs and it landed with a loud boom. "The doors!" called Joab, and the men turned to pull on the heavy doors of the gate. Sibbechai stepped back from the gate and pulled a horn from his belt. With all of his breath, he let out a sharp blast.

Shammah grabbed the inside handles of the two heavy doors. He leaned backwards and pulled, driving with his strong legs. As they slowly opened, he could see the center of the Israelite front line marching over the crest of the steep hill that looked down on the Kidron valley. King David was in the lead, his sword raised above his head as he rushed the gate. A flood of arrows fell alongside him, but none so much as touched the king. Behind him the Israelite ranks came on in a fury. Panicking, the Jebusites began hurling themselves at the gate, trying to close the doors. For a few seconds, the heavy doors stalled as Joab's men and the Jebusites pushed against each other in a life and death game of tug o' war. Then the massive weight of the Israelite formation crashed into the gateway, pressing the doors wide open. The army flowed into the city with David at its head, the king slashing his way through the Jebusites like butter.

Abishai stood close behind the king, shouting commands. "Take out the archers!" he called to Uriah, and the Hittite led his company up onto the wall. Others followed him, and soon the turrets around the gate were crawling with Israelites. Then the captain sent his own bowmen to replace them, and the Israelites fired down upon the Jebusites from their own posts.

Eleazar had led his men right down the main road of the city, leaving a path of fallen Jebusite soldiers in his wake. Far ahead, the swordsman could see Adonizedek fleeing further into the city, surrounded by a squad of his guards. "My lord!" he called out to David. "There he is!" he shouted, pointing with his sword.

"With me!" the king responded. David took off at a run followed by Eleazar and his men. Few now opposed them, as most of the soldiers had either run or been killed. Adonizedek and his men fled into the bottom of the temple, slamming the doors shut behind them. Reaching it, Eleazar stepped up and kicked the doors open. As his men spilled into the room, they found the Jebusites waiting. The two groups set at each other, filling the lower rooms of the temple with blood and violence. David and Eleazar ran through the rooms, looking for the Jebusite king. Finding a set of stairs, the pair ran up until they found a door that led out onto the roof. There stood Adonizedek, with his back up against the statue of his evil god Molech. The tall king had a crazed look in his eye and held a long sword in his hand. Its blade was red, and blood ran from his arms, a final plea of self-mutilation to his demon-lord.

"Come now, David!" cried the king, raising his sword overhead. David came forward slowly, his eyes on the wicked king. Suddenly, Adonizedek rushed him in a madness trying to bring the long sword down on David's head. David ducked and stepped to his left, aiming a stroke of his own sword at Adonizedek's belly. The Israelite's blow landed, and the tall Jebusite folded at the waist and fell to the ground, moaning in pain.

"Hear me, Adonizedek. Your city has been given to me by the Lord Almighty because of your great wickedness," David said as he looked the king in the eyes. "Eleazar, strike down that accursed statue."

"Yes my lord," said the Israelite. Eleazar strode over to the statue and raised his sword. With one swift stroke, the bull's head crashed down, landing in the ashen pit below it. Knocked off its balance, the body followed suit, both arms breaking off as it hit the ground.

As Adonizedek took his final labored breaths, David left his side and walked over to the edge of the building. Looking down, he could see his army marching through the streets. Already they controlled most of the city. Only a few small pockets of resistance remained. There were long shadows on parts of the ground, but the setting sun shone brightly on much of the city, making it appear almost the color of gold. Weapons and armor below glittered as the sun's rays reflected off them. Eleazar came and stood beside the king. David spoke to him without turning.

"The Lord debases the proud, Eleazar, and exalts His people, whom He loves. He has placed us here in this great city. It shall be the royal city of Israel."

"You will rule from Jebus, my lord?" asked Eleazar.

"Not Jebus," answered David. "Jerusalem."

17

"We will chase these heathen out of the cities of Israel. Too long have they remained on the land God has given us." David stood looking downhill at Baal-perazim, a small town on the western side of the great central highlands of Israel. It had long been in the hands of the tribe of Benjamin. But after the death of Saul, it had been taken by the Philistines, along with many other cities along the border of the two nations. It had been three days since the Lord had delivered Jerusalem to David. Small groups of escaping Jebusite troops had made their way to join the Philistine army, swelling the already full ranks with eager fighters. Achish had ordered his men to march toward Jerusalem, and now they occupied the valley to the west of Baal-perazim. The town itself had become a defensive post, full of Philistine soldiers waiting for the Israelite advance.

Behind David, the army of Israel stood assembled on the slopes of the lowering hills. It had been a long time since he had faced the massive Philistine war machine with all of Israel at his back. Twenty years had passed. Then he had been a lean teenager, wearing dirty rags and armed with a slingshot. Today the king was in full armor, with his great sword sheathed on his back and a crown upon his head. But David knew it was not due to him. The battle had been the Lord's that day, and it would be the Lord's today.

"We cannot advance everyone at once," said Joab, looking down at the king. "The road is far too narrow." The big captain was right. The road that ran into the town had a steep rise on both sides, and was only wide enough for eight or ten men abreast at the most.

"We will send archers to the top of those," said David pointing to both hills along the road. "They will fire before we march on the town. The road opens up just as you reach the town. Each company will just have to move quickly to reassemble there. The town is well defended, but I do not think they have enough soldiers on the ground right there to overcome us. In any case, the Lord has said to go up, so we will go up."

The big man nodded. "Very well, my lord. I will gather the commanders and give them their orders." David nodded and Joab stomped off, calling his troop leaders forward. The big man had completed his task at Jerusalem, and David had kept his word, reinstating Joab over the army. Abishai had willingly stepped down. As he waited for Joab to give out the orders, David prayed silently to himself.

My Lord, if we have found favor with You, walk before us today. Make our hands as strong as brass, and our feet as swift as deer. But do not bring us glory from this battle. Bring glory to Yourself, that all of the Philistines may know that there is a God in Israel. Bow the heavens and come down. Make the hills tremble, and shake the very earth. Make Your voice to thunder, and scatter them with lightning. Deliver we Your people from these heathen that are too strong for us.

The Philistine army was nearly four times the size of David's. If he met them in the valley below, Israel stood little chance. But this was the purpose for which God had raised him to the throne. David was to protect God's people, and cleanse the land of heathen gods worshipped by other nations. God had spoken, and David would obey.

Joab returned to the king's side. "All ready my lord. When we begin the march, two companies of archers will swing around and climb the hills. They have orders to stay out of sight and not to fire until we reach the end of the road. We will not be under fire from the Philistines until then, for farther down the hillsides block their view. Then each company will move in, as you said. Abishai is over the first thousand men, and the front companies are led by Eleazar and Shammah. They will get the job done."

"Very well," said the king. He looked up at the bright sky above. It was the middle of the morning, and the sun was starting to get hot. "Let's get on with it then. No need to be quiet, they can see us already."

Joab nodded. He turned around to face the army, spread out on both sides of the road. It would take a while to get all these men in line moving down the road. All the troops were quiet and looking forward. "Ready!" he shouted. "Forward, Israel!" called out Joab, and David stepped off, followed by the big captain and the first of the companies.

Baal-perazim was nearly a mile away, plenty far enough for the Philistines to make themselves ready for the Israelites. From the starting point, the army was in full view of the town, but the hills rose as the road descended and David soon lost sight of it. Before long, the companies of bowmen had split off to make their way into position. Joab sent a company of line soldiers with each, hoping they would be able to descend the steep hills after the archers had done their work, getting more troops quickly to the front. They were moving downhill and the pace was quick. In only a quarter of an hour David came within sight of the town at the end of the road.

Joab noticed the Philistine watchmen moving around, and thought he could hear them calling to one another. "They see us," he said lowly to the king. "We need to speed up."

"Call for the archers," David replied. Joab raised a small trumpet to his mouth and blew. It rang loud and clear in the morning sky. After a moment, an answering horn could be heard, and Joab could see a great commotion in the town ahead as the Israelite arrows started raining down.

"Ready my lord?" he asked the king.

"Ready."

Joab drew his big sword and held it out in front of him. "The Lord fights for Israel! Forward!" Joab and the king took off at a run, followed by the soldiers behind them. It was only a minute or so when they came to the end of the road. The hills fell away on both sides and the road opened up into a wide flat area, large enough for half the Israelite army at least. In the middle stood several groups of buildings made from brick, mostly small houses and stables. Crop fields bordered the town to the left and right. On the far side stood a large well made of stone, and then another wide space that sloped away toward the valley below. Baal-perizim had been abandoned earlier that day over the threat of war, and now was inhabited entirely by Philistine soldiers.

Joab blew his trumpet again, signaling to his archers to cease firing. As the volleys of arrows stopped, the Philistines also sprang into action. In an effort to bottle-neck David's army at the road, three companies of swordsmen rushed forward in disciplined formation. Another company also came forward from either side, having hidden under the edge of the hills. There were more of them in the town than David had first thought, and for a moment the king felt as though they would be overwhelmed. David and Joab crashed into the oncoming Philistines, with Eleazar and his men right behind them. With speed that surprised even Joab, all of the first company was on line in a matter of seconds, and Shammah's men were just as quick. Israel's front braced against the Philistines, refusing to be pushed back. They were definitely outmanned, but they were gaining troops every second as men filed in from the road. As Joab pushed forward in the center, he realized many of the Philistines had been directed away from the road. His line companies had made their way down the steep hillsides and jumped into the fray, attacking the Philistine flanks. Meanwhile, the Israelite army continued to pour out of the roadway. In short order Israel had gained quite a bit of ground, driving nearly to the buildings of the town itself.

The Philistines were experienced though, and had many troops to spare. They sounded their own horns, calling for reinforcements. All the soldiers left in the city had formed into line, and pressed against the Israelite advance. Joab spread his men out to cover the entire open area. Eleazar had led out to the left, Shammah to the right. Israelite soldiers continued to fill in the space behind them. But the Philistine horns did their work. In only minutes, hundreds more soldiers came rushing up the hill behind the well, fanning out to meet the Israelite front. Soon the entire area was full of bodies, as each side fought for more ground. The tide began to turn in favor of the Philistines, and Israel's forward movement stopped. Only about two-thirds of David's army had been able to file into the town, the rest were stuck on the road behind the mass of troops. If David was going to press through the town, he needed the rest of his men.

Joab sounded his trumpet again, and the archers resumed firing, aiming far beyond the front line at the oncoming Philistines. For a moment, it gave Israel some breathing space. The Philistine commanders at the front pulled the entire line back beyond the far side of the buildings, trying to gain some cover. As their targets pulled away, the archers ceased firing. Eleazar and Shammah pushed their men further alongside the town. In the center of the line, Abishai had brought another two companies in among the buildings, looking to deal with any Philistines that had managed to hide. Joab had called for the outside companies to halt, waiting for Abishai to come up even with them. It took longer than the big captain liked, for his brother had many rooms to search.

During all this, the Philistines did not remain idle. Reformed at the rear of the town, they brought their archers to the front and unleashed their arrows against the men on the sides of the town. The Israelites were caught out in the open, and forced to cover themselves with only their shields. Using that as a distraction, a company of swordsmen crept up through the buildings to surprise Abishai and his men. Soon the middle of town had erupted into bloodshed. Abishai was a skilled leader, but he took a heavy loss before he was able to push the Philistines back to their lines.

Meanwhile, David had been moving up and down the front lines, fighting and giving orders. "We need to push them completely out of the town," he said as Joab came up. "Put them in the open, and take it as a defensive post. We still have men in the road that are unable to join the fight."

"Abishai is handling the center," answered the big man. "I'll call for the archers. That'll make the Philistines shoot high, and we can advance. From what it looks like, they are only holding the last row of houses in the rear."

"Good. Call the archers and let's get moving," said the king.

Joab blew his trumpet again, and once more the Israelite bowmen started firing. The Philistines in turn tried to return fire, aiming high above the heads of the Israelite front line. "Forward, Israel!" boomed Joab, and the front line started moving, trotting across the fields toward the Philistines. In less than a minute, Joab sounded the trumpet again, calling for the archers to cease. By then the Israelites were at a run, charging into the Philistine front lines. The two armies crashed together, swinging with swords and striking with spears. The tide had turned back to Israel, and soon the Philistines found themselves in a retreat, unable to muster the heart to push their enemies back.

As the front lines moved into the open space behind the town, Joab called for a halt. All of the troops had made it into the town now, and they filed into a great formation split by the buildings as they watched the Philistines pull back over the hill. Joab gave two short blasts with his trumpet, calling for the archers to rejoin the army. The remaining Philistines had retreated into the valley to fall in with the main force of their army. The men would rest and regroup, and soon they would march down into the valley to meet the Philistine war machine.

First, however, there was another matter to deal with. A group of defiant Philistines, thirty at the most, had refused to return to the valley. They stood around the well, cursing Israel loudly as they brought up water for themselves. One of them, an exceptionally large soldier carrying a huge war axe, stalked in front of the others boldly as if daring an archer to shoot him.

"Do not think you have defeated us, you cursed dogs!" he shouted. "The might of the Philistines is behind me! You will all run red with blood before this day is through!" He continued stomping about in anger. "Where is your king? Your dog of a king? Tell him to come out like a man and fight."

David had no standard above him as many of the Canaanite kings did, making it harder to recognize him. As the big Philistine cursed, he strode forward from the lines, without saying a word. Standing alone, his crown glittered in the bright sun. It caught the man's attention.

"There you are, David, son of a dog! You are a traitor, and will die for your crimes! Come to me! I killed the last king of Israel, and I will kill you as well!"

Joab came up behind David, followed by Eleazar and Shammah. "Let me go kill the fool," boomed Joab. "He cannot speak that way of our king and live."

"I worry less about his words to me than I do about the well." It was hot, and Israel would need that water to keep the soldiers going. "A drink of that water would taste sweet just now."

That was all Joab needed to hear. "Come you two," he said to Eleazar and Shammah. "We will slay this fool and bring water to the king." The captain started forward, but David held out his arm.

"No Joab, I'll not lose my commander over this. Send a company to deal with these worthless men."

"We can do it, my lord," piped up Shammah in his deep voice. The big man raised his own war hammer. "I'll plant this in his skull."

"You can lead, but take a company. As I said, I'm not losing my leaders over foolish actions."

"Yes, my lord," answered Shammah. "On me!" he shouted to his men, and he took off, followed immediately by Eleazar. A company of men flew out of the ranks, flocking to Shammah. The big man rushed with such quickness, the Philistines were not prepared for him. With one brutal blow, he crumbled the skull of one unfortunate soldier. Eleazar joined the fray, hacking and slicing with his sword. In only seconds Shammah's men joined the fight, and David could no longer even see any of the Philistines. Moments later the fight was over, and the big Philistine was in a heap on the ground surrounded by his men. Eleazar drew a cup of water from the well and carried it back to the king.

"For you, my lord," he said as he bowed his head.

David took the cup, and bowed his own head. "Far be it from me to drink this, oh Lord," he said aloud. "Is it not by the blood of these men who risked their lives for this? I ask, oh Lord, that You accept this as an offering of what they have risked for Your people." With that, the king poured the water onto the ground, letting it pool itself into a small divot. David looked up at Joab standing next to him. "Have the men water and rest. We must prepare for the next assault."

"Yes my lord," nodded Joab as he walked away to gather the other leaders. A company was moved forward to the edge of the hillside beyond the well as a watch, and the rest of the soldiers sat at ease, drinking from the well in turns and eating what they could find. David visited the well and drank the cool water, thanking the Lord in his heart. Refreshed, he strode over to the hillside by himself to take a look.

Along the edge of the hill stood several meandering rows of mulberry trees, shielding the town and the well from view. On the other side, the bare ground sloped away gradually for several hundred feet. At the bottom, it spread out for miles in either direction, running north and south. Nearly half a mile to the west the ground rose again, leveling out into a plain that reached all the way to Sorek miles away. The sun was high and the sky bright and cloudless, and the king could see a great distance in every direction. It was an impressive view, but what caught David's breath was not the valley but what it held. The entire floor of the valley was black with men. Thousands and thousands of Philistine troops moved about below, preparing for a final clash with David's small army. A steady noise rose to David's ears, sounds of marching and horse hooves and shouts of men. As he looked on, David's heart sank. Even after losing so many soldiers in the town, the Philistines were still close to ten thousand strong, far greater than the army of Israel. Any attempt against them seemed like suicide.

Heavy feet crunched the ground behind the king as Joab stepped up alongside him. The big captain stood silent as he took in the sight.

"How are the men?" asked the king.

"Nearly ready," came the answer. "Do you have a plan?" Joab was a skilled battlefield commander, but he had no idea how to approach a force this size.

"I'm working on it," replied David.

"Maybe we should wait for nightfall," offered Joab.

"No," answered David. He knew the Lord had said the Philistines would be delivered into his hand, and God was as good as His word. "The Lord fights for Israel, Joab. No army can stand against Him, no matter how large." Just as he finished speaking, more footsteps approached from behind. The pair turned around to see Abishai approaching with Gad the prophet next to him. The tall lean man was breathing heavily as if he had been running.

"My lord," said the prophet as he reached the king, "the Lord fights for Israel."

"He does, my friend. What word do you have for me?"

"That is the word. The Lord will fight for you. Not through you, but for you." Gad was speaking excitedly, very unlike his normally reserved attitude. "Stand still, and see the salvation of the Lord. You are to wait behind the tree line until you hear the sound of the Lord's army marching to battle. He will go forth before you and slay the Philistines. Then you may follow Him into battle. Today the Philistines will know there is a God in Israel."

David stood almost uncomprehending the words of the prophet. Stand still, and watch the Lord fight the Philistines? It seemed so strange.

But the Lord was as good as His word, so David would obey. "Very well. We shall stand and watch the Lord's deliverance."

Suddenly a soft breeze swept through the still, hot air. Gad looked up and scanned the sky. Far in the distance clouds had appeared. "It is almost time," said the prophet hurriedly. "Prepare your men."

"Assemble the army," David said to Joab. "Move them into formation here along the hillside. Quickly."

"Yes my lord," said Joab, and he and Abishai trotted off toward the army. A trumpet was blown, and the troops tightened their armor and picked up their weapons as they fell into formation. Joab ran to and fro, shouting orders to move the men into position. The trees began to sway as the breeze picked up, and the clouds had grown closer and more numerous, casting a shade on the valley. The sky in the distance was turning dark blue.

It took only a few minutes for the Israelite army to assemble. The entire force stood spread out along the hillside. The tree line was not thick, and the soldiers in the front could see the valley beyond filled with Philistines. Joab stomped to the front next to David and let out a blast from his trumpet, calling out to the Philistine army. Down below, the Philistines had been called to attention, blowing their own horns and drawing weapons as they waited for the Israelite attack. In the center, just beyond the front line David could see Achish, raised up on a great chariot. His high standard flapped proudly in the wind.

"The Lord comes," called out Gad as he looked at David. The sky grew darker every minute. The wind had become a gale, bending the trees and flowing through the valley like a mighty wave. Dark clouds covered the sun, thunder sounding in the distance but growing closer with each rumble. David's chest pounded with energy, and his heart soared. *The Lord comes!* he thought. The king turned around and faced the Israelites, raising his arms and shouting out to them over the wind.

"Let the Almighty arise!" he called out. "Let His enemies be scattered! See, the Lord bows the heavens and comes down! Let the earth shake and the hills tremble! Let Him roar with thunder and strike with lightning! He is our Rock, and our Fortress, our Deliverer! See now, Israel! The Lord fights for you!"

Through the howling wind, David could hear the sounds of marching and the mighty beat of hooves. It was so loud and clear, so close. Above him the trees parted, bending outwards against the wind as if forming a gateway. The sound of a great trumpet pierced the wind, sharp and beautiful and full of power. David felt as if a great host was passing by ready for battle. As the sounds died away, the trees snapped back together. David looked out over the Philistine army with awe, breathless with expectancy.

With a mighty crack, a bolt of lightning shattered the sky, searing through the dark and striking the ground before the Philistine line. The sky boomed with thunder, and hailstones fell from the clouds. The Philistine charioteers held tightly to their reins as the horses reared up in panic. More lightning crashed in the sky, and the Philistine soldiers shook with fear. The wind blew into the valley from all directions with such force it knocked many of the shaky Philistines to the ground. With cries and shouts, they were overcome by madness. Horses trampled men in their haste to escape, and the soldiers attacked each other in mass confusion. Chaos reigned on the valley floor.

Up on the hillside, the Israelite army stood in amazement. David shouted in joy. "The Lord! The Lord fights for Israel!" The king drew his sword and held it high. "Come now Israel! Let us join in the victory of the Almighty!" Next to the king, Joab blew his trumpet. "Forward, Israel!" yelled David as he rushed down the hillside. Israel erupted in shouts as the troops charged after their king. They swept down into the valley and fell upon the Philistine army, slashing their way through the madness. Already in a panic, the Philistines fled. Every man dropped his weapon and ran for all he was worth, some escaping further down the valley and some retreating up to the higher plains before Sorek. The Israelites gave pursuit, chasing them completely out of the valley. Soon no living Philistine remained where only a short time before a massive army had stood. Joab sounded the trumpet, calling for the men to reassemble. The hail and lightning had stopped, and the wind began to die down as the Israelites returned from being spread out across the valley. The clouds started to dissipate and the sun shone through. As quickly as the storm had come up, it melted away. Soon the sky was clear and bright again, shining down on the re-formed Israelite army. As David made his way toward the formation, he looked down to see a golden object shining on the ground. He stooped over and picked it up, holding it out in front of him. It was the heavy crown of Achish, fallen from its master's brow. No more would he threaten the Lord's people.

David dropped the crown and went to stand in front of the troops. He was covered in dirt and blood, but his heart was bursting with gladness. Never had he seen the Almighty show Himself with such power. "How great is our God, Israel! He has delivered us today from the hands of our enemies!" he called out, and the soldiers shouted in agreement. David turned his sword upside down and plunged the blade into the ground. Then he raised both hands above his head and shouted, "I will praise You, my God and my King! I will bless Your Name forever! Great is the Lord, and greatly to be praised! I shall declare Your mighty acts and Your glorious majesty to all men! My mouth will speak praise to You, oh God, and may all men bless Your holy name forever!"

Epilogue

The night sky was clear and the moon was bright. A gentle breeze blew through the air. It was nearly midnight, and the city was still and quiet. David stood on the roof of the king's house in Jerusalem, taking in the night air. It had only been a few months since he had moved his capital here from Hebron. It had been peaceful during that time, the Israelites finally free of the constant harassment from their neighbors. The Philistines had a new king, and they had moved back near the western coast, keeping clear of Israel's territory. The Jebusites no longer existed as their own nation. Without a ruler, most had simply assimilated into the other peoples of Canaan. Some had chosen to dwell with the Israelites, knowing the new king was serving a great God. After seeing the impressive display of power, a handful of Philistines had also decided to reside with Israel, led by a man named Ahuzzath. David had welcomed the former enemies, knowing the Lord grants forgiveness to all who repent. So long as they were sincere in their worship of the Almighty, there would be room for them in Israel. There were still many foes to be dealt with, and in time troubles would arise. Yet David was now secure as the king of Israel, the most powerful man in the region. Jerusalem was the most defensible city of Canaan, and the Israelite army was experienced and growing. For now God's people had rest and security.

David looked out to the east. The moon was bright enough that he could just see the outline of the great mountain that stood facing the city. For some reason, it had been catching his attention recently. Every time the king had been within its view, he had felt almost as if it was calling to him. Earlier today he had spoken with Nathan the prophet in this very spot. Nathan had shown the king the word of the Lord, that David's line would not fail to reign over God's people. A king from David's descendants would forever rule on the throne, and the kingdom of God would be established. He had been speechless. Nathan had departed, and David had spent much of the day in prayer. All evening he had been restless. Unable to sleep, David had finally returned to the roof, hoping the warm air would help him relax. Still in awe of God's promise to him, the king dropped to his knees and bowed low to the ground. With a heart full of joy and gratefulness he prayed.

Oh Lord God, how great You are. Who am I, Lord, that You have brought me here? What is my father's house, that I should be placed on the throne? You have made a promise to Your servant for many days to come. For the sake of Your word, and for Your name, I know You will make these things to be done. For there is no God like You, so great and powerful and merciful. You have brought Your people up from Egypt and placed them in this good land, that You might redeem them to Yourself, and have confirmed them to You forever. For the sake of Your great Name, oh Lord, establish this people, and establish this throne, that Your name may be magnified forever, and the nations will know that there is an Almighty God in Israel.

As David prayed, the sky began to lighten. He looked up and saw again the outline of the mountain, but it was more than an outline. Above and beyond it, a great brightness was growing, as if the sun was rising behind it. Had he tarried so long on the roof? David leaped to his feet and watched. The brightness continued to grow, consuming the night sky and making everything as bright as day. Soon David could hardly bear to look at the mountain for the brightness. Then without warning a great figure from the air descended upon its peak, bright as fire, hurting David's eyes. The figure had the form of a man and shined like the sun in its strength. He shouted with a voice like thundering waves. As His feet touched the mountain it trembled, and with a great crack it split in two, half moving away to the north and half to the south. The Man descended into the Kidron valley, the earth shaking beneath His feet as He walked. Suddenly David found himself at the east gate of Jerusalem, looking down into the valley. When the Man reached the valley floor, the waters of the brook ceased flowing, separating before Him and allowing Him to step across on dry ground. The hill leading up to the gate flattened out and rocky steps sprung up, and the Man climbed up toward the city. From above David's head came the sound of trumpets, and the king looked up to see the sky full of shining creatures, thousands upon thousands of them. Most were also in the form of men, though none so bright as the Man, and they shouted and cried for joy as He drew nearer the gate. David trembled with fear, and yet his heart was full of joy as he watched the Man approach. As

He climbed the last step before the gate, the brightness became so great and painful David fell to his knees unable to look.

Immediately the sounds of trumpets and shouting died away, and all became silent. The brightness disappeared and the night returned. David looked up and found himself once again on the roof of his house, alone. He stood up and looked to the east, seeing the outline of the mountain, standing as it had been in one piece. Except for the moon, the sky was empty and dark. David's heart was racing. He ran to the stairs and rushed down. All were asleep as he hurried through the hallways, back toward his chambers. He went in a small room that he used for study and lit a candle. Finding an empty scroll and a pen, he bent over the unrolled paper and began to write. As he finished, he held it up close to the light to read:

The Lord said to my Lord, "Sit at My right hand, till I make Your enemies Your footstool." The Lord shall send the rod of Your strength out of Zion. Rule in the midst of Your enemies! Your people shall be volunteers in the day of Your power, in the beauties of holiness, from the womb of the morning, You have the dew of Your youth. The Lord has sworn, and will not relent, "You are a priest forever according to the order of Melchizedek." The Lord is at Your right hand, He shall execute kings in the day of His wrath. He shall judge the nations, He shall fill the places with dead bodies, He shall execute the heads of many countries. He shall drink of the brook by the wayside; therefore He shall lift up the head.

Now I saw heaven opened, and behold, a white horse. And He who sat on him was called Faithful and True, and in righteousness He judges and makes war. His eyes were like a flame of fire, and on His head were many crowns. He had a name written that no one knew except Himself. He was clothed with a robe dipped in blood, and His name is called The Word of God. And the armies in heaven, clothed in fine linen, white and clean, followed Him on white horses. Now out of His mouth goes a sharp sword, that with it He should strike the nations. And He Himself will rule them with a rod of iron. He Himself treads the winepress of the fierceness and wrath of Almighty God. And He has on His robe and on His thigh a name written:

King of Kings and Lord of Lords

Revelation 19:11-16

**I am the Root and the Offspring of David,
the Bright and Morning Star**

Revelation 22:16

Even so, come Lord Jesus

Author's Note

I would ask that any who read this book also take the time to read the real story in the Bible. It can be found in the books of 1st and 2nd Samuel, though I have used references from throughout the Bible. It is an amazing story, as is the entire story of God's plan of redemption for His people, of which we know only in part. It is my sincerest hope that all who read this book find the salvation which is provided only through the blood of Jesus Christ. If you have not turned to Him for forgiveness, please know that no matter who you are or what you have done, He desires to give it to you, and if you would only ask it of Him, you will have it.

Printed in the United States
By Bookmasters